Jo Thomas worked for many years̶ producer, including time at Radio 4's *Woman's Hour* and Radio 2's *The Steve Wright Show*.

Jo's debut novel, *The Oyster Catcher*, was a runaway bestseller and won both the RNA Joan Hessayon Award and the Festival of Romance Best eBook Award. Her recent book *Escape to the French Farmhouse* was a #1 bestselling ebook and in every one of her novels Jo loves to explore new countries and discover the food produced there, both of which she thoroughly enjoys researching. Jo lives in Pembrokeshire with her husband and three children, where cooking and gathering around the kitchen table are a hugely important and fun part of their family life.

Visit Jo's website: jothomasauthor.com/books
or follow her on:

🐦 @Jo_Thomas01
📘 @JoThomasAuthor
📷 @JoThomasAuthor

Also by Jo Thomas

THE OYSTER CATCHER
THE OLIVE BRANCH
LATE SUMMER IN THE VINEYARD
THE HONEY FARM ON THE HILL
SUNSET OVER CHERRY ORCHARD
A WINTER BENEATH THE STARS
MY LEMON GROVE SUMMER
COMING HOME TO WINTER ISLAND
ESCAPE TO THE FRENCH FARMHOUSE
FINDING LOVE AT THE CHRISTMAS MARKET
CHASING THE ITALIAN DREAM

Ebook short stories:
THE CHESTNUT TREE
THE RED SKY AT NIGHT
NOTES FROM THE NORTHERN LIGHTS

Jo Thomas

Celebrations at the Château

CORGI BOOKS

TRANSWORLD PUBLISHERS
Penguin Random House, One Embassy Gardens,
8 Viaduct Gardens, London SW11 7BW
www.penguin.co.uk

Transworld is part of the Penguin Random House group of companies
whose addresses can be found at global.penguinrandomhouse.com

Penguin
Random House
UK

First published in Great Britain in 2021 by Corgi
an imprint of Transworld Publishers

A CIP catalogue record for this book
is available from the British Library.

ISBN
9780552176873

Typeset in 11/14pt ITC Giovanni by Jouve (UK), Milton Keynes.
Printed and bound in Great Britain by Clays Ltd, Elcograf S.p.A.

The authorized representative in the EEA is Penguin Random House
Ireland, Morrison Chambers, 32 Nassau Street, Dublin D02 YH68.

Penguin Random House is committed to a sustainable
future for our business, our readers and our planet. This book
is made from Forest Stewardship Council® certified paper.

To the Romantic Novelists' Association,
for the faith and friendship I have found there.
And for all of those who have a dream
and are brave enough to do it!

1

'It's like . . . Hogwarts!' I say, peering through the early-morning autumnal mist. At least, I think it's me who says it out loud. Tiredness and shock has mashed my brain and blurred my vision. But I'm pretty sure it's what we're all thinking, for once, all on the same page, as we sit inside the hire car.

'I'm waiting for Frank-N-Furter to come and meet us,' says my eldest sister Nellie, short for Elinor, but no one calls her that and she doesn't mind.

'Who?' I ask, questions whizzing round my brain, like eggs in a blender, turning to froth.

'Never mind, you're too young!' says Lizzie, my middle sister, short for Elizabeth, but no one calls her that and, yes, I think she does mind.

'Er, not that much younger than you!' Nellie reprimands.

'It's fine,' I say. 'Let's just find out where we're supposed to be and what's going on.' And they both close their mouths, like bickering children who have been silenced.

'And Hogwarts is a lot bigger,' says Nellie, but quieter. She would know, bringing up three boys.

'But just as creepy,' says Lizzie. 'This is . . .' She carries on staring at it from behind the steering wheel, through the big metal gates.

'This is a joke, right? Someone's idea of a practical joke! Wait until I find out who's responsible for this!' Nellie shakes her head.

But who would do that? Especially not now, not with our grandfather only just buried. Tears, which seem to have been constantly ready to spill for the last month, prickle again.

'Or someone's got their facts wrong, which is more likely!' Lizzie likes to have facts and answers. She works on logic. 'An overnight ferry crossing, on choppy waters, then driving on the wrong side of the road for over an hour in a hire car for a wrong address!' she says, sounding fearsome. I just know that someone is going to be in big trouble if this turns out to be the case.

We sit in the car, the heaters blowing on our cheeks, looking at the listing iron gates and the long tree-lined drive to the left, covered with fallen late-autumn leaves. And beyond that, shrouded in mist, is what I can only describe as . . .

'It's a castle.' I say what we're all thinking.

'A château,' Lizzie corrects.

'Yes, a château,' I agree. 'I've seen one on television with Dick and Angel.'

'Who?' Lizzie asks.

'Daytime telly,' Nellie confirms.

Lizzie tuts and purses her lips.

Neither of us says any more. Lizzie doesn't do daytime TV. In fact, I don't think she does telly of any sort. She just works and she isn't happy about taking time off to be here. We all sit and stare through the gates.

Lizzie grips the steering wheel. 'Check the satnav again,' she instructs, jabbing a short painted fingernail at my phone.

I do as I'm told. 'You have arrived at your destination. You have arrived at your destination,' it repeats, grating on our nerves.

We all look around and behind us, but there's nothing else. Just these gates, the long tree-lined drive, a field of brown and white cows to the right of it and a farmhouse with lights on. And, beyond the gates, this building, glowering at us with a Gallic glare. Suddenly, there is a flickering of lights from a window in the turret closest to us – there's one on each side of the building. Again they flicker and go out, flicker and go out.

We look at each other nervously.

'Are you sure we own this?' I ask again, hoping there's been a big mistake.

'That's what the solicitor said,' says Lizzie, eyes narrowed.

'We've even got a key.' Nellie holds it up.

'Well, we'd better find out if it fits, and then we'll know for sure.' I want to sort this once and for all – and quickly. The lights in the window flicker furiously.

'Fliss!'

I snap my attention back to Lizzie. Fliss, that's me, short for Felicity and I've always preferred it. 'You do the gates,' instructs Lizzie, staying put at the wheel and pointing.

'We'll both do them,' says Nellie, pushing open the car door tentatively, clearly having as many reservations as I am. But there's no way this can be the place. It can't be. If it was, we'd have known about it way before now. Way before our grandfather died.

We lift and push back the gates with effort. The quicker we can find out where the place we're looking for is the better. This is definitely not the holiday home in Normandy we were expecting when we set off yesterday and travelled through the night. There's clearly been a mix-up on the address. Maybe someone here can help us, I think, as we get back into the car and continue our journey slowly down the potholed drive. The lights in the turret flicker on and off again, quicker this time, and a shiver runs down my spine as I get the feeling we're being watched.

2

'It fits!' Nellie says. We look at the key in the big lock as we stand at the top of the stone steps, leading straight up to the big wooden door, with its ornate stone surround.

I know I should feel elated, like Cinderella when the shoe fits, but I don't. Nothing about this fits. And I feel the same as my sisters: confused. The heavy early-morning mist, hanging in the air around the building, not only makes the place seem eerie but damp too. Even our hair is wet. We stare at the huge key in the lock again. Having tried knocking, Lizzie had been bold enough to try the key. And, yes, it fits! But none of this makes any sense. I knew him!

After our dad died when I was young, Mum married Martin and they bought a smallholding together. Grandpa was on his own in his little rented terraced house,

5

where he lived all his married life with Gran until she died, when I moved in with him to keep him company and keep an eye on him. It suited us both. It still suits me. Living in a small coastal town that's alive in the summer with holidaymakers and second-home own- ers, but as quiet as can be in winter, may not be for everyone, but it suits me and my life. And I loved living with Grandpa. I miss him. Tears prickle again.

We're not what you would call a close family. In fact, I can't remember the last time we three sisters were together. It's not that there was any big falling-out, we just went our separate ways. Well, Nellie and Lizzie did. Nellie moved to a cheaper area. She couldn't afford a place to live in the town where we grew up: small houses and cottages are snapped up by second-home owners. She needed somewhere to bring up her three boys, on her own, after her ex left her with a load of unpaid bills and debt collectors knocking at the door. Lizzie moved just over two hours away, to the middle of Cardiff with her fiancé. They have a flat down the Bay. She works in a big accountancy firm there. I stayed with Grandpa. It's where my life is, or was, until recently: there's Ty. My head swirls. I'm not sure what my life with Ty is right now. Or how to explain to my sisters what's going on, because I don't really know. We're all busy. We all have our own lives, jobs – or I did until really recently, but I don't want to think about either of those things right now.

So, it's rare for the three of us to be together, like someone's set us up on a date, insisting we get to know each other again. But I still don't understand. Grandpa wasn't a rich man. He lived modestly. No one ever mentioned a house in France, let alone a château. I know his older brother died in the D-Day landings, but that was the only connection to France I'd ever heard mentioned. So when the solicitor said a house in France had been left to us, we were expecting something altogether different. A small cottage, an apartment, a patch of land with some fruit trees and a pile of stones where a house had once stood. Not this!

'He must have said something to you,' Lizzie says, as if I'm daft, and Nellie is looking at me with the expression of a teacher asking a pupil one more time for the truth. Honestly, they treat me like I'm still the baby of the family, not a grown woman with her own life and a partner . . . of sorts. A job . . . of sorts. But I'm cross as I get a flash of what they're seeing, someone who hasn't really got life together. Just because my life is different from theirs, less pressured. It was how I liked it, I repeat to myself. I was happy with Ty, handsome, smiling Ty. My soul-mate . . . or so I thought.

'Nothing, not a word, I swear!' I hold my hands up and this time tears tip down my cheeks. I sweep them away.

'I mean, did he win it in a card game, or inherit it? Win the lottery? Why didn't we know about it?' Lizzie's determined to get some answers. She always was driven, at school and university, and now in business: she's planning to set up on her own when the time is right and she'll do it brilliantly, I know. She's focused. Unlike me. I have a million different ideas running round my brain of businesses I'd like to set up but I've never been able to settle on one. Besides, I don't think I'd be very good in business. Too much paperwork and organization. I'm better working for other people.

'Like I say, I don't know,' I say firmly, and take a deep breath. The familiar feeling from when we were kids, getting scratchy with each other, is rising. I rack my brains for any mention of a place in France. Now I think of it, he loved French cheese, and if he made supper for me it would usually be cheese on toast or bread and cheese, and he always called '*À table!*' when it was ready. But that was it. We holidayed once in France as a family, a campsite near a beach in Normandy – it can't have been too far from here – Grandpa, Mum, Martin and us. But I don't remember much about it, except that trying to pee in a Portaloo at night was a nightmare, and there were moles that dug themselves out of the ground under the tent. But that was it.

'*Bonjour?*' A deep, abrupt voice behind us makes the three of us jump and turn with our backs to the door, covering the key, as if we've been caught red-handed breaking in. Droplets of water from the mist scatter from our hair, like glitter, and slide down our foreheads and necks.

'Um, hello,' says Lizzie, standing tall and taking charge.

The man, with dark curly hair, is also covered with diamond droplets and has dark stubble around his chin. He's wearing scuffed leather boots and an old wax jacket, with a ripped pocket, and carries a thumb stick, even though he can't need one because he's no older than Nellie. Despite his appearance, and his furrowed brow, he is extremely attractive, I notice. I think my sisters may have spotted it too, judging by the looks on their faces.

'He must be the caretaker, or the sitting tenant the solicitor told us about,' Nellie whispers.

He stares at us, then at our hands covering the key, and back at us.

'We're . . .' Lizzie clears her throat and speaks loudly and slowly. 'We've got a key.' She takes it out of the lock and holds it up. He says nothing. 'Is this Des Arbres?' she says, as if Des were a person.

'Château des Arbres. *Oui!*' He nods sharply, just once.

'Château des Arbres,' Lizzie repeats, and still doesn't get it quite right. But it sounds to me as if we're in the right place. 'We are . . .' She carries on as if she's speaking to someone hard of hearing, still in English.

'*Nous sommes . . .*' I think back to my GCSE French. 'We think we might be the new owners,' I blurt out, interrupting my sister, who frowns at me.

Once again, the man stares at us, then gives another sharp nod, turns on his heels and walks away, driving his stick into the ground forcefully with each step.

We watch him march down the drive, fallen leaves hiding its potholes and danger points.

'How rude!' says Lizzie.

And we certainly can't argue about that.

'Perhaps he's got a problem working for women,' says Nellie.

'Well, we'll certainly be having a word about his attitude and the state of this place if he thinks he'll be staying on here, supposedly looking after it.'

'Staying on?' I ask.

'Well, just until we sell it,' Lizzie says, and Nellie nods. For once the Hope sisters are in agreement. If this place really is ours, the only thing we can do is sell it.

'And if we do sell it,' says Lizzie, a smile tugging at her lips, 'imagine how that would help us all out.'

We look at her, then at each other.

She could be right.

'It's like we've won the lottery,' says Lizzie, squinting up at the gargoyles over the stone pillars of the big front door.

'This could be the answer to all our problems.' Tears spring to Nellie's eyes. She needs help more than Lizzie and I do right now.

'A fresh start for us all,' I say quietly, feeling something stir inside me as I take in the intricate carved stonework.

Lizzie turns to the door, puts the key back into the lock and tries to open it.

'Here, let me,' I say, giving the door a shove with my shoulder, once, twice and, finally, it gives. I push it open, curiosity pulling me over the ancient threshold.

3

As we step inside, our eyes are automatically drawn up the long flight of stairs, beyond the huge tiled hallway, to a massive window where the stairs split and continue to either side of it.

'Wow!' I turn on the spot, looking up at the high ceilings. Although there is peeling paint, a musty smell and it's colder inside than it was out, it takes my breath away. None of us speaks as we all take in the enormity of the place.

'What on earth? It's in a state!' Lizzie says eventually.

'Gives me the creeps,' says Nellie, shivering.

'It's beautiful,' is all I say, as, despite the cold and damp, the ivy creeping round the door, I see how this place must once have been. The original ceiling rose is still in place, with a chandelier and ornate cornices.

The craftsmanship that had gone into building the place is stunning. I'm in awe.

There are doors off the main hall and we wonder which one to open first and what we might find behind it. The other two look at one another, then at me.

'Hello?' calls Nellie, in the direction of the stairs.

'Nellie, there's no one here. We just met the caretaker.' Lizzie tuts. But we feel strangely as if we're trespassing.

I pick a door, grasp its mottled brass handle, and glance at my sisters, wondering what we might find. They grab each other's hands, then mine. I nudge the door with my shoulder.

We tumble into the big room together, then untangle ourselves and straighten up. The walls are a beautiful barely-blue, with gold on the doors and around the panelling. A high ceiling, and a huge fireplace, with marble surround and blackened back behind a wrought-iron grate. There is furniture: a long table, with chairs and candlesticks by the look of it, covered with sheets and blankets. Beyond that, there's another room, a snug, perhaps, with a baby grand piano, and then the turret. I open a door to it, and a staircase spirals all the way to the top floor. A curved door leads down a few steps to what must be the kitchen.

We return to the hall and go into the billiard room – I think that's what you'd call it – and then, the drawing room, with another beautiful fireplace and doors out to a moss-covered patio. There's a big sideboard and a table with what looks like an antique gramophone, with a trumpet speaker. We walk across into the library: books fill the shelves and dust sheets cover the furniture, as if someone has just locked up and walked away.

'This can't be right,' says Nellie, ever the worrier. 'This can't be the right place. We should leave before someone finds us here.' She tugs at my sleeve.

'But we have the key,' Lizzie says firmly. 'It fitted, remember? Why would the solicitor give us a key to a house that he says we own if it wasn't the right one?' She has a point.

I walk up to the French windows to look out at the patio, with ivy-covered urns on plinths, leading to a lawn and what looks like a swimming pool. Beyond that there's a hedge, and I can see cows on the other side. Despite the cold, abandoned feel of this place, it has a wonderful elegance and faded beauty. Like a glamorous Hollywood actress who has grown old gracefully, holding her head high despite the wrinkles.

'Honestly, I'm not kidding, this place gives me the creeps,' Nellie repeats.

'It must be worth a fortune,' says Lizzie, ever the numbers woman. I can see her doing mental calculations. 'Even in its current state. First, we need to find that caretaker and ask him exactly what he has and hasn't been doing around here. When the solicitor said a tenant was in situ, I assumed it would have been looked after,' she says, grimacing at a windowsill littered with dead flies.

'Mind you, we never expected anything like this place, did we?' I say, my eyes dancing with excitement as I wonder who might have lived here.

'Typical you! Always seeing the romantic side of things! Imagine the upkeep, the repairs . . .' Lizzie tuts.

'Imagine the heating bills,' says Nellie. 'It would cost a fortune to run.'

'But why?' Lizzie looks at me and Nellie. 'Why did he buy this? And why have we never known about it until now?'

I glance down at my phone to check the time. It seems like we've only just arrived yet it's nearly midday.

'Look, let's get something to eat,' I suggest, thinking it's the only practical thing we can do right now. 'We'll go to the nearest village or town. Have an early lunch. Find out if anybody knows anything. If anyone knew our grandfather.'

They nod eagerly, clearly keen to get out of the place.

I take a final look around the room and poke my head into the others while my sisters wait in the hall, ready to leave as quickly as they can.

Outside, I shut the door, giving it a sharp tug – the wood has swollen in the frame, I suspect – and lock it with the big key. The low autumnal sun has finally come out, filtering through the branches that hang over the tree-lined drive, creating shadows but also shafts of bright light. I can feel it warming me after the chill of the château. Somehow I can't move, imagining what the place must have been like in its glory days.

'Come on, Fliss,' Lizzie calls, opening the car with a blip. Reluctantly, I move down the steps, looking back at the stone façade, my hand running down the lichen-covered balustrade. At the bottom, I turn back to the château. I'm buzzing with questions and curiosity. I want to see it all. I want to find out who lived there. How my grandfather ended up owning it. Find out everything about it, before we have to say goodbye to it and go home.

For once, the thought of home doesn't fill me with the warm glow it usually does. I don't mind putting off going back just a little longer and seeing how things are when I get there. If the pieces are all in the same place . . . Or not. I can see Ty's face and his expression before I left for our Channel crossing last night. I have no idea why I suddenly chose to say what I did. Maybe it was because summer has gone, which means he will be going away again. It's the same every year. He teaches skiing and snowboarding in France during the winter, then goes to his family's summer house to teach surfing next to the beach café where I work. Or worked.

I'm used to it. It's how it's always been. But this time I wished it wasn't. This time I wished he wasn't going.

Maybe it was the mood of the evening, the wine, but I did the thing we've always promised we'd never do. We were happy. Why change what we had? We had more than a lot of people find in a lifetime, we knew that. It was just that . . . What if he didn't go? What if we stayed just as we were in that moment? I couldn't help saying what I did. Maybe it's because Grandpa has gone and there's a huge hole in my life, which hurts. Perhaps being here for a day or two is just what I need for things to settle, see if they go back to how they were. Why change what isn't broken? But something inside me has shifted, something between me and Ty. And I don't think things will go back to how they were.

I swallow the memory, get into the car and slam the door. That's the moment when I realize Ty and I may not have a future together. I look back at the impos-ing building as Lizzie drives away, and I could swear I see something move in one of the upstairs rooms, the lights flickering on and off again, I catch my breath. What was it?

From a distance, I can see the caretaker again, stand-ing at a gateway as we turn on to the tree-lined narrow road, soggy leaves banked up in the hedgerows. He's watching us with interest – and a hefty dollop of disdain. Clearly not impressed with us. But I doubt we'll be his employers for very long, I think, with a tinge of regret, as I look back at the beautiful but neglected château as we drive away from it. I can't help but wonder, though, who made the movement I saw in the window if the caretaker was at the end of the drive? My heart beats just a little faster.

4

We park as near as we can to the centre of the town before the cobbled streets get too narrow. And I have a strange feeling of déjà vu, a dream maybe. It's as if I've been here before. A vague memory scratches at the back of my mind. That family camping holiday and a day trip to a pretty town. Just like this one.

We leave the car in the practically empty car park, under the bare plane trees, and head for a narrow cobbled street that may lead us into the heart of the little town. The brightly coloured, half-timbered houses, with window boxes, seem to trigger more of a memory – the red and black timbers making crosses and lines on the front of the buildings, up to their pointed roofs, the last of the red geraniums, a final burst of colour before winter sets in, hanging in pots from hooks by timbered doors, the dark wooden balconies and the twisted bare branches of wisteria winding around door frames. There are big square lanterns on wrought-iron brackets and a strange silence in the little town as we walk up the slow incline, following the cobbles around the bend as it opens, under a light stone arch, into a small square, filled with the autumnal sun.

I spot the old washhouse, with its large wooden pillars, open-sided with a tiled roof, and hear the gentle trickle of water from an ornamental fountain. There is a church, with a clock tower, and houses, with small paned windows and pointed moss-covered slate roofs. There's an *épicerie* with awnings in striped cream and brown to match the half-timbered walls of the shop front. Outside, wicker baskets are for sale, with boxes of fruit and vegetables – large red tomatoes, green beans, courgettes and strings of onions. Inside the shelves are packed with jars and tins, and from the doorway I can see an old-fashioned set of scales with a big metal bowl. There's a *boulangerie*, with baguettes stacked in baskets, a chocolate shop and a florist, all with full windows but very few customers even though it's lunchtime. There is even a hairdressing and beauty salon, but the door is shut and the lights are off.

We stand and look around and then, as one, see what we're looking for and head for the low doorway in a timber-framed building, the walls the colour of *café crème*, and a sign over it: 'Crêperie'. The smell draws us in, as much as its old-world picture-book charm.

As we step inside, dipping our heads through the low doorway, on to the worn flagstone floor of the low-ceilinged bar and restaurant, a few men in flat caps are sitting at a high bar, drinking and staring at us, like we've got three heads each.

'Why are they looking at us?' Nellie asks quietly.

'Staring, more like!' Lizzie says loudly.

'Perhaps this wasn't such a good idea,' says Nellie. She seems a lot more nervous than she used to be.

'We said we'd come and see if anyone knew anything about our grandfather,' I say firmly.

'Yes, come on,' says Lizzie. She lifts her head, swings her hair over her shoulders, pushes back her shoulders and walks in, like the professional she is. Nellie follows, then me.

The barman looks at us with interest and when Lizzie asks, in sign language and clear, loud English, for a table for three, he leads us to one by the huge fireplace, just beside the door to the kitchen and opposite a window, looking out on the neat little square. As we follow him, all eyes from the bar and a couple having lunch by the window follow us. He hands us a menu each, taking his time, then returns to the bar.

'Now what?' whispers Nellie.

'Just pick up a menu and look at it!' says Lizzie.

'I can't read it. It's all in French!' Nellie frowns.

The owner comes over to the table holding a note-pad and pen over his large belly.

'Er . . .' My two sisters look at each other.

'Um.'

'*Galettes, s'il vous plaît, fromage, jambon, pour trois.*' My school French comes back to me in a rush.

'And drink?' he says abruptly.

'The house wine,' I say, hoping it will be just fine. '*De la maison,*' I attempt clumsily.

He nods and heads to the kitchen, the smell making my stomach rumble.

'What did you say? What did you ask for?'

'Pancakes. For three. And house wine.'

Once again, I feel as if I've been here before, eaten crêpes and left feeling happy, full and sleepy.

'It smells heavenly, whatever it is,' says Nellie. 'The boys would love pancakes!' She smiles and I can tell she's missing them. Jason is sixteen, and when I asked on the journey over how he was doing and what he was up to, a worried frown appeared on her forehead. And then there are the twins, heading into secondary school next year. 'Even Jason,' she goes on. 'He might be a sulky teenager, but he'd like them as much as the twins would! Just hope he's managing to look after them okay. It's not ideal leaving your uncommunicative teenager with his younger brothers.' She sighs.

She and Lizzie get on their phones and check in on life back home. I take a quick look at mine and see there's a message from Mum, checking we got here safe and sound, but nothing from Ty. I reply to Mum to let her know we're fine and push it back into my bag. I'm trying not to think about Ty and how we left things. I look around the restaurant, at the huge wooden beam over the fireplace, the pile of logs throwing out heat. Behind the bar a woman with bright red lipstick, pinned-up hair and heels that clack over the flagstone floor appears – from an upstairs flat I assume – links her arm through the barman's and asks, without much subtlety, who we are.

'Maybe holidaymakers?' He shrugs.

'It's been a long time since this place had visitors.' I think that's what one man perched on a bar stool says.

'Why would people holiday here?' says the other, shrugging.

'Maybe it's more second-home seekers, looking for a bargain,' the woman says, her red lips pulled down at the corners.

The barman prises himself free from the clutch the woman has on his arm and carries a terracotta jug and cups to our table. Not quite what I was expecting.

'The house?' I question.

'The house,' he confirms firmly, with a nod.

We watch as he pours a slightly murky liquid into the cups and places them in front of us.

The men at the bar are still watching us – like Mum watches *EastEnders*, glued to the screen.

'I'm not sure any of them will be able to tell us about our grandfather and why he owned that place,' whispers Nellie. 'I'm not sure I want to ask.'

'Or why we didn't know about it,' says Lizzie.

Nellie picks up her cup and sips. 'Ew . . . that's harsh!' she says. 'I thought Normandy was supposed to be cider country.'

'Clearly not around here,' I say.

'It tastes more like vinegar to put on my chips!' says Nellie.

I can see the men at the bar out of the corner of my eye: they turn their mouths down beneath their moustaches and say something to each other as we attempt the tart, sharp cider again and try to get used to its taste.

The tall barman returns from the kitchen with three large plates and a smell that is like a huge hug, wrapping itself around us as he puts down the big plates. We stare in awe at the large folded pancakes, garnished with parsley, and the mountain of fresh, dressed salad on the side, with rocket, walnuts and beetroot, and breathe in deeply. I try to remember when I ate last, not counting the packets of Hobnobs and Pringles we shared in the car, which Nellie had brought along. We smile, even Nellie, who seems less worried about her boys back home.

The barman returns to the kitchen as we pick up our knives and forks, relishing the pleasure these plates of food are about to give us. It's been a long and tiring journey, and the house is nothing like we expected it to be, but this meal will make things feel better, even if the cider doesn't. Just then the barman returns and puts a dish of thin, crispy, glistening French fries in front of us and our smiles widen.

'*Merci*,' I say, and he says something back from behind the bushy moustache.

'*Pardon?*' I try again with the French pronunciation.

'You want ketchup?' he says, with a sniff. He says it with scorn, clearly reserved for visiting British holiday-makers.

'*Non merci*,' I reply, and he gives a slight nod – of appreciation, I hope.

'Actually . . .' says Nellie, and he half turns.

'No, we are not having ketchup,' I hiss at her, in a rare moment of leadership – I'm the one who doesn't run a business or a family, but the look I gave her clearly told her I meant it.

'We have everything we need,' Lizzie says loudly, as if that makes her English easier to understand, glaring at me.

'*Merci*,' I say again, with a sigh of relief. As if we wanted to stand out any more than we do already. Ketchup might have seen us marched into the square and pub-licly outed as heathens.

I cut into the savoury pancake, and smile. I take a mouthful. My eyes close as the soft smoky ham and delicate creamy cheese reach my tastebuds. My sisters are silent and ketchup-gate is clearly forgotten. We open our eyes at the same time and have the same 'wow' look on our faces. There is a smokiness to the galettes, a heartiness and nuttiness in the buckwheat flour, a sweetness in the butter they're cooked in and a creaminess in the cheese as it strings from the plate to our forks and mouths. The galettes may be the closest we've come to a welcome around here.

'I'm going to make these when I get home,' says Nellie. 'The boys will love them.'

'I'll have to diet for a week after this!' says Lizzie, who doesn't look as if she'd ever need to diet as she sucks in her stomach and pats it. Lizzie doesn't like anything to be out of her control, including her weight.

I just have a feeling of contentment and comfort, and even the cider doesn't taste as bad as it first did. I'm also feeling an odd sense of connection here, in this place, but I have no idea with what. But all the worries that followed me here, which I've been turning over and over in my mind, seem to have practically disappeared. The answer, I think, lies somewhere between our arriving here and this meal. I'm just not sure what it is. I just wish Grandpa was with us.

We finish the galettes, salad and *frites* in relative silence. Then we mop up the remains of the cheese, butter and dressing with the sliced baguette from the basket that the woman with red lips and high heels dumped on our table. We sip the cider, which, although still harsh, seems less offensive with the glorious flavours floating around my mouth.

We sit back as one, with a contented 'Aah.'

The barman appears at the table and at first says nothing, then, looking at our empty plates, gives a nod with a downward pull at the corners of his mouth. 'You want dessert?' he says, picking up the plates with ease.

Lizzie holds up a hand, the other clutching her stomach, and shakes her head.

Nellie looks bright-eyed and eager, and I'm full but intrigued as to what dessert might be.

'Crêpes?' he enquires.

'*Oui*,' says Nellie.

'*Chocolat?*'

She nods eagerly.

'*Et vous?*' he asks me.

'*Oui*,' I say, feeling I'm being challenged somehow. With that, he turns and walks to the kitchen. There was no menu and I've ordered a chocolate crêpe, like my sister. I'm feeling a little miffed. I would have liked to make my own choice, but clearly he thinks all British customers are incapable of choosing their own food. Although we may have shown him we're the exception.

His partner with the red lips is standing at the end of the bar, not taking her eyes off us, a cat keeping an eye on a mouse, like the two men at the bar.

We're lost in our thoughts when the kitchen door reopens and the barman returns with two plates. He puts one in front of Nellie. Three triangles of thin pancake, drizzled with warm dark chocolate and sprinkled with hazelnuts, a pot of cream on the side. The smell as she pours the cream over them is heaven. Then he puts down my plate. Not the same as my sister's and a small smile is tugging at the corners of his mouth.

'Our speciality . . . for the non-ketchup lover.' The smell is like Christmas, home and belonging all in one big hit, filling my head and my heart.

'Apples, cinnamon, apple brandy and cream,' he says, but doesn't move away. I know he's waiting for me to try it so I pick up my fork and spoon. 'You are on holiday?' he asks.

I shake my head and wonder if this is our moment to find out about the château and our grandfather. 'We're here for the château,' I say, cutting into my crêpe.

'Château des Arbres?' He tilts his head, as do the three others at the bar.

'Yes.' I take a bite, chew and blow out hot steam from the sweet cinnamon apples. 'Our grandfather owned it.'

'Your grandfather?' he asks, looking up at the bar as I place another mouthful of the sweet thin pancake in my mouth. I shut my eyes again and imprint the taste on to my memory, where there seems already to be a memory, taking me back to my childhood and that camping trip with my grandfather.

'Yes, our grandfather,' I say, as I open my eyes, but he's gone, back to the bar and washing glasses. His partner is now glaring at him, tapping a pen furiously on the counter, a hand on her hip, clearly cross with him for getting too friendly with us.

I finish the dessert, smile and nod my appreciation, then hold my hand over my mouth to disguise a tiny burp and suppress a giggle. 'Excuse me,' I say, at my sisters' scolding looks, realizing I'm being told off. I just don't think they'll ever take me seriously as a grown-up. I try to smile at the barman's partner. There must have been a reason my grandfather bought that place ... Maybe it was the apple and apple brandy crêpes, I think, imagining how much he would have enjoyed that dessert. It certainly wasn't for the cider. I look at the cup, its contents as sour as the barman's partner's face. Clearly the news about us being related to the man who owned the château hasn't gone down well.

5

'So, we need to decide what to do,' says Lizzie, leaning in and speaking quietly, as the plates are cleared and we're asked if we'd like '*Café? Digestif?*' I say yes. Lizzie raises a hand and shakes her head, ever business ready. I sit back, look at the flames in the log fire and enjoy the glow of possibly the most perfect lunch ever . . . except for the cider and the barman's partner. But right now, it's a long way from where Ty and I were and it's exactly what I needed.

'Well, it's not the holiday home we were expecting, with a live-in caretaker, that we can rent out on Airbnb,' says Nellie, which had been the plan we came up with on the ferry and car journey.

'Phfff! It's certainly not that,' says Lizzie, indicating to the restaurateur that she would like 'coffee *au lait*' as he puts little shots of espresso in front of me and Nellie and small round glasses that release a glorious boozy apple aroma. I take a sip. It's glorious! Apple brandy! It reaches into the corners of my mouth, tickles them to wake them up, then warms as it slides down my throat. With the coffee, a full-strength hit of caffeine, it's a heady mix that takes away the taste of the cider.

A row seems to break out behind the bar, the restaurateur's partner chastising him. If I'm not mistaken, he's given us the wrong drinks, the wrong bottle. I'm not sure what the problem is, but she's waving a bottle from the bar and shaking her head at the one he's opened. He returns the shots she's fired and shoos her out from behind the bar with a wave of his hand. He shakes his head and, after some hissing and steaming from the machine, returns with a large coffee and hot, bubbling milk in a jug on the side.

I'm lost in my thoughts, wondering what Ty would make of this, what he's doing now and, frankly, what will happen to us now we've realized we're not on the same page. Is that it? Are we over for good? Or on a break? Avoiding each other in Swn Y Mor will be hard as there aren't many places to go. But hopefully he'll be off on a surfing job soon, taking private parties to warmer waters, then snowboarding for the winter.

'So what are we going to do?' asks Nellie, having drunk her apple brandy in one. For a moment I think we're returning to my sisters' favourite topic of conversation: my unconventional love life and semi-single status, which now looks to be hanging in the balance. I open my mouth to explain that Ty and I were happy as we were, but things have changed. And, no, I don't know what's happening from here and I don't have any plans yet. In fact, I'm still in shock about it, when Lizzie cuts in and I realize we're talking about the château, not me and Ty. It's a welcome relief.

'There's only one thing we can do. We're agreed on that,' says Lizzie, looking between the two of us. 'Sell it. And the sooner the better.'

I see the restaurateur's partner craning her neck as she clears the table of the couple in the window and offers them coffee, while trying to hear what we're saying. We lean in closer and lower our voices.

'Yup, we all agree,' says Nellie, with a nod, her cheeks shiny, like red apples, probably caused by the fire, tiredness and apple brandy.

For a moment I feel sad that I won't see more of the old place, discover its history and watch it come back to life, but I know they're right. It's the only thing we can do. And I drain my glorious glass of apple brandy. I never even knew I liked it . . . or even what it was. Calvados, I'm thinking. Whatever it was, it was delicious, like the meal.

'Fliss, are you listening?' I bring my attention back to Lizzie and she starts again, as if she's holding a meeting, which, I suppose, she is.

'Okay. It would be best if one of us stayed on and got it sorted out quickly,' says Lizzie, glancing between me and Nellie. 'I have to get back to work on Monday morning, so it can't be me,' she says, draining her coffee cup and putting it down.

'I can't stay,' says Nellie. 'I have to get back for the boys. Who knows what kind of trouble they'll have got themselves into by now?'

'But Jason's there,' says Lizzie.

'Don't remind me,' says Nellie, checking her phone, her worried look returning. 'People think babies are hard work. You wait until they're teenagers.'

I feel a pang, a twist in my stomach and in my heart. If only waiting was all I had to do. Right now, I'm not sure I have a partner, or not one that wants a family.

'That's when all the trouble begins, and the sleepless nights, believe me.'

'I do know about young people. I was that age too once,' says Lizzie.

'I know,' says Nellie.

They look at me.

'I . . .' I'm not sure what I'm going to say.

'You could stay,' states Lizzie. 'You're the only one without a full-time job.'

'Well, not actually without—'

'You said you'd finished in the café, now the season's over, and after that row you had with Brian, the owner, over giving out too-large slices of cake and top-ups of cream . . .'

'He said mine were the size of two slices . . . small ones!' I protest. 'I couldn't serve it like that. It looked mean! And these were regular customers. Surely he wants people to enjoy visiting his café, instead of never coming back. And as for giving people extra cream . . . It's just a bit of cream! You can't charge them for it!' I'm enraged all over again. They stare at me. I shrug. It was a matter of principle.

'So he sacked you?' asked Lizzie.

I shrug again.

'We agreed I'd finish. As you said, it was the end of the season anyway.'

'What else have you got on?' asks Nellie.

'Well, I can probably pick up a few shifts at the pub.'

'But that's quiet too until the tourists come back for Christmas and New Year,' says Lizzie.

I can't help but agree. 'I'll find something.' I try to smile brightly.

'And Tyler? He'll be off soon, won't he?'

'Ty and I are . . .well, taking a break. Working out what we both want. Seeing if it's the same thing.' Tears fill my eyes. I don't want to do this right now. I'm not ready. I haven't had time to take it all in, or worked out where we go from here, if anywhere. I take a deep breath.

'So you're free for a bit, aren't you?'

I bite my bottom lip and think about me and Ty, our last night together, and rub the little shell necklace I always wear. The look he gave me when I knew everything had changed.

This is how life is with Ty and me. It's how it's always been, since our school days, ever since we'd first met on the beach when he ventured away from his family and braved coming over to talk to me and my friends, taking over the rocks, looking down on the sands, the holiday-makers and second-home owners, as if we were claiming it as our own, the locals. He'd invited me for ice cream and at first I'd refused. We didn't mix with well-off second-home owners. But his charm won me over. To the giggles and jeers of my friends, I agreed, grabbed my towel and joined him for a 99. I had an oyster, with marshmallow at the bottom and chocolate dipped in coconut. But I insisted on paying for it. We walked and talked and teased as the sun started to set and he had to go home. After that, I met him every day of the holidays. Much to my friends' chagrin. From then on, it was always the same. He would arrive at the start of the summer, before my school had broken up . . . well, private schools always finish earlier, don't they? He unleashed his surfboard from the top of his parents' car and unloaded his belongings into his grandparents' holiday home, and that was summer sorted. Ty and me. Never out of each other's company. We'd spend the days surfing, catching waves, and the evenings barbecuing on the beach.

35

And that's how it stayed. He'd be back for the summer, when the surf was good, and away again in the winter, following work and the surf, around the globe. For years he'd been entering competitions, making a name for himself on the international circuit – with sponsors too. He worked on his branding online and hoped to still have a shot at the world title, despite his accident two years ago. But more and more these days, he's stuck with teaching, surfing in the summer and snow-boarding in the winter. The competitions are thin on the ground, a bit like the branding, not that Ty will admit it. He just gets frustrated when he sees younger, more high-profile surfers coming on to the scene, and invitations to him to enter competitions are slowing. Everything changes . . .

That's what started me thinking. I mean, this can't be for ever, can it? At some point he'll have to stop. That was all I was thinking when I said what I said. What will happen when he stops? I wondered aloud how old our children would be when they got their first boards. He stopped rubbing my feet and looked at me. There was something in his eyes I couldn't identify. Some-thing that made me suddenly question where he and I were at. It's always the same. He comes back for the summer and then he goes again. I've accepted that. But I also assumed that some day it would be different. Peo-ple would ask whether we were going to marry, settle down, but our answer was always the same: 'Why try to fix what isn't broken?' But when he broke his back in an accident, came back to his grandparents' house and I moved in to nurse him, I could see that, one day, things would be different.

I think about Ty's shut-down look when I mentioned our children. I was reminded of the pledges we'd made to each other, years ago, that we were enough for each other, didn't need anyone else. But that was then and this is now. Time is moving on. Grandpa dying has made me realize that. We can't just stay as we were for ever – we're not teenagers any more. Life moves on, and Ty needs to grasp that. I'm not saying I want children straight away, but I would like to talk to him about what the future might hold for us. Finding out that my grandfather had Château des Arbres, that there was more to his life than I knew, has shown me that I want something more. I'm just not quite sure what it is yet.

'I love you,' I said, suddenly feeling the need to hear it. As if the rope I'd been anchored to all these years was gently slipping from my hand.

'Love you too, sweetcheeks,' he'd said, as he stood up and ruffled my pixie-cut hair. That wasn't what I was hoping for or needed. We want different things. I can see that now. I just need to work out if there's still an us in it.

I look at my sisters. Maybe this is what I need, and what Ty needs right now: me not to be there when he's expecting me. Maybe, just maybe, me being away for a few days, a week tops, will give him time to think. Just so he knows I'm not waiting around moping about him. He's not the only one who has places they need to be. Maybe he just needs to realize that everything changes at some point. He needs time for the idea to settle. Then maybe he'll see things differently and realize that, actually, we should look to the future. We both need to consider our situation, and I may as well do it here.

'Okay,' I say, painting on a smile.

'You'll do it?' says Nellie, beaming.

'You'll stay?' says Lizzie, looking concerned.

'Yes. Like you say, it's just for a few days, a week max.' I smile again, this time with more meaning. 'What's not to love about spending time in a beautiful old château in France?'

Their expressions show I've surprised them.

'I'd love to have some time to get to know it.'

'Are you sure?' says Nellie.

'Well, you *are* the only one with nothing to get back for,' repeats Lizzie, looking to Nellie for back-up. Nellie frowns at her and gives a sharp little shake of her head. 'I don't mean that in an unkind way, just that, with Ty leaving soon . . . I'm sure you'll work things out.'

'I meant about staying here on her own!' Nellie glares at her.

'It's fine,' I say. 'And I know what you meant, Lizzie. I *am* the only one with nothing to rush back for. Like you say, with the holiday season over, work's drying up. The café and ice-cream kiosk are only opening at weekends and the car parks are quietening down so they don't really need attendants. I probably won't get much work now until the Christmas season starts. And Ty will be off again.' And this may indeed be the little jolt Ty needs to realize I'm not always there. I can't just wait around for him: I need to find a life of my own, a future, and Ty has to decide if he wants to be part of it. 'Besides, like I say, it'll be nice to view the whole place and try to find out why Grandpa ended up with it.'

They nod in agreement.

I try not to think about the look Ty gave me. How something has shifted inside me.

We okay? Ty had texted, with a winking emoji, as I was on the way to France. But I know we're not. Something's changed. Like the shift from summer to autumn. I don't want to be as we were. I want more. I want it to be 'us', a future, a family. The only problem is, I'm sure now that's not what he wants. He wants 'as we were', but that's the thing: 'were'. I'll be thirty next birthday. It's like someone has set a clock ticking inside me and I'm yearning for something I can't quite reach. Do I wait for Ty and me to want the same things, hoping that some time apart means we end up on the same page, or do we both want completely different things now?

'I could always see if there's something at the supermarket with me when you get back,' says Nellie, interrupting my thoughts again. 'Talk to the supervisor and see if there are any shifts going.'

'Or you could think about going to college and retraining,' says Lizzie.

Is that it? A new job? Or college? Is that what I'm yearning for? Is that what's missing in my life?

I shake my head. 'Thanks, but I was never one for written work. We know that by my non-existent exam results from school.'

'You were always the practical one,' says Nellie.

'You could train in something practical!' says Lizzie, keen to put everyone in their box, neat and ordered. Just like her job in the accountancy firm, where she has all her clients, their businesses in neat files, ordered and in their place. She's never been able to understand my inability to settle to one thing. But I've never found the one thing I wanted to do. I want to do it all! That's why life suits me as it is: working at the café and ice-cream kiosk in the summer, with shifts at the beach car park in Swn Y Mor, then waitressing and bar work in the winter at the hotel. Sometimes I help Mum and Martin on their stall at the farmers' markets, selling home-grown vegetables and honey. But there isn't really enough work for the three of us. I just help out when one of them needs to stay at the allotment at harvest time.

'We just worry about you,' says Lizzie. 'You don't seem to have any kind of plan! You should have taken over the beach café when you had the chance.'

'I would have mucked it right up! Ended up with everyone losing their jobs. You know what I'm like, trying to decipher big documents.' I remember having to stand up in class at school to read out a passage of Shakespeare, the words blurring, my eyes stinging, the laughter getting louder as I stumbled over the words. I'm far better as a member of the back-up crew than heading up the workforce. Nowadays I like to turn up, do my job and go home, without having to ask for help. School felt like torture. Getting out on to the beach for the summer, working in the café, serving ice creams, being with Ty, that's where I was happy.

'I had a plan. It didn't work out,' says Nellie, quietly.

'But you've got the boys,' I say, hoping she doesn't regret the choices she's made.

She shakes her head. 'Wouldn't change it for the world. But I'd like to be more intellectual, like you, Lizzie, so I could get a job that pays better. Move us out of the area we're in. I worry about my kids. If I'd planned it better I'd have had a partner who stayed with me and could afford to live somewhere I'm not terrified the boys are going to be sold drugs or mugged every time they go to the shops or out to play with friends. I wanted a family but I wish I'd thought things through and could give them a better start in life. You had a plan from the word go, Lizzie.'

'And I'd like to be able to cook like you,' says Lizzie, smiling for a change. It suits her. 'You can make a meal out of nothing.'

'Comes from necessity.' Nellie laughs. 'And you were so good at so many different things, Fliss,' she says to me.

'Just not really good at one thing in particular,' I say quietly. 'Really I'm happy doing what I do, a bit of everything.'

'Our Jack of all trades!' Lizzie rubs my hair, making it spiky, like Ty did, and I wish she wouldn't.

'Master of none,' I finish for her but with a good-natured smile. I don't want to spoil the mood. This has been nice, if a little strange. Here we are in Normandy, trying to work out how we've come to inherit a château. 'I wish Grandpa was here to share this with us,' I say.

'To Grandpa.' Nellie raises her cup of rough cider – we still haven't finished it – and her eyes fill with tears, as, surprisingly, do Lizzie's.

'He would have liked to see us together like this,' she says, and we clink cups and brave another sip of cider, taking a moment to think about Grandpa, the hole he's left behind.

'So, back to business.' Lizzie returns to the matter in hand. 'Nellie and I will head back in the morning. You'll stay here, speak to the estate agent and get it on the market. Agreed?'

'Agreed!' we all say.

'So, you're sure you're happy to stay here . . . on your own.'

'Yes, fine.' I think about the château. I'm keen to explore the place . . . and the flickering light in the turret, I think, with a leap of excitement. And I need to be away from Ty, for him to consider our future, my future, and whether or not he wants to be in it. I take a deep breath. It's just for a few days anyway.

'Right. I suggest we grab a bottle of wine from the shop in the square and work out where we're sleeping tonight,' says Lizzie.

'Fine. And we might be able to find out why we never knew about this place,' I add.

'And what we can do once we sell it,' Nellie's eyes glisten. 'I dream of a house with a garden and a working bathroom.'

'Is the ballcock still sticking in the loo? I could have done it if you'd said,' I say. Being in charge of the loos in the public car park has made me very good with ballcocks.

'I got Jason to have a look, but I think he might have broken it for good.'

Poor Nellie. She works so hard. Our inheritance could change her life.

'I'm going to take a holiday,' says Lizzie. 'A proper one. Who knows? I might even have time to plan a wedding!' She smiles. James is Lizzie's partner. He works for the civil service.

We all give each other a bit of a squeeze.

'What about you, Fliss?'

'I have no idea.'

'Maybe you could set yourself up in a business, like the café?' says Lizzie.

'Or go travelling.' Nellie warms to her theme. 'You've never left Swn Y Mor.'

'Because you didn't want to miss Tyler coming back for the summer,' says Lizzie. 'Maybe it's time.'

'Maybe,' I say. But, right now, I don't know which direction I'm turning in.

'I bet you could get work in other cafés or bars. Take some time to work out what you want to do in life,' says Nellie.

I smile, grateful for her understanding. And although we may not know why we've inherited this house, or why it was bought, I have a feeling this is going to change everything, for all of us.

6

We pay the bill with the man at the high bar, while his partner glares at us. Frankly, the meal was worth way more than we paid, apart from the awful cider and the scowling woman. I have no idea why she's quite so unhappy about us being there, or why the men at the bar haven't taken their eyes off us. But I don't think we should ask questions. We turn to leave, feeling like exhibits in a country showground, being assessed by critical eyes from the ringside.

'*Merci*, Monsieur,' I say, and leave a healthy tip, to improve relations and maybe get some more information at some point.

Lizzie starts to say, 'That's far too much,' as she always does. She may be an accountant, but I'm a waitress and I know that you can never leave 'too much'.

I nudge her. She tries to give me 'the look' but I manage not to catch her eye and turn to leave, pushing my purse into my bag, slung over me, like a poacher's.

'Really, Fliss! With you not working, you're really going to have to manage your money better,' she hisses, as if I'm a teenager. My sister thinks I'm foolish with money, men and work. Maybe she's right. Maybe I have been foolish, thinking life would just work out, and that one day Ty and I would be different. We've always just said, 'We'll see how things go.' But basically that's just a relationship without a title. I need to be a girlfriend, partner, fiancée. Or maybe I need a job as a chef or café owner that gives me enough satisfaction. Or, maybe . . . The words muddle in my brain. Maybe I need to be part of a family, my own family. A mum. That's what being here has made me understand. Ty and I are not okay as we are. We need to change. It just looks as if Ty doesn't see things as I do.

'Now what?' Lizzie asks. 'I'm thinking we should find somewhere to stay for the night.'

'We could always stay at the . . .' I struggle to say the words without sounding ridiculous '. . . the château.' The eyes from the bar are on us.

My sisters stare at me as if I'm mad.

'I think there was a small hotel across the square,' says Lizzie, pointing to the 'Auberge' sign on the half-timbered building there. And I know it's not a suggestion. I turn to the door just as it opens inwards, catching me off-guard, and stumble back, crashing into my two sisters behind me. It's the caretaker from the château.

He steps back and apologizes, his face set, holds out a hand and lets us leave, while seemingly glaring at someone in the restaurant.

'We'll talk to him later,' Lizzie says, into my ear. 'In private.'

As the restaurateur and the barflies watch us go, I have a feeling we're the subject of conversation. From the look on the caretaker's face, he has something on his mind, and we hurry off to the *auberge*.

7

'And you're sure you'll be okay?' says Nellie, hugging me tightly, as we stand at the bottom of the worn stone steps leading up to the front door of the château. Once again, early-morning mist is rolling down the long drive, weaving between the tree trunks and creeping up the overgrown lawn from the woods.

We'd all slept like logs in the comfy beds at the *auberge* last night, after an afternoon walking around the town, taking in the little streets, shops and church, followed by cheese and wine in our bedroom, watching *Emily in Paris* on Lizzie's iPad. Breakfast was a delight of *café au lait*, croissants and baguettes with beautiful unsalted butter and homemade apricot jam. The elderly owners eyed us with interest, polite, and said very little, but I'm sure they were wondering who we were and what we were doing there. They had the same look of curiosity tinged with suspicion as they moved as fast as their arthritic hips would let them to serve breakfast. I was tempted to offer them a seat while I made the coffee but Lizzie gave me one of her looks. Clearly, having guests, making beds, cleaning are hard work and I felt for them. I know how much my feet ache at the end of a day in the café.

'You'll speak to the agent, get it on the market, then work out the best way back, right?' Lizzie confirms.

'Yes, I'll be fine,' I reassure her.

'And you'll speak to the caretaker, will you? Tell him our plans and that he needs to tidy the place up. And explain there'll be new owners coming in. You'll have to be firm with him – he's obviously been allowed to get away with murder. He needs to know it has to be put right,' she fires at me.

'I can do that,' I reassure her.

'I can speak to him before I go, if you like. Maybe I should,' she says.

'I can do it. Really! You'll miss your ferry!' I wish she'd just hurry up and leave now. I'm dying to look around the place.

She looks doubtful. 'Okay. If he gives you any problems, get a mobile number from him and I'll speak to him. Same with the estate agent,' she says firmly.

'It'll be fine, don't worry. Now, go!'

'Yes, yes!' They climb into the car and shut the doors, then wind down the windows.

'And you're sure you're happy to stay here? Not in the *auberge*?' Nellie asks.

'Yes, I told you, I'm looking forward to exploring the place!'

They both look at each other.

'It's ours, we might as well use it! Much cheaper than staying in the *auberge*.'

'Are you okay for money? Here – have what I've got!' Lizzie empties her purse of euros into my hands.

'And make sure you eat!' says Nellie. 'Go back into town and find the shop!'

I take a deep breath. I'm twenty-nine and my eldest sister is telling me I need to make sure I eat. The middle one is handing me change from her purse. It's like I'm still twelve! Just because I haven't gone anywhere, it doesn't mean I haven't grown up.

They look back at the front façade of the château.

'I have no idea why he bought it, but all I can say is thank you, Grandpa.' Lizzie smiles. 'This is going to change everything. Finally, I'm going to set up in business on my own! My own business,' she repeats dreamily.

I can't help but smile back. It's what she's always wanted.

'And you'll be looking for somewhere new too,' I say to Nellie.

'And a new place to buy instead of rent if this place gets anything like what I think it could fetch!' says Lizzie, with a final look around.

We all take a moment to gaze at the château and feel very, very grateful. Suddenly my eye catches a movement, again, in what must be the east wing. A light flickering on and off. And then, as I look more closely, it stops. I definitely didn't imagine it. It's been three times now. I look around. Or maybe the low sun rising through the mist and the trees, lining the drive, burning off the rain from last night, made it look like that. The slowly rising sunlight bouncing off the panes of glass in the windows.

My sisters don't seem to have noticed anything untoward and are busy resetting the satnav. I turn back to the window but there's nothing. It must have been the sunlight, I tell myself firmly, not my mind playing tricks on me at the thought of being here on my own for a day or two.

With a final wave my sisters set off down the long drive, past hedgerows to one side, laden with berries, which, if my grandfather is to be believed, is a sign of a harsh winter to come. Hopefully, by the time it does, I'll be somewhere warm, either hot and sunny, or enjoying a fire in a log cabin on the ski slopes. Nellie and Lizzie wave out of the car windows as they pass the fields to the left on the way to the gates at the end of the drive. 'Don't forget to open the clutch slowly,' I call through cupped hands, 'to stop it stalling!' The car stalls and Lizzie restarts it. Nellie opens the gates and shuts them, waves and they drive off down the lane, with a toot-toot and bit of kangarooing.

Lizzie barely drives these days, now that she lives in the city but she insisted on taking the wheel on this trip. Either Nellie or I could have driven, but Lizzie likes to feel in control. Nellie drives her boys everywhere, in a clapped-out old banger that I've helped keep on the road for years. Grandpa always looked after his own car, and it was something I grew up doing.

As I hear the car's engine fade down the lane, I stand and listen. Silence. It's just me, and the mooing of cows from the field running along one side of the drive and behind the château, silhouetted in the sunlight. It's just me, and this huge house. I turn, and could swear I see a light flickering again, but the sun is now through the branches and on the windows. I unlock the door with the huge key and push it open. Just as before, my eyes are drawn up the wide wooden staircase to the big window on the half-landing. I put my hand on the smooth, worn, wooden banister as I start to climb the stairs. I can't help but think about the hands that have held it over the years before me, the stories in the wood, in the worn treads of the stairs. I have an overwhelming urge to make sure I see every room before I leave, so I have a memory of this place and why it might have ended up in our hands. I feel I owe it to the château to know it before we sell it on.

At the landing I stop and look out of the window, as far as I can see, fields of cows, white with brown, like they've been drizzled with melted chocolate. The morning autumn mist curls at their feet and around the base of the trees dotted across the fields, their leaves floating down in the morning light. My nose is practically pressed to the condensation on the big panes, with coloured glass in the corners. I'm dying to see more of this place.

I look at the corridor to my left and then to my right. I decide to go left, and open the first door I come to. I look up at the ceiling and the ornate plasterwork, then at the faded paper on the walls.

How did my grandfather own a château in France and none of us knew anything about it? The question goes round and round in my head. And how could he have allowed it to become so neglected? Why didn't he live in it instead of in a rented cottage on his own until I moved in with him? It seemed to make sense at the time. Grandpa liked the company after Grandma died. He had downstairs, I had upstairs, and Ty could come and go between his grandparents' house by the sea and Grandpa's cottage when he wasn't away. And there was this, just standing here.

I feel an overwhelming sense of sadness. The man I loved and looked up to as a father figure after Dad died, perhaps I never knew him at all. I thought we were close. I thought we shared so much.

I move on down the long corridor from room to room. It's like the place was just locked up and left, bedclothes still on the beds. From the servants' rooms on the next level, the attic floor, with its small windows, there is a separate staircase, spiralling down the turret to the curved kitchen door. I step inside to find a wood-burning stove, coffee and cups in the cupboards, plates, cutlery, everything you'd need to cater for a big house like this. Everything is in its place as if time has stood still. And in the basement, there is a sink, and a door that leads straight out on to an overgrown vegetable patch. Grandpa loved gardening. He would have loved this, wouldn't he? So why hadn't he lived here and tended this plot?

There's a laundry down here too. And more storage rooms that are really dark. I pull out my phone to use as a torch. One is full of barrels and I'm not going into it now.

It would make a fantastic place to get married if Lizzie was serious about wanting to do that. Although, knowing her, she'll probably decide on a Caribbean island, in a hotel, with every modern touch.

Back in the kitchen, I catch a glimpse of the caretaker in the field behind. It's as good a time as any, I think, and take a deep breath.

'Excuse me! *Excusez-moi!*' I move outside the back door and wave from the steps there, then make my way down them to the hedge and get caught in brambles. 'Monsieur!' I call, through the hedge of deep green holly, with red berries, and hawthorn. Maybe there would have been a better time and place to have this conversation.

He stops, surrounded by cows, and turns to me as do the cows. I shuffle along the hedge, fully loaded with red berries of various types, and take that as another warning of an icy winter to come. If I think it's cold in the château now, imagine what winter will be like. We must make sure the pipes don't burst. That's why the place has a caretaker, right?

I find a dip in the hedge and am once again surprised by how attractive the stony-faced caretaker is. His face is set as he looks at me, not in the least welcoming. A bit like the icy winter to come. Cold and frosty.

'*Excusez-moi!*' I repeat and then, having exhausted my French, switch to English, hoping he'll understand. 'The house, the château,' I correct. 'We are the new owners. It's in a very bad state. It needs lots of cleaning and clearing up. Could you start, do you think?' And when he says nothing, I try to channel my inner Lizzie. 'I don't need to remind you that you live here rent-free and we need to see some effort. By the look of it, there hasn't been any for a long time. So . . . if you please.' I'm feeling quite proud of myself for taking control of the situation.

The caretaker stares at me and then says, 'If you are the new owners, I suggest you put in some effort yourselves!' He walks away, followed by the herd, like security surrounding a cabinet minister, separating him from the general public.

'Er . . . excuse me!' I call again, and I'm not sure what I'm more surprised by: his reply or his excellent

English. 'Maybe if you stopped looking at cows and actually did what you were paid for!' All control of the situation slips away from me as I watch him walk away. Well, really! Rude, I think. Now what am I going to do? I can't tell Lizzie I've tried to talk to him and he told me to do it all myself. Perhaps I should go round to the farmhouse, a more suitable place for a discussion, and find out what his problem is. Although I suspect, like the woman in the crêperie, he doesn't want people from the UK here, snapping up 'bargains'. Not that I think the château is a bargain. As Nellie said, it must cost a fortune to run. As I turn back to the house, I think I hear a piano playing. I stop. It stops. Like the lights going on and off. Could this place have a ghost?

I walk back up the steps to the kitchen and along the short corridor, through the arch into the main hall, up the stairs again, this time wondering what I'm looking for, nervous and excited at the same time. I go along the corridor in the opposite direction this time, to the east wing, until I reach double doors, with ornate worn gold trim all around them. I try to open them, but they're locked, or stuck.

I go up the next flight of stairs to the attic floor and more small rooms, full of junk, or maybe treasure: I pick up small figurines, and run my hand over an old cot.

Then I walk back down the stairs to the first floor, wondering how many people have used them before me, wondering if one was Grandpa, as I listen for the piano again.

I look out of the window, then turn back to the landing to go downstairs to the main hall and suddenly jump back, my heart lurching. I feel as if someone has thrown a bucket of cold water over me.

'Gah!'

I hold my breath. There's no such thing as ghosts, there's no such thing as ghosts, I repeat. But now a ghost is standing right in front of me.

8

'I thought you'd gone!' says the ethereal figure standing with the light behind them, on the landing, looking not unlike Cruella de Vil from *The Hundred and One Dalmatians*. A white streak in otherwise dark hair piled on her head. A long lace-covered dress, heavy make-up, with pale powder that makes her look almost translucent. Oh, and a cross-looking pug cradled under one arm, her other hand, with painted nails, resting on its head. Again, I'm shocked, not least that she's speaking perfect English.

'Who – who are you?!' I demand, despite the quiver in my voice, a mix of excitement and fright. My heart is trying to return to its normal beat.

I hold the banister tighter, as if trying to keep a grip on reality. There's no such thing as ghosts, I repeat, like a mantra. Not talking ones anyway, with a pug under their arm.

I take in the pale dress, the long chain necklace with the charm at the end, the piled-up hair, the fair skin, the ornate buckle on the belt and the decorative chains hanging from it, with a key, a pair of glasses and a small pair of scissors.

'I am Madame Charlotte Cadieux,' she says, lifting her chin and head as if announcing herself to an awaiting audience. But I am no clearer as to who she is.

'The chatelaine here at Château des Arbres,' she says briskly. 'And you are?' She tilts her head slightly and looks at me through narrowed eyes.

'I'm Felicity Hope,' I reply, as if I should reply as formally as she introduced herself, then quickly follow it with 'Fliss, Fliss Hope,' not sure why I gave my full name. No one calls me Felicity, not even Mum. But nothing about this feels normal. In fact it's surreal, standing in front of this thin, gaunt yet immaculately dressed woman.

She nods, letting me know she understands.

'Sorry, the chatel . . . ?'

'The chatelaine. I am the mistress of the château,' she explains. 'And you?' She juts her chin at me, as if disapproving of everything about my appearance. I seem to be the one under interrogation here, when I should be demanding to know why she is in my grandfather's property.

'My, erm . . . my grandfather owns – owned this place.' My mouth is dry and I can't help staring at the elderly woman, with paper-thin pale skin on her hands and neck. And I realize she's doing the same to me. For a moment neither of us speaks.

Then she says, 'And if you are here . . . ?'

'He died a month ago.' My voice wobbles. I'm still finding it hard to believe that he's gone. Let alone that I'm standing in a château in France telling a woman I've never met before about my grandfather. 'In his sleep . . .' I add.

She lets out a sob and her legs seem to give way. I only just catch her as she falls.

'And you live here?' I help her to drink the glass of water I've pressed into her cold, shaking, bony hands, after guiding her to one of the deep wooden window-sills on the landing, then being directed through the previously locked door to a large neat apartment, with views over the drive and the lawn to the woods from a beautiful ornate, gold-framed chaise longue in front of the window. I poured water from the carafe beside the ornate bed, brought it back and handed it to her.

'All my life.' She sips the water gratefully, holding the glass in one shaking hand and rubbing the charm on her necklace with the other. 'And my family before that.' She sips again and it seems to be helping.

'I thought for one moment . . .' She swallows. 'You – you look like him.' She puts down the glass, pulls out a lace handkerchief and lifts it to her nose. 'Your short hair, like a boy's . . . Forgive me.'

'And you knew my grandfather?'

She clutches the handkerchief in one hand and her necklace in the other, smoothing it with her thumb. 'I do . . . did,' she says. 'I thought, for a moment, you were him.'

'You were expecting him?'

She shakes her head. 'No,' she says flatly.

'But you knew him?'

She nods, but seems to clam up and sips the water.

I run my hand over my short dark haircut, still wondering how this woman knew Grandpa. She seems as frail as a bird. But not a ghost. All real. A chatelaine, who lives in the château. Where else would a chatelaine live? I wonder how she'll take it when I tell her we're selling the place. But I have to. I take a deep breath.

9

'So, the agent said . . .' I'm standing at the back door of the big kitchen, after waking early and visiting the estate agent in town. I spent the rest of yesterday finding a bedroom to sleep in, up on the top floor in the servants' quarters. It didn't feel right to occupy one of the bigger, grander rooms on the first floor, and I felt keeping my distance from the chatelaine would be my best bet. After all, it's not every day a stranger moves into your home, even for a short time. I found bedding in the laundry room and sent photos to Mum, trying to find out if she had any idea how we came to own this place. But she was as shocked as Nellie, Lizzie and I were. Then I took a long, slow walk into town for some essential food shopping, mulling over the crossroads that Ty and I are at.

I'd hoped the walk and some shopping would take my mind off things, but with all of the looks I was getting, I didn't linger. Clearly, people want to know who I am and why I'm here, but I'm not really sure myself.

I'm leaning against the door frame, looking at the overgrown vegetable patch and on to the fields behind, still full of the white and chocolate cows. One hand is pressing a mug of coffee to my chest for comfort and warmth, the other holding my phone up to get a better signal so that I can see my two sisters, eagerly waiting to hear my news.

'Yes?' they say in unison, peering at me from the screen.

I let out a long sigh. It's not what they want to hear, I think, as I look out on the yellow, gold, orange and red of the falling leaves, trying to snapshot this almost perfect autumnal day.

'He said,' I take a run at it, 'that it will be impossible to sell.'

'What?' Lizzie is the first to react. 'What do you mean "impossible to sell"? That can't be right!'

'Is that because of the, um, chate– the old lady living there?' asks Nellie.

'The chatelaine. Madame Charlotte Cadieux. *Oui* – I mean yes,' I say, surprising myself with my French.

'But surely if we made her some kind of offer,' says Lizzie, already crunching numbers.

I shake my head. 'Really, she's not going anywhere.' I bite my bottom lip. 'Her family have lived here for generations. And there's something else you should know.'

My stomach knots. Why would lovely Grandpa do this to us?

The sky outside the back door is darkening and so is my sisters' mood. I stand back to close the door and can see all the cows lying down in the field behind the house. That looks ominous.

'Fliss, what is it? What else could there possibly be? We've got a house.'

'A château,' I correct.

'A château, with a sitting tenant, that the estate agent says we can't sell! Of course we can. We'll just offer her a deal, a cut of the profit, to move out. Surely—'

'It's not just that.' I stop her. 'She's not just a sitting tenant, the property was sold as *viager occupé*.'

'What's that?' asks Lizzie, sharply.

'It means she has a right to stay here until she dies. Then the house belongs fully to the owner, for them to sell on or whatever.'

'Right. And how old do you think she is? How well is she?'

'Lizzie!' Nellie and I exclaim.

'It was just a question. I'm being practical! I can't be the only one thinking it!'

I clear my throat. 'She's – I don't know – late seventies maybe? And I have no idea about her fitness, although she is very slim, and doesn't seem to have a problem with stairs. But the point is,' I say, trying not to be distracted by Lizzie's questioning from what I need to get across, 'not only does she have the right to stay here,' I'm trying to remember everything the estate agent said, 'but when the owner, the landlord so to speak, bought it they would have paid a small sum, a deposit on the château.'

Writing it down wouldn't have helped me. I'm much better at remembering things. Ask me to write it down or read aloud and the words jumble themselves. Letters too can get mixed up. I've had special glasses and tinted paper, and if I really concentrate I can do it, but if I'm trying to read quickly, I can't take in what's in front of me. I like to get patterns in place where I'm working. Use tills that add up. Being dyslexic has meant I've always had coping mechanisms, and in my workplaces, I have my techniques. It's new situations that present problems.

'So, not the full amount?' Lizzie asks. I can see she's taking notes.

'That's right.'

'Well, at least we know Grandpa didn't have a secret stash of money he ploughed into this place.'

'He would have paid a deposit,' I confirm, 'and then a monthly sum to the tenant. Like an income.'

'A what?'

'An allowance?'

'How much?'

'If I heard the figures correctly, it's not peanuts,' I say uncomfortably.

'Okay, I'll email the solicitor,' says Lizzie, used to taking over in matters like this, 'and find out why we didn't know. Really, someone should have explained this.'

I hear my sister tapping on her keyboard.

'So what you're saying is,' says Nellie, slowly, 'we have to pay this lady a monthly allowance. We're paying her to stay there.'

'Correct,' I confirm.

'And where is the money supposed to come from?' she says, processing the news with a shake in her voice.

'Okay, I've googled *viager*. Jeez!' says Lizzie, staring at her screen. 'She's right. There's a monthly allowance due. Wish someone would pay me that for doing nothing!'

'Where does it come from?' Nellie's panicked now.

There's a moment of silence before Lizzie cuts to the chase: 'The château owners,' she replies. 'Us!'

'But I can barely pay for my groceries each month! I've got a third-hand Android phone and an electricity bill I can't pay. I've had to cancel the internet. How on earth am I supposed to pay "an allowance" to a woman I don't know living in a château in France?' Nellie sounds close to breaking point.

'The money from Grandpa's bank account isn't going to last long,' says Lizzie. 'We'll need to think of something.'

'Don't panic. I'll find a way, I promise,' I say, trying to reassure Nellie. And then a thought occurs to me. 'Maybe there's something here we can sell. I mean, there's a lot of furniture.'

Lizzie lets out a long sigh and taps a painted nail impatiently on the desk in front of her. 'But it's not just this month's payment that's due. This is like, for ever, until she dies,' she says, in her usual blunt manner.

We stare at each other.

'And what happens if we don't pay?' Nellie asks, her voice shaking.

'The property will revert to the original owner and their family,' I say calmly.

'So if we can't pay the allowance each month, we lose the lot,' Lizzie says, clearly frustrated. She slams a pen on to her desk, then hits the keys again. 'She's right. It's a legally binding contract. It says here that if we don't pay, the property reverts to the previous owner.'

'And we'll get nothing?'

'Correct,' I say. 'That means Nellie won't be able to move. Lizzie doesn't get her business and the chance to plan her wedding. And I won't be able to stay on in Grandpa's cottage unless I find a job I can actually stick at.'

'What are we going to do?' says Nellie.

I swallow. 'There's something else,' I say, though I can barely speak.

'Yes?' they say expectantly.

'Something the estate agent thought I should be made aware of.'

'A buyer? Someone willing to take it over with a life-long tenant?'

I shake my head. 'We'll owe taxes on the property too. As the owners, we'll have to pay land tax on the first of January. The bigger the house, the more you pay.'

We've fallen into a deep pit of despair – or into the money pit that Grandpa has left us with.

10

Having finished the call with my sisters, and promising I would see what we could sell to meet the tax bill and the monthly allowance, I clutch my head in despair. There must be something. A room of hidden treasure, a cellar full of expensive wine . . . If not, the château returns to the family.

Right now, I need to try to help mine.

I grab my coat off a chair, head for the back door and some fresh air to clear my head. I walk down the steps to the vegetable plot. It's a mess but I can see a few surviving vegetables. There may be onions, butternut squash too . . . Beyond the vegetable plot, in the field, all the cows are still lying down and the sky is very dark. I walk out of the vegetable plot to the front of the château and stare across the overgrown lawn. I decide to walk along the boundary of the château, then to the woods. The more I'm walking, the more I won't be sitting still, wondering how we came to be in this mess and, more importantly, how we're going to get out of it.

I pull my phone out of my pocket and take a picture. I contemplate sending it to Ty, but decide against it. He'll contact me when he's had time to think. I send the picture to Mum instead.

I think again about my conversation with Ty before I came here. Those words tumbling out of my mouth. I could tell the next surfing trip was on his mind, his next job, not what I was talking about. Ty will always find a way to get to the waves. He's a free spirit. That's what we liked about each other. So, what on earth made me come out with my comment about 'our children'? We've never discussed having any, and I have no idea where it came from. It just seemed natural. I'd felt a change in me, a slow shift, as the summer passed and autumn rolled in. Watching families on the beach, still braving the sea in wetsuits, walking dogs and playing games, wondering if this would be us one day. Would we have grandchildren who would come to Swn y Mor for holidays with their surfboards, and have lessons with Ty? Would I have a grandchild who loved me like I loved Grandpa?

The wind whips up, making me tuck my arms tighter around myself. There is a change in the air. Is it Grandpa passing? Everything seems to have shifted. I mean, clearly this place, and trying to work out what to do with it. But also a sort of yearning inside me for something. Tears spring to my eyes and I don't know why. Maybe it's all tied up with Grandpa, the stress of being here. But I can't help thinking about what I'm going home to. It can't be more of the same, waiting for Ty to come back to his family holiday home and picking up where we left off. Time seems to have stood still for Ty and me: nothing has changed since we first met. And now a clock is ticking inside me. Somehow being here has shown me that time is slipping through my fingers. I don't want to be left on an empty beach, waiting for Ty to return. I wonder if he is thinking about us. If he'll see this, too, and get in touch. Maybe he'll come out here and surprise me, tell me he wants the same things I do. Maybe this break is just what we needed.

Something rustles in the hedge and suddenly I see a huge white head poking through it, making me stumble back. It's the biggest horse's head and neck I've ever seen. I don't know much about horses but I did help out at Pony Club Camp in the summer holidays a few years ago, but that was more plaiting manes and tails and helping with the fancy dress costumes and gymkhana games, including finding sacks for the sack race. The riders had to gallop up the beach, jump off into sacks and race back to the finish line. I had to come up with stuff for the obstacle race, potatoes and spoons for the 'egg' and spoon race, that kind of thing. Brian from the beach café wasn't happy when half of his spoons went missing for the afternoon. I'm surprised he had me back after that. I'm not sure he will this time. But I don't want to go back to working for people who are too caught up with their profit margins to make the café a nice place to visit. Part of me wishes I'd taken it over when the old owner retired and offered me the lease, but I didn't think I could.

Once again, there is a shift inside me. The easy-come-easy-go life I've lived for so many years seems to be getting harder. Work is getting tricky to find, especially when keen young students, mostly second-home owners' children, are looking for cash-in-hand holiday jobs. And with Grandpa gone, I have a feeling it won't be long until the rent goes up on the cottage. The owner knows he can get much more for it as a holiday let. The horse rolls back its lips, showing its big teeth, and whickers. I jump again and laugh.

'Hey, you gave me a start!' I stretch out a hand for the horse to sniff, then run it over his neck. It's so thick, he's like the bodybuilding champion of the horse world.

'Hello,' I say. 'Or should that be *bonjour*?' I smile as I pat the solid neck. 'And what's your name, eh?'

'Pegasus,' comes a deep reply in a thick French accent.

I glance around and laugh, putting my hand over my mouth. 'Well, *enchantée*, Pegasus,' I say, patting the horse and wondering where the voice came from.

'*Enchanté*,' says the voice, making me smile and then a head appears, a human one this time, beside Pegasus, and my smile drops. It's him. The one I thought was the caretaker. My cheeks burn.

'*Bonjour*,' he says, a smile tugging at his lips. He's laughing at me. I bristle. It's a familiar feeling, when I mess up, when I can't get things right in my head, numbers or words. A feeling of being laughed at, like in school. I couldn't wait for the holidays and for Ty to be there, taking me to a life where these things didn't matter, and the ice-cream kiosk where I had all the prices rounded up and written down so I wouldn't get into a pickle. It was a well-practised routine.

I clear my throat and, hopefully, my thoughts. 'I, um, look, I meant to say, about yesterday.'

'Yesterday? *Hier?*' He looks at me as if he's going to prolong my agony by asking me to remind him.

'When I,' I clear my throat, 'mistook you for the . . . uh-hum . . . caretaker.'

'Ah, yes, when you said I needed to spend less time looking at cows and more doing the job I'm paid to do.'

I cringe.

'Well, like I say, I'm sorry about that. I realize now, having spoken to the estate agent and meeting Madame Cadieux, that you're not the sitting tenant in the property nor the caretaker of this house.'

'No,' he says, putting a head collar over the big horse's soft grey nose, which twitches.

I stroke Pegasus's neck for distraction as much as comfort. 'I'm Fliss by the way.'

'Jacques.' He nods.

'He's enormous,' I say.

'He is. He's a Percheron.'

'A what?'

'A Percheron. One of the heavy horses. They come from Normandy. Workhorses, like the shires you have.'

'Ah, yes.'

'He weighs a tonne.'

'I'm sure.'

'No, literally, a tonne. That's his weight.' He flicks a strap over the horse's head, behind the ears, and catches it expertly, then buckles it. 'Only he doesn't know his own strength. Keeps pushing down fences by leaning into them when he wants to say *bonjour*,' he says, clipping a leading rope to the underside of the head collar. 'He always wants to be a part of things. Doesn't like to be left out.'

'Ah.' I realize I'm leading him astray.

'He is, as you say, a gentle giant,' he says. 'He will do anything for apples,' and the big horse snuffles at his pockets. I think about the rough cider we drank at the restaurant, but also the beautiful apple brandy.

'*Viens!* Come!' He gently tugs at the rope and the horse reluctantly allows himself to be led away.

'So, as I say, sorry about the – um – misunderstanding,' I repeat, just to make sure there's no bad feeling left.

The farmer stops and turns back to me. 'And now?' he asks. 'What are your plans?'

I shrug. 'Now we know about the sitting tenant, *en viager*, and the money this place has to make just to keep going, I'm not sure . . . See what I can find of value to sell from it, I suppose.'

'Not everything around here is for sale,' he says, and walks away with the horse.

As I stand there, perplexed, big fat raindrops begin to fall.

By late afternoon, there is a break in the rain and, with nothing to eat in the house, I step out into the vegetable garden and the tangle of weeds. I find some comfort in it, as if I'm at home with Mum and Martin on their smallholding. I weed all afternoon and find the makings of a soup I can cook for dinner.

I take the vegetables inside, switch on the lights in the kitchen and put them on the side. The lights flicker on and off. And I wonder if the chatelaine is playing with them. I must ask her about that. Then I go back outside to the pile of logs and collect some to light the wood-burner. It looks like the model Grandpa had, but bigger. The dark clouds roll in once more and the rain comes heavier than before. The lights flicker again. I wonder if they'll go off altogether. They do. I sigh. Where's the fuse box? When I see it, high on the kitchen wall, I grab a broom, pull up a chair and flick the trip switch. Just like I had to in Grandpa's cottage when something tripped. Then I jump down and run outside for more wood, just to be on the safe side. As I stand up, my arms full, I see people walking along the drive. It's a couple and they're carrying something.

They spot me and wave.

'Hello! *Bonjour!*' the man says, holding a little boy's hand while trying to shield the woman, who has a toddler in her arms. I put down the wood and hurry towards them down the drive.

The rain gets heavier. I can barely hear him. With my spare arm, I wave them towards me to take cover. 'Come in, come in!' I call, as the rain lashes down, waving them towards the front door.

They rush up the steps to the door as I hold it open. Once they're in, I shut it. The lights flicker again.

The man and woman are dripping wet, clearly grateful to be out of the rain. The little boy is shivering as the family slide off their hoods, and the woman sets the toddler on the floor where he hugs her legs and scowls at me.

'Sorry, um, *excusez* . . .' the man begins.

'Oh, I'm English,' I say. 'I'm Fliss. Are you two okay?' Pools of water are gathering at their feet.

'Come into the kitchen,' I tell them, leading the way. 'I'm lighting the fire.'

The couple look around the hall.

Suddenly, as one, they catch their breath and step back. Now the toddler hides his face in his mother's legs. I wonder what's stopped them in their tracks and step back into the hall.

'Ah, Madame,' I say to Charlotte, with a nod. 'The chatelaine of the château,' I tell the family and see them relax a little as she nods, tilting her head.

'We have some visitors sheltering from the rain,' I tell her, and she seems as curious about them as they are about her . . . and the flickering lights.

'Our car broke down at the end of your drive. We hit a pothole. A tyre blew out,' the man tells me, as I take their coats and hang them by the fire in the kitchen. 'I'm Tom, and this is my wife, Niamh.'

'It was all a bit frightening and I'm afraid this little one's had enough of travelling. He threw up everywhere,' says Niamh, who's about my age, 'didn't you, Arthur?' She smiles, picks him up and he cuddles into her.

'We were looking for somewhere to stay the night. We're on our way back to the ferry port.'

'Well, there's an *auberge* in the town. I could try to find a number,' I say, as Charlotte joins us in the kitchen. It's the first time I've seen her downstairs. '*Mais non*,' she says, and tuts. 'Is too far on foot, with the little ones.' She gives Arthur a little smile and reaches a hand to him. 'And in this weather.' She tuts again.

'You're right. Let me check we have hot water and you can get cleaned up. You're welcome to stay – if I have bedding that is – until the mechanic can fix your car.'

'Sometimes in life we have to make the best of where we are,' says the chatelaine, with a slow nod. 'And who we end up with.' I presume from this that she's as unhappy about me being here as I am at finding out her status in the place. But this sounds like an olive branch.

'I phoned a breakdown service, a local mechanic, from the car. But he said it will be the morning now before he can get to us,' says Tom, a smile spreading across his face. 'Are you a B-and-B, a *chambre d'hôte*?'

'No,' I say.

'Bedding and towels in the laundry room,' Charlotte says quietly but clearly to me, holding up a neatly polished nail and pointing to the room off the kitchen at the back of the house. 'Where the boiler is. Oh, *la*, the boiler! I hate that thing,' she says, sitting down.

'Right,' I say, taking a deep breath and heading into the laundry room. When I come back, I tell them to follow me. 'I'll show you to the bedrooms you can use, and a bathroom.'

When I've shown them the main bedroom, the room next door and the bathroom opposite, the family thank me again.

'Really, it's fine,' I say, as I hand them towels, whip off dust sheets and start making the beds, with Niamh's help. Tom runs back to the car to bring in a bag and gets soaked again.

As they head off to have hot baths, and the big beast of a boiler rumbles out of hibernation and into life, I go about making soup. 'It's all I have,' I say, looking at Charlotte for help.

'Perhaps you could get some milk from next door. Jacques, the farmer? For ze little ones. His cheese is very good too.' She raises her pencilled eyebrows.

'Next door?' I say.

'Yes, next door. At the end of the drive.'

'Um, I don't think the farmer will want to help me.'

She shrugs. 'The shops are all closed now.'

Have I any other options? The lights flicker but stay on.

'Madame,' I say, 'about the lights in your apartment flickering yesterday?'

'Ah, you have caught me out. It has been a long time since anyone has visited this place. I thought you were nosy buyers, wanting to get a cheap property out here. It happens. People see the house and think they can come in and look around.'

'So you act like it's haunted?'

She smiles. 'It has worked.'

I can't help but smile too. 'But why?'

'This place was shut up to visitors a long time ago.' Her smile slips.

'And now?' I ask tentatively, thinking of the family in the big main bedroom on the first floor.

Her smile returns. 'It is nice to hear their voices,' she says. 'And Jacques, next door, tell him I sent you.' She lifts her chin high. 'This place was always full of people. We were the heart of the town. It is good to hear laughter again,' she adds, as we hear the family upstairs running the bath. 'Jacques will make sure you have enough.'

Well, it's worth a try, I think, with a sigh. I pull on my chunky boots and still-wet coat, pull up the hood, and walk along the dark, potholed drive, shining my phone torch.

11

It's cold, and I'm shivering. The rain is pelting down, stinging my face, dripping from the ends of my short hair, and the wind joins in to punish me further.

I knock at the front door of the farmhouse, the golden glow from the lights inside spilling out onto the puddles that are quickly forming. For a moment I think no one will answer. I'm about to leave when the door opens with a creak, as if it's rarely used.

'*Oui?*' he says, and then, seeing it's me, frowns.

'I . . .' I'm tongue-tied. How do I explain I've taken in some people who needed somewhere to stay but have no food for them, and could he give me some? 'The car, at the end of the drive, it's broken down.'

'*Oui.*' He nods.

'The mechanic is coming in the morning.' I pull my

collar tighter around my neck as the rain splats down on it. I take a deep breath. 'The chatelaine sent me.'

He opens the door wide and invites me through the warm living room into a big kitchen with a soft old sofa and another wood-burner.

I look around for any signs of anyone else. There is a colourful rucksack on the table. A woman's coat by the back door, boots too. But he is on his own in the kitchen.

'You say the chatelaine sent you? Is everything okay? Does she need something?'

I nod. 'Oh, yes. It's just that the couple who have broken down have a little boy and a toddler. They're getting cleaned up in the château. I have made soup but . . .'

'You need cheese, bread, too. Maybe.' He walks into a pantry, coming out with his arms full, a round of cheese, a baguette, what looks like a bottle of cider, an apple cake and a small jug of cream.

I take the bread from him. 'It's so much fresher than the one I got from the *boulangerie* in town,' I say, and frown. The baguette I bought when visiting the estate agent had been hard in no time.

'Ah,' he says, with a knowing nod, and I wonder what he's not telling me, but he busies himself filling the basket.

'This is very kind of you.'

'They have children. We will do what we can. We are a welcoming town,' he says, adding a jar of chutney to the basket.

I feel suddenly miffed. Not to me they're not. I haven't felt in the least bit welcomed. 'Is that homemade cheese?' I ask.

'Yes. It's what we do here, on the farm. Make cheese, with the milk from the cows.' He hands me the basket.

'I can pay,' I say, pulling out euros.

He holds up a hand. 'Like I say, we're a welcoming town. We want people to come back here.'

'Just not me, or my family,' I say slowly.

He looks straight back at me, his dark eyes the colour of the autumn leaves that have been falling. His hair is curly and wild, with a dark beard. And something about him feels familiar.

'*C'est compliqué,*' he says.

'Why?' I push. 'Why is it complicated?' He clearly knows something.

He says no more and hands the basket to me. 'Your guests will be waiting,' he says, with a firm look.

'Why is it *compliqué*? Tell me!' I persist.

Suddenly, the lights flicker on and off.

'It happens. In the rain.' He shrugs. 'Sometimes they go out altogether.'

I bite my lip and roll my eyes. 'Not a ghost, then?'

'No.' He gives a sardonic laugh. 'Not a ghost. Just the weather.' And I bristle.

'Of course!' I say, pulling myself up from my shoulders. 'Everyone knows there is no such thing as ghosts.'

He gazes at me steadily. 'Ghosts,' he says, 'come in all

different forms.' I'm a bit taken aback. What does he mean? I open my mouth to ask, but before I can he says, 'Now take these. Your guests will be waiting.'

Holding the basket I slip back out into the wet, dark night, 'Why?' still buzzing in my head. Why is it complicated for me and my family to be here? What does he know?

12

That night, I lie in my bed in the small attic room, up the staircase in the turret, above the kitchen. I can still taste the cheese we ate in front of the fire in the dining room, with the candles lit, and the delicious cider – which was nothing like the one we drank at the crêperie.

What are we going to do? We can't sell the place by all accounts. And I'm not sure selling the furniture is a good enough plan.

Madame Cadieux's words from last night keep rolling around my head: *Sometimes in life we have to make the best of where we are . . .*

As morning comes, I've barely slept. There is a chill in the air. A change as the wind outside puffs through the long windows.

I get up, put on as many of my clothes as I can, and prepare to go down to make my guests coffee. I hope they don't find the place too cold. First, though, I stop to look out of the windows in my little room, at the mist rolling up from the lawn, the old formal gardens with urns on plinths, the old swimming pool, the patio and the cows beyond.

I pull the sleeves of my sweatshirt over my hands, wrap my arms tightly around myself and head down the servants' staircase to the kitchen. It still feels warm in there from last night. When I open the door to the wood-burner, it's stayed alight. The embers glow cheerfully at me. All those years of learning to keep in the old wood-burner at the village pub and in my grandfather's cottage seem to have paid off. I toss another log on to the glowing embers as the last falls apart. The wood is dry and catches straight away. The orange flames lick up and around the log and I shut the cast-iron door with a squeak, open the vents and let the flames grow with the air and in confidence.

I dust off my hands and look at the fire basket, knowing I'll have to go out and refill it to keep the place warm today. 'Breakfast first.' I wonder what I can offer my overnight guests. It's not as if the *boulangerie* is just down the road and I haven't any transport.

There's bread from last night I can toast. And the amazing butter. Apples, cheese, all from the basket Jacques sent me back with. I start to gather what I can find and lay it on the kitchen table, next to the wood-burner, rather than relighting the fire in the dining room. I fill the big kettle and put it on top of the wood-burner to boil. I have chocolate, too, and break it into pieces to go with the toasted bread, just like we did when I was a child on that camping holiday. We would have fresh bread from the bakery, and chunks of chocolate broken up in it. And dip it in hot chocolate. I decide to heat some milk for my guests, maybe warm milk and melted chocolate.

As I'm thinking this, the door opens and there stands Madame Charlotte Cadieux, looking as if she has been up for hours, her hair neatly piled on top of her head, her dress worn but clean and starched, wearing the necklace she always wears and her belt around her waist.

'I thought I heard noises.' She stares at the laid table and the kettle.

'I'm just making breakfast for our guests. Would you like some?' She looks like she never eats, she's so thin.

'*Non*,' she says, in her clipped tones. 'Just some coffee, *merci*.'

She's talking to me as if I'm the housemaid, but I make the coffee and hand it to her. Will it live up to her standards? How can I tell her I'm not a housemaid and that I'll be leaving soon? Once we've worked out what to do with this place.

'*Merci*,' she says, lowers her nose to it and inhales. Then, slowly, she tastes, and gives a nod of satisfaction. I feel strangely pleased with myself. Years of knowing how much customers enjoy their coffee at the café, and not listening to how I'm told to make it in the most cost-efficient way, might have paid off. I smile.

Madame Cadieux picks up her cup, stirs in some cream, then makes for the door. 'I shall take this in my apartment,' she says, her head held high. 'Next time you go to the *boulangerie*, make sure you get the fresh bread, not yesterday's. That bread he sold you yesterday was *dégueulasse*! Disgusting! Never settle for anything second best in life!'

She opens the door as the family appear on the other side of it. Tom and Niamh, their older son Harry and little Arthur, tucked into his father's legs and staring incredulously at Madame Cadieux, who wishes them 'Good morning'. She walks steadily into the hall and up the huge staircase to her apartment, in the east wing. As she goes, she turns and winks at Arthur.

The little boy's eyes are wide with wonder.

'Dad, are you sure there's no such thing as ghosts?' asks Harry.

'Do you want there to be?' whispers Tom, with a smile.

'Oh, yes! It'd be so cool when I get back to school.'

'In that case, I'd say definitely!' Tom laughs and Harry beams.

'Ghost!' says little Arthur, who smiles and waves at Madame Cadieux.

Although Madame Cadieux barely moves her head as she drifts up the stairs, I swear I see a mischievous smile on her lips.

'Come in, come in,' I say to Tom, Niamh and the boys, waving them in front of the warm fire. They look refreshed. So, despite the loud clanking of pipes, I'm presuming the boiler worked well enough for them to wash.

'How did you sleep?' I say, pulling out cups and saucers, in beautiful patterns, from the glass-fronted dark-wood dresser and rinsing them under the warm water of the tap as they gather around the table. I put another log on the wood-burner and shut the door. 'There's coffee, and I've warmed some milk, from next door's cows,' I say, wondering how I'm going to thank Jacques. He may not want me here, but clearly he's not all bad. I show them to the table where I'm laying out plates and butter.

'Really, you don't need to . . .' Niamh goes to protest, little Arthur snuggled into her side. My body aches with a previously unknown yearning, for a sense of belonging, to a family, a unit, a couple, as a gust of wind blows autumnal leaves at the window in the back door.

'It's fine, just leftovers, I'm afraid. I haven't got a car to get to the *boulangerie*. And I doubt the bread van has visited here for years.' I busy myself, making more coffee and heating more milk, and sliding the plate of broken chocolate towards the little boys, whose eyes light up. 'Dip it in the milk,' I say conspiratorially, and we all smile at each other.

'Now, anything else I can get you?' I say, as they dunk their toast, loaded with butter, into the hot creamy coffee.

'No, really, you've been amazing, thank you,' says Tom, and Niamh agrees.

'I don't know what we would have done without you,' she says.

'Is there anything we can do to return the favour?' says Tom. 'Spread the word, write on Tripadvisor?'

'No, no.' I laugh. 'I'm not—'

'You are going to be setting up as a B-and-B, aren't you?' says Tom.

'This place is amazing. So many original features. People will love it.' Niamh lifts her phone to photograph her coffee and toast, then the wood-burner. 'And you're such a great host. Have you always been in hospitality?' she asks.

'Um, no, well, not really – just the local café, and the ice-cream kiosk, a bit of car-park attending, and occasional shifts at the local pub.' The words are tumbling out of my mouth. 'Well, I was sacked, sort of – laid off – from the café. Always giving out too big portions,' I finish.

'But you're going to set up a B-and-B here, aren't you?' she persists.

'Oh, no. We were hoping to sell it. But it's complicated,' I say, remembering Jacques last night.

'But you have to!' says Niamh, as her boys happily eat their toast with the warm chocolate milk.

I think about Madame Cadieux's words, how this house was always filled with people, fun and laughter.

How it was the heart of the town. Well, clearly that's not true any more. But maybe it could be full of people again. I can feel it somehow – coming back to life. A home . . . the family home it once was. It's in the walls of the place.

'Please do think about it . . . and if there's anything we can do to help . .' Tom slides his card across the table, along with several folded euro notes.

'Oh, no! Really!' I try to hand him them back but he holds up his hands.

'We're very grateful. We've loved being here – with the cows, Madame Cadieux and her piano playing last night after dinner.' He smiles. 'And we want to say we were your first paying customers. But now we should get going. The mechanic was out early, the car is fixed and we have a ferry to catch.'

'Thank you again,' says Niamh, and looks as if she'd like to hug me but Arthur is wrapped around her, sitting on her hip as they stand to leave. Once again, I feel a twinge, a pull, a yearning in me, like roots searching for water . . . yet I have roots, back home. I feel a fizz of excitement as my guests leave through the big front hall, taking in the ceilings, the wood panelling and paintings as they reluctantly leave, thanking me all over again, telling me that little Arthur loved watching the cows.

'Mooo!' he said, and nuzzled his mother's neck.

I stand on the wide step at the front door, waving, as the heavily laden car weaves and bounces down the long drive, past the line of trees. The mist is rolling across the lawn, down to the woods, and I glimpse what may be a deer. I turn to the huge ornate door. I think of Madame Cadieux gazing out of the window at the guests leaving, how she and the house had seemed to come alive again . . . I look up at the château. Could I pull this off? Is there any other way to make this place pay?

I go back into the house, smiling at the memory of Arthur and the cows, and open the back door to fetch fuel for the ever-hungry wood-burner. The cows. I smile. And stop smiling very quickly. The cows are all over the recently weeded vegetable patch. All over the vegetables!

'Hey!' I shout, grabbing and waving a tea towel at them, but the more I shout, the more they move in different directions, trampling the vegetables I worked to save.

'Jacques!' I see him from a distance, still riled by his welcoming of last night's guests and his avoidance of my questions, his loaded comment about ghosts coming in all forms. Well, two can play at that game. If he won't tell me what he knows about Grandpa and his connection to this place, he can keep his cows off my land. 'I need a word with you! *Un petit mot!*' I shout, through the trampled opening in the hedge between the château and the field. Fallen leaves swirl at my feet.

*

'But you said the little boys loved the cows . . . and the ghost!' He smiles, like he did when I was talking to Pegasus. It's a nice smile. Shame he doesn't produce it more often instead of the scowl he seems to wear permanently. Or maybe that's reserved for me. It seems everyone round here is welcome except me.

'That's not the point.' I put my hands on my hips. 'The point is the cows, roaming around on the château grounds.' The more I think about it, the B-and-B is the only answer. And I can't do that with his cows trampling all over the château's gardens.

'Pegasus must have pushed down the fence again,' he says, as he guides the animals back to the field.

'Well, fix it!' I say crossly. 'I have a business to set up here!' Suddenly I'm totally fired up about the B-and-B idea. I think of the folded euro notes on the table. It's a start in paying off what we owe on the place: the chatelaine's allowance and the tax bill. At least if we keep it going we have something . . . and, yes, maybe one day it will be ours to sell.

'A business?' Jacques crashes into my happy thoughts again, like an unwelcome guest at a party. Like Pegasus through the hedge, creating chaos.

'Yes, a business! This château needs to help pay for itself.'

Jacques narrows his eyes. 'And you know a lot about châteaux and château life, do you?'

I feel like I've been doused in a bucket of cold water, all my warmth gone. He's leaning on his stick, judging me, as the cows amble into the field.

'Well, as much as anyone who's never lived in one before,' I throw back at him. 'Anyway, what do you know about it? You're a farmer.' He's a cheese-maker . . . and there's no denying it, a really good one. But he has as much experience in running a château as I do by the look of it. And why should he care? It's not like I'm suggesting I set up a dairy herd to go into competition with him, 'I'm just trying to do what I can here.'

But my confidence starts to wobble. He's right. What do I know about château life? Nothing. Only what I've seen on the TV. I'm only here to work out what to do with the place.

My phone pings. It's Nellie ringing. I press decline. I take a deep breath and refocus on Jacques. My phone pings again to let me know I have a voicemail.

'Whether you like me being here or not, I am here. And I'm going to be setting up a business. Now keep your cows off the château gardens!' I turn to go.

'Like I say, it's impossible for you to run a business here at the château. You don't know anything about châteaux or château life!'

'Well, maybe more than you do!' I snap. My heart is thundering. I turn back to Jacques with a fire in my belly that only flares up when I think back to that day in school when I had to read aloud and everyone seemed to be laughing, making me feel useless. Well, right now, this is the only answer I have to pay the bills and I'm going to do all I can. If it means staying longer than I intended, that's what I'll have to do.

'The château. Things here are—'

'Complicated. I know! But I will be doing this, whether you like it or not.' Perhaps doing what I know how to do, make teas and coffees, make beds, will help us all. And what would I be going back to if I went home? An empty cottage with the memories of a grandpa I apparently didn't know at all. Trying to find work to pay the rent and waiting for Ty. Well, I'm done with waiting.

He glares at me. 'Let's hope the mayor approves of your plans.' He raises an eyebrow. 'You know you'll have to visit him. All new arrivals do, especially those who want to run a business here. It's the same over most of France,' he says, as if I should know that.

'Fine. I'll go and see the mayor.'

'Make sure you take a gift. An expensive one,' he calls, as I march back towards the château to get my bag and go to the town hall. If Ty wants a life with me, a future, he'll have to come and find me. As for Jacques, he'll just have to accept I'm here to stay.

Madame Cadieux is in the hallway. 'Is everyzing okay?' she asks. 'You look . . . how you say?' She waves a lace-trimmed hand. 'Flustered.'

'Oh, just . . .' I take a big breath. 'Madame, you should probably know, I'm going to try to run this place as a B-and-B, a *chambre d'hôte*. I'm sorry if you don't like—'

'How exciting!' Her eyes sparkle and I see an altogether new Madame Charlotte Cadieux in front of me. It seems a night with our guests has transformed her. 'It will be wonderful to have people in ze house again!' She clasps her hands. 'I must practise the piano.' She turns towards the big salon.

'But, Madame, you're going to have to stop pretending to be a ghost. Stop flickering the lights and playing the piano late at night.'

She looks at me.

'It's the only way I can get your money to you, Madame.'

'Just a bit of fun,' she says. 'I used to have fun.' She gives me a naughty smile.

'Well, you have to stop so I can open as a B-and-B.'

'Of course, but the lights, it happens anyway when it rains. The piano playing at night, I agree to stop. And please call me Charlotte. I have a feeling we are going to be friends,' she says. 'Now, have you spoken to the mayor?'

'On my way to see him now,' I say picking up my bag.

'You'll need to. And take a gift. Something homemade,' she says.

'Homemade?' I say.

She nods. 'Something that will appeal to the mayor . . . a tarte Tatin maybe. Apple pie.'

I put down my bag as Charlotte goes off singing to

herself, a gentle lullaby. I'm sure I hear her talking to someone or probably to herself – there's no one else here after all.

I pull out my phone and remember the missed call from my sister. I press play and put the phone to my ear to listen to the voicemail.

I ring her straight back and she answers just as quickly. 'Nellie?' She's crying. 'Nellie! Don't cry. It'll be okay,' I say. 'How's Jason?'

'How can it be okay, Fliss?' she asks. 'It's not okay. He's been excluded. Not just suspended, excluded.'

My heart twists.

'I don't know what to do. He won't speak to me at all. He's just shut himself in his room. Won't go out. Won't talk. I don't know what's going on! They just said he was caught with a large amount of drugs in his bag in school. Others said he was dealing. I had no idea . . .'

My poor sister. I think of her in the flat, working and bringing up the boys . . . 'Nellie,' I say, before I've had time to think, 'send him over here. Put him on the train. I'll meet him. He can help me. I need extra hands right now. He'll be doing me a favour.' Suddenly it makes complete sense. This will get Jason away from whoever he's mixing with. He can help me set up the B-and-B.

There's silence at the other end.

'Nellie?'

More sobbing. Then, 'Really?' says Nellie, still crying.

'I mean it. Send him over. I need him,' I say firmly.

'Thank you, Fliss,' she says, with a tight voice. 'I owe you.'

'And I need your help now. How do I make an apple pie?' She sniffs, and laughs, as do I. It's a release.

'I'm serious!' I say, still laughing. It may just be the answer to my problems. That . . . or the start of them.

Outside, just down from the vegetable patch, there are windfall apples. I rush out and collect some from a tree among brambles.

Once I'm back in the kitchen Nellie talks me through making the apple pie over the phone. She knows I wouldn't be able to do it by reading a recipe. And I talk her through my idea for the château. She seems happier now that Jason is going to come out to join me and is slowly recovering from her meeting at the school on her only day off from the supermarket.

'And how's Jason in himself?' I ask, when the pie is finally in the noisy oven.

'You know,' she says, and I do. He's always been quiet, not like his brothers, who are boisterous and quite a handful. It's taken all Nellie's energy trying to keep the three of them on the right side of the tracks. If only she could move away from that school and the crowd he's been hanging about with.

The apple pie seems to be working as a distraction for us both.

*

It's much later in the day than I wanted it to be when the pie is finally ready and I'm set to walk into town. As I'm about to leave, I open the cupboards to see if there is a bottle of anything I can take. An expensive gift. I'm in luck . . . apple brandy! Not just one but a case full. I take one and the pie, with a cloth over it, and call to Charlotte that I'm off, then make my way out of the front door and down the big stone steps towards the town.

'Oh, the mayor doesn't see anyone without an appointment,' says the young receptionist, wearing bright red lipstick and big wire-framed glasses, like a stern school mistress.

'Oh, but I—'

'Perhaps you could come back next week,' she says, looking at the computer screen and tapping on the keyboard.

'Next week? Oh, but surely I could see him or her sooner. *S'il vous plaît*,' I add. I need to show I'm trying to speak French.

'I'm sorry,' says the receptionist in English, making me feel like the incomer I am. 'Not possible.'

'But—'

'It's okay,' I hear a voice call from the office next to the receptionist's desk. She purses her lips, clearly unhappy with having been overruled.

'Come in,' says the voice, a voice that makes me frown and my heart slowly slide into my boots.

She points to the door and I tentatively make my way there, carrying the pie and the bottle. I push open the door, stand on the threshold and stare. My suspicions are confirmed and my hope of setting up my new business, saving and salvaging what we can from this situation, shatters before my eyes.

13

'You!' I can't hide my dismay. 'Of course.' I'd throw my hands up if I wasn't carrying a pie in one and a bottle in the other. 'You're the mayor.'

'I am,' says Jacques, with a nod.

'Right,' I say, not sure where to go from here. Actually, I am. I turn to walk away, still holding my bottle and wishing with all my heart I wasn't holding a home-baked apple pie that looks like a good effort but nothing like his apple cake the other night.

'Please, sit down,' he says and, surprised, I stop and turn slowly. He's holding out a hand to the leather seat on the other side of his dark-wood desk, in front of the long window. Much the same as the château's I think. It has the same twist and turn handle that took me ages to get the hang of but now I love. The windows open inwards and somehow let in the outside world.

'Please,' he says politely but firmly.

Even the château's tiniest details fascinate me. The ornate brass door plates and handles, the marble fire surrounds, the push-button bells in the big rooms that ring in a wooden box in the kitchen for service, the intricate carved coving and faded gold trim throughout the ground floor. It's like . . . like slowly falling in love, and makes me smile.

Then I look at Jacques's set face and sit down on the polished leather chair, the office smelling of beeswax. I must buy some for the hall in the château, I think. There I go again! Thinking about the château! I have to stop because, with Jacques as mayor, I can't see it happening. But, I tell myself, I just have to try. What have I got to lose? This business is the only chance we have of holding on to the château and finding out why Grandpa bought it in the first place. I don't have a plan B. This has to work. I don't want to walk away from it. Right now, it's my happy place. I can't give up on it.

As I sit, so does he and we stare at each other, him waiting for me to speak. But I have no idea where to begin. He knows exactly why I'm here.

I clear my throat and try to smile. I may not like being here and feel as uncomfortable as if I were sitting in a bath of cold custard, but I have to do this, for my family and for me, for the château.

I cough. I feel hot and my mouth is like sandpaper. I try to speak but my tongue sticks to the roof of my mouth. He indicates the water bottle and glass in front of me. I put down the bottle of apple brandy and the pie, pick up the water bottle and pour, despite my shaking hand. I can do this, I tell myself, as I hear the laughing voices from that classroom ringing in my ears. I drink the water and put down the glass.

'So,' I say, taking a deep breath. I think of Charlotte, raise my head as she does and drop my shoulders. And suddenly, in a moment of clarity, the words come.

'My name is Fliss Hope. My two sisters and I are the new owners of Château des Arbres.' It feels so weird saying that, as if I've been catapulted into some parallel universe, a sliding-doors moment. But it's true. And at the moment it's not like the lottery win I'd imagined. It's a very big money pit, a black hole we're staring into. We have to find a way to make it pay for itself. Like a totally unsuitable boyfriend who has a good heart, I have to get everyone else to love it and my plan. And the farmer next door, even if he is the mayor of the town, isn't going to stand in my way.

'*Bonjour*, Fliss, *et bienvenue*,' he says formally. 'My name is Jacques Cadieux. I am the mayor here, a dairy farmer and cheese-maker. I am very proud of the produce we make in the town,' he says.

I pick up the bottle and the pie and clutch them to me. He looks at me and then at the gifts in my hands, guiding me through the ritual of meetings like this. A small smile is tugging at the corners of his mouth.

'Oh, yes.' I really wish I hadn't made the apple pie, had stuck with the 'expensive' gift. 'I brought you this.' I hand the bottle of apple brandy to him.

He takes it from me as carefully as if it was a new-born baby and stares at it. 'A very good year.'

'You know it?' I ask.

'*Oui*,' he replies, then looks at the pie covered with its cloth. 'And what have we here?'

'Oh, this . . .' I don't want to expose my culinary attempt to this man's scrutiny. I was expecting a whole different meeting. Someone who might enjoy my efforts not judge them. Why did I listen to Charlotte? The bottle would have been fine. 'This is . . . I found some windfalls . . .'

He takes the pie and pulls back the cloth. 'I'm sure it will be delicious, with cream,' he adds. 'So, tell me your plans now that you are here in our town. All of them.' I feel as if I'm sitting in front of my headmaster, with him asking what I'm going to do with my life. My palms sweat and I run them down my jeans to my knees, feeling as if I'm being asked to act out a scene. Jacques the farmer knows exactly why I'm here.

'Well, as I said, my name is Fliss Hope. My sisters and I have found ourselves in the unusual position, of, er, being the new owners of Château des Arbres. And now that we are, and we've found out it's *viager occupé* . . . with a tenant,' I add, in case I've mispronounced it, 'we need the château to earn a living for itself.'

'And you have no idea how you came to be the own-ers of this château?' he asks, with pursed lips, this time looking at his desk and tapping a pen.

I frown. 'My grandfather bought it. I don't know how or why or when, and now he's d-died,' I stumble over the word, 'it's come to me and my two sisters. And as we gather we can't just sell it, as it has a sitting tenant, Madame Charlotte Cadieux . . .' I stop. 'Wait, sorry. What did you say your name was?'

'Jacques. Jacques Cadieux,' he says slowly, looking straight at me with those hazel eyes, the colour of the leaves that line the drive at the château. The château, again. Like a feeling I remember from when I first met Ty. Falling in love. Always in my thoughts, only right now it's a château. And I get the feeling Jacques could be a jealous ex.

'You're related to Madame Cadieux?' I ask tentatively.

'My *grand-mère*,' he says.

'Your . . . ?' I look up at him.

'My grandmother.'

'Charlotte is your grandmother.' I breathe in deeply, the smell of beeswax calming my rattled nerves.

He nods.

I bite my bottom lip, feeling the shift in atmosphere between us, as if the man opposite me has just moved in with his knight on the chess board and removed most of my remaining pieces.

'So you . . .'

'My grandmother and my father grew up there. As did I. Both my parents have passed away. Now it is just me and my grandmother. The château was in my family from the eighteenth century.'

'Wow! And I was worried I hadn't moved far from the home where I grew up!' I joke nervously. 'But you don't live in the château? You're not a sitting tenant too, are you?' I try to clarify.

'No, the *viager* agreement at the château will end with my grandmother. I live next door. As I say, I am a dairy farmer, and I have milking soon,' he says pointedly.

I clear my throat. 'I was told that I should introduce myself to the mayor. But as we've already met this is a waste of time. And to tell you my plans—'

'Your plans, yes.'

I sigh, frustrated now with his game-playing. I need to crack on. 'To set up a B-and-B,' I say.

'At the château?'

'Yes.' I want to say, 'Where else?' but hold my tongue.

'A B-and-B, like a *chambre d'hôte*? You want to turn my family home into a theme park?' he says, eyes widening. 'You want to turn the château into a cheap motel?'

'Yes! I mean no! A business, yes. The guests last night loved the place. They think it would work as a *chambre d'hôte*, not as a theme park or a cheap motel!'

'My family home has always been just that, a home,' he says firmly.

'Well, now it needs to be a business and pay its way,' I say, just as firmly.

'But why a *chambre d'hôte*? We already have an *auberge* in the town.'

'It's very small, and can't take many guests,' I say. 'And the owners are very elderly.'

'It has served the community well, and I'm not sure we need any competition.'

'It's not competition! It's another business, bringing visitors to the town. I've had some guests. You know I have! They can help bring more guests . . . And the chatelaine, your grandmother, loves the idea too.'

'Forgive me, it's milking time. The cows wait for no one,' he says, sliding off his glasses, closing his computer lid and putting the bottle of apple brandy into his battered leather briefcase. He picks it up, the apple pie balanced on the other hand, and makes for the door, nodding to it for me to leave first.

'But my plans, the château . . .'

'I'm sorry, but I really do have to go. I can't see that this is necessary for the good of the town right now or the château.'

As I don't move, he does, wishing his receptionist a good afternoon and leaving me standing there.

Now what am I going to do?

14

'Charlotte!' I call, as I get back to the château and start peeling off my coat, then change my mind: it's as cold in the main hall as it is outside. 'Charlotte!' I call up the huge staircase.

'*Oui*,' she says, coming out of the east wing, with Percival, her grumpy pug, under her arm. I wonder if it ever gets put down on the floor.

'I've just been to see the mayor!' I say crossly, as if I'm talking to a naughty child.

'Ah,' she says, floating down the stairs with the dog still tucked under her arm. 'Did he like your gift?' She raises a pencilled eyebrow, her eye twinkling naughtily.

'Why didn't you tell me it was him? Jacques, the farmer next door, your grandson.'

'An excellent cheese-maker!' she adds, with another twinkle, not answering my question. 'Jacques. He was always a hard-working child. Took his studies very seriously. Anything he turned his hand to, really.' Still avoiding answering me.

'Well, he's certainly serious about not letting me open a B-and-B here.' I throw my hands into the air and head through the archway to the kitchen.

I sit down at the big scrubbed-wood table and put my head into my hands. I hear Charlotte's footsteps following me. I look up to see her at the big dresser pulling out one of the bottles of apple brandy. She takes a glass from the cupboard above and gives it a rinse under the tap, which gurgles. She dries it, holds it to the light to check for smudges, then pulls out the cork, pours a good measure into the glass, then places it on the table in front of me.

Then she takes down another glass, rinses and dries it, pours another large measure and sits at the table. '*Santé*,' she says, raises the glass and takes a good slug. I watch her, then follow suit. I shut my eyes. It tastes surprisingly good.

I sigh. 'He's not going to agree to this becoming a B-and-B,' I say, running my fingers through my hair. 'And now I know why! *Phhhfffff*.' I take another swig of the apple brandy.

'Jacques . . . he is too serious by far. He needs to enjoy life more, have some fun. He never smiles any more. Not since his wife left him.'

'He said I knew nothing of château life. And I don't!'

'He is being pompous. French people can be!' she says, making me laugh. 'He wants to keep this place like a museum. But it needs to be lived in. To feel alive again. Not just people coming to stare at it. It needs to be loved. We all need to be loved,' she says, and drifts off to somewhere else in her thoughts. And then, 'He feels that this place is the family home,' she says, 'and that it should have come to him. He feels his inheritance was stolen from him, or maybe,' she shrugs, 'that is what his wife thinks, before she left him for Alphonse, the crêperie owner.' Ah, I think. The woman at the crêperie. That explains a few things.

'She runs the local beauty salon and hairdresser. She thought this place would become theirs. But it wasn't possible. She didn't find that out until it was too late and she had married him. But he wouldn't have had the money to keep it up. This place is a money pit.'

'You don't say!' I laugh.

'But you, you have the ideas and clearly the va-va-voom!' She grins and I laugh louder.

'But if Jacques wants it can't he buy it? From us?'

She sips her drink. 'Sometimes we can't always have what we want.' She has that faraway look in her eyes again. 'And sometimes the memories are enough. You can waste a life wondering what might have been,' she says, dropping her head. I wonder if now is the time to talk about my grandfather and what she knows, but before I can she says, 'I have been the chatelaine here

110

for many, many years now, since I was a young woman, and I have watched people come and go from my life. Some good, some bad, some just scared of change. I have spent my life waiting for what might be . . .'

I try to push thoughts of Ty from my mind. Is that what I've been doing, waiting for what might be but never will? Thinking we were happy as we were. Do I just have to accept that things change whether we want them to or not? Grandpa dying has made me realize that. I take another sip of the apple brandy, a big one.

'I do know that as chatelaine, running a house like this, being its custodian, you are the person who has to make things happen, one way or another, using whatever skills you have.'

'Like you pretending to be a ghost to keep people away?'

She smiles. 'It has worked in the past. And when I saw you, well, I didn't want to believe he was gone. If you were here, he *was* gone. Just because we want something badly, it doesn't mean we can turn back the clock. Nor should we. We should cherish what was and what we have. It doesn't stop us hoping, though.'

'Charlotte,' I say, fortified by the apple brandy, 'why did my grandfather buy this place?'

'Because I asked him to,' she says, and stands to leave. 'He was a good man.'

I think for a moment. 'But if I can't get this place up and running and paying for itself, if I default on your allowance and can't pay the tax bill in January, the château will revert to the original owner. You.' I take another deep breath, finally fitting the piece of the problem into place. 'And, in turn, your grandson.'

'*Oui*,' she says. 'Like I say, not everything that was is meant to be,' she says. 'I think you will do a fine job of bringing this place back to life and looking after it for the generations that are to come. None of us own a place like this. We are just its custodians, as it is of us. All you have to do now is work out how to get Jacques to agree. But I have a feeling you will. Sometimes, although something is forbidden, it often tastes the sweetest and we can't stop ourselves following our hearts and ignoring our heads . . . however wrong it may feel at the time. Remember, there is more than one way to cook an egg.'

She turns to leave, taking her glass and Percival with her.

Is she saying I should just go ahead and do it? The mayor's own grandmother? But surely she wants the house back in the family. Surely she doesn't want a stranger here running it as a business. Or does she?

'Charlotte, I have my nephew coming to stay. He's . . . going to help out with a few jobs around the place.'

She stops. 'Good. We could do with more young people around here. Just what we need.' She departs.

The conversation whirls around my mind. *He wouldn't have the money . . . You have the ideas and the va-va-voom!* It sounds like she approves of my plan. But what about the mayor, her grandson, the man due to inherit the place if I can't pull it off? And as much as I don't want to be 'stealing' his inheritance, my grandfather bought this house in good faith and paid for it. Right now, I need it to help Nellie and Jason. It's what Grandpa would have wanted, and Charlotte seems to have given me her blessing. But what was that bit about eggs?

15

The next morning I'm waiting at the station. Claude from the local taxi company has driven me here, dropped me off and will return when the next train arrives. Jason's had strict instructions on how to get here.

I flick through the messages on my phone while I'm waiting, checking with my worried sister that he knows which station to get off at. He's already been on the wrong train and had to start again. I'm hoping this time he's got it right.

I look at the approaching train.

It stops and, for a moment, no one gets off. My heart lurches. He's missed it. I walk quickly up and down the carriages, then jog alongside them, looking through the windows, wondering if he's fallen asleep, but I can't see anyone. Then the train moves off and I panic. How will I tell my sister I've lost Jason? I look down at my phone for any messages from him and berate myself for not ringing him just before he got off the train. I'm wondering what on earth I can do now as Claude arrives back, and then I spot him. Right at the far end of the platform. At least, I think it's him.

'Jason?' I call, to the lone figure standing beside a sagging rucksack as the train disappears from sight. I jog back up the platform. I recognize him as I get closer. He's a very different figure from the boy I used to babysit. He raises a hand, clearly relieved to have got off at the right station. I let out a sigh of relief and text my sister to say he's here. She sends an emoji back.

I wrap him in a hug, but he stays stiff and upright, not returning it. 'The taxi's waiting. Let's go,' I say, suddenly nervous. Have I done the right thing in bringing him out here? He doesn't look happy about it. We get into the back of the car.

'*Ça va?*' Claude asks.

'*Ça va!*' I smile and attempt to put on my seatbelt as he takes off from the station, throwing us both backwards.

'So, how was the journey?' I ask Jason.

'Fine,' he replies, glancing down at his phone.

I can't help but wonder whom he's talking to and whether he really wants to leave his life back home right now.

'Are you hungry?' I try again.

'No.' He shakes his head, not telling me whether he's eaten en route, but I suspect Nellie packed him food for the journey.

'How's Mum and your brothers?' I try again.

He shrugs. 'Y'know.' His face tightens.

I do know. Times are tough for Nellie, for all of them. He starts tapping into his phone. I wonder if I should take it from him, stop him having contact with his gang back home, but how would that help anything? He'd only resent me. I want him to want to be here.

I decide not to ask any more questions and look out at the bare trees instead. I catch Claude's eye in the rear-view mirror, sensing the elephant in the car and the chasm between Jason and me.

At last, after what seemed like the longest journey ever, I see the entrance to the château. 'We're here,' I tell my nephew. He lifts his head and, with total bewilderment, stares at the château and the parkland as we pass through the gates.

He looks at me as if I'm joking.

'This is it,' I say, opening the car door. He does the same, stepping out and staring up at the château in awe, just as I did on that first morning.

I pay Claude, thank him in French, and then, as he drives off, I watch Jason watching him go, as if confirming that this isn't a joke. 'Follow me,' I say, beckoning him up the stone steps to the front door.

'That's Pegasus.' I point to the horse pushing his head over the hedge to get a look at who's arrived, never wanting to be left out of any action. '*Bonjour!*' I call up the stairs to Charlotte to let her know I'm back from the station.

Jason shivers.

'Do you want something to eat or shall I show you to your room?'

'I'll, um, just go to my room, thanks,' he says, as Charlotte appears at the top of the staircase, as pale as ever in a long lace-trimmed dress, the chains on her belt rattling, and Percival under her arm. Jason takes a couple of steps back, alarmed.

'Jason, this is Madame Cadieux,' I say, and Charlotte slowly descends the stairs, holding out a thin, pale hand to Jason. His mouth drops open, but he says nothing.

'*Enchantée,*' she says, as Jason raises a hand to her and eyes Percival suspiciously.

There is another moment of awkward silence. Jason looks as if he might just turn and run.

'Let me show you your room,' I say brightly. 'You're up in the servants' quarters with me.' But as he shuts the door on the attic room I've made up for him he looks anything but reassured by what I've said.

I return to the kitchen, feeling anxious. Should I take the bull by the horns, ask him what's been going on and why he did it? Confiscate his phone?

'Give him time,' Charlotte says, seemingly reading my thoughts.

'Yes,' I agree, and make him a plate of food, some cheese, bread, crisps, then climb the servants' staircase and stand outside his door. I'm about to knock, but first find myself putting my ear to the door. I hear nothing. I wonder what he's doing. Maybe I should just ask him about it all, get it out in the open.

And then I hear Charlotte's words in my head: *Give him time.*

I knock and take a deep breath. 'I've got some food for you, Jason,' I say. There's no reply so I bend down and leave the plate outside his door.

16

'Oh, no! Not again!' I'm in one of the top-floor bedrooms at the front of the house with my mop and bucket, washing the floor, having scrubbed the skirtings, polished the windows, taken a broom to the cobwebs in the corners of the ceilings and cut back the intruding ivy. I push back the shutters, and one drops off its hinges. I sigh, making a mental note to add it to my to-do list. Then I wave my hands out of the window, in the cold November air, shouting, 'Shoo! Shoo!'

The brown and white cows don't give me a second glance and are busy working their way up towards the kitchen garden – the *potager*, as Charlotte corrects me – trampling over the lawn, bushes and brambles.

'No, no, no, no!' I run towards the stairs, noting that the croissant and bread I left outside Jason's room, replacing the untouched meal from last night, is still there. I wonder if he's embarrassed about what's happened. I hesitate and tell myself again to give him time. I run down the main stairs, waving a mop in one hand and a feather duster in the other. I pass Charlotte serenely walking along the corridor from her apartment, with her dog, and launch myself into the main hall, on to the herringbone parquet floor that is next on my list to clean and polish, and throw open the big front door.

'Hey! No! No! No! No! No!' I shout at the slow-moving herd.

I run down the stone steps to the right, still waving my mop and duster.

'Shoo! Shoo!' I say, trying to head them off before they reach the *potager* where I spent yesterday afternoon straightening and picking anything left after their last unexpected visit.

I see the cow in the lead, a determined look on its face: if I can head it off, I may stop the others. It's a bit like when I worked on a summer play scheme back home, organizing daily rock-pooling safaris. If you could get the pack leader involved and steer them away from trouble the others would usually follow. I remember one girl in particular: Flo. She had amazing red hair and a spark in her eye. There had been a moment when I thought I'd lost her interest but caught her attention and had her back onside, thinking rock-pooling was the coolest thing ever.

'Hey!' I shout, and the lead cow – I've mentally named her Flo – hesitates. I pick up a windfall apple from the grass, where I found the ones for the apple pie, and throw it just in front of her, then another. She stops as the second falls at her feet, bends to sniff and then eat it. The other cows stop, and I take my moment to run ahead of the herd and turn them back the other way, waving my mop and feather duster. For a moment they all stand still, and I think they've won, but Flo looks at me, then around her for more windfalls, turns and walks in the other direction. The others begin to follow her. Sometimes you just need to get the pack leader onside and the rest will follow, I think, with a smile.

Now all I need to do is work out where they got through. At that moment Pegasus sticks his head through the hedge and whinnies, clearly not wanting to be left out. The cows jump, scatter, then run, bumping into each other, leaping and scurrying, crashing through bushes and undergrowth, clearing a path where there wasn't one before. There seems to be no stopping them as they career down the boundary towards the woods. I watch them go, feeling helpless.

All of a sudden I hear a whistle.

Jacques!

The cows seem to slow down. My hackles rise. 'This is château property! Get your cows out of the garden!' I shout furiously.

He whistles again, barely acknowledging me, and I wonder if he's done this on purpose to try to scare me off.

'I mean it!' I'm not going to be bullied. 'You may think you can get rid of me and my family easily but you can't! Get your cows off my land now!' I say, with a surge of anger.

He nods politely, compliantly. 'Of course. My apologies. I will fix the fence. Pegasus has been at work again.'

'Has he? Or maybe you let Pegasus into these fields so he can push down the fences and help you get rid of the fly in your ointment.' I put my hands on my hips and glare at him. 'I have no idea yet why my sisters and I have ended up with the château. Not really. Or why we never knew about it. But I do know I'm not going to be bullied out of it by you because you think you've been cheated of your inheritance!' I feel like I'm riding the crest of a wave, just like when I was surfing, adrenalin pumping through my veins, not knowing when the fall will come but enjoying the ride while I'm there. Not that I've surfed for years. Not since I took a bad fall. But right now I'm back there, riding high, not caring about the consequences.

'You may be mayor in the town, but that doesn't make this right!' I march towards him.

'Of course,' he says again, and whistles, this time louder. The cows slow and this time stop, looking over their shoulders. Another whistle and they seem to be turning and walking towards us. They're moving much slower this time but definitely towards us, up what must have once been the manicured lawn, past the side of the house to the back, splitting up to walk around the empty swimming pool, across the moss-covered terrace, up towards the drive on the other side of the house where they gather and mingle.

Jacques turns to me, looks briefly over my shoulder and then says, taking me by complete surprise, 'My apologies.' He whistles again and sets off down the long drive, the cows walking obediently behind him, back to their home on the other side of the hedge.

I watch them go, tails swishing, strolling down the drive in a swirl of autumnal golden leaves falling and dancing in the low sunlight. Calm, after the sudden burst of excitement.

Finally, as they turn the corner at the end of the drive, back into the farmyard, I see Charlotte standing at the front door, also watching them go. It's the closest I've seen her to a door and the outside world. I wonder if that's who Jacques looked at when he glanced over my shoulder. Perhaps that's what caused his sudden change of attitude. Not me telling him to get his cows and go, standing up for myself and my family. Now I've fallen off the wave, and the weight of it all is too much. I look at what must once have been a beautiful lawn, now overgrown and trampled by a herd of cows. I put my hands over my face. I can't set this place up as a B-and-B, even if the mayor did allow it. There's so much to be done. The wave is dragging me down, pounding me. Just like the last time I took to the water, when I was riding high until I wasn't. If Ty hadn't dragged me from the swell, who knows what would have happened? I'd crashed into him, knocking us both off our boards. My board hit me, knocked me out for a moment and I was disoriented. Ty pulled me out. It was my fault he damaged his back and I couldn't have felt worse.

Charlotte has disappeared. Back inside, I presume.

As I gaze at the château, I'm imagining what it would have been like full of people, life and laughter. And up in the attic room, I see Jason at the window. He seems to be eating a croissant. I allow myself a little smile.

I turn back to the mess on the lawn, the woods beyond and the trail the cows have left and something catches my eye.

17

I walk slowly past the worn red-brick boundary wall that leads down the side of the lawn towards the woods at the bottom that curl up and round to the château, running along one side of the driveway, opposite the cows' field. Just beyond where the cows have trampled through the brambles I can see what looks to be a brick arch. I'm intrigued.

I use the mop and feather duster to beat down the rest of the brambles. The stones here are different from the rest of the wall, and as I stamp on the brambles, I realize there's a door. I'm out of breath, my hands snagged and torn, when I see the handle. I lean into the wood and push. It doesn't budge. I put my shoulder to it, like I did with the front door when we first arrived here, and push harder. I rebound off it with a yell of pain, and frustration with the cows and Jacques. I try the door again. It still doesn't budge.

'What are you doing, Auntie Fliss?'

Jason is standing behind me, frowning. Pleased to see him out of his room and hear him calling me Auntie Fliss, just like he always did, I smile, despite the pain in my shoulder. 'Hi!' I say.

'I saw you from my bedroom window,' he says, his long fringe hanging over his eyes. I wonder where the old Jason has gone, the one I babysat until he grew too old for babysitters and became this Jason, hiding from the world, withdrawn and sullen.

'You saw me chasing cows and didn't come to help.' I give a little laugh. What a sight I must have looked, chasing cows with a mop and a feather duster.

'They looked scary!' he says. 'So did you!'

I gesture to the door. 'Well, now you're here, could you give me a hand with this?' I point at the door. 'I'm trying to open it.'

He shrugs. 'Sure,' he says. I glimpse the little boy he used to be and resist an overwhelming urge to rub his head, like I did when he was younger, on nights I'd babysit while Nellie worked every hour she could. I can feel him waiting for me to say something. I can practically feel his embarrassment. I hear Charlotte's voice again: *Give him time.*

'Let's have a try at this door. I just need to work out how to unlock it,' I say, wondering how to climb over the wall.

Jason steps towards it.

A moment later: 'Where did you learn how to do that?' I'm staring at the door, open, its lock picked.

'At school.'

I can see why Nellie's been so worried about him.

'Does everyone . . .' I stop. This is about a new start for Jason. I decide to bite my tongue and say no more, other than 'Thank you.' If he wants to tell me about everything that happened to him, I'm sure he will. He needs time.

He steps back and I'm suddenly nervous. I have no idea what I'm going to find behind the door. But the fact that it's been locked for years tells me it's not going to be good. Something behind it has been hidden and my curiosity won't let me walk away.

I take hold of the rusty ring handle – Jason looks as interested and apprehensive as I think I do – give it a shove and it opens.

'Whoa!' says Jason. We look at the mist creeping around the trees in the space. They're laden with apples on the branches, and there are more on the ground. There are brambles but it's not overgrown, like the kitchen garden was, and it's not Narnia either. I'd been imagining all sorts.

I take another step inside. Jason is right behind me and I'm happy he's with me. He may not be saying much, but I like him being here.

'So, it's an apple orchard,' I say, stating the obvious, picking up a couple of windfalls. That must have been

why I found some on the lawn – some of the trees over-
hang the wall. There are thousands of apples here, and
in one corner, there are buildings: a gardener's cottage
by the look of it, a potting shed and an open-sided barn.
I'm presuming this is part of the château but have no
real idea. I know someone who will, though.

18

'Charlotte,' I say, when she appears in the kitchen, Percival under her arm, with his usual condescending stare. She pushes him out of the back door, where he pees against an ancient urn, then hurries back inside. She quickly shuts the door, keeping the outside out.

'Charlotte,' I say, washing the apples I picked up in the orchard under the noisy tap. 'About the orchard . . .'

She looks at the apples I'm holding and her face pales. 'The orchard?' She seems shocked, and put off her stride. Usually she's so measured, like she was on the day I arrived even after her initial shock at hearing Grandpa had died. Now her cheeks flush pink.

'Yes, the orchard. The one just there. The door was covered with brambles and locked.'

She reaches for the back of a chair, scoops up Percival and holds him tightly to her, much to his chagrin.

'Does it belong to the château?'

'You've been in the orchard?' she says slowly.

'Yes. Is it the château's?' I ask carefully.

This time, she nods.

I don't know what answers I'm looking for, but it seems strange and a waste that it's shut up like that, and odd that it isn't as neglected as I would have expected to find behind an overgrown locked door.

'Does anyone else have access to it?'

'Nobody has been in ze orchard for . . .' she swallows '. . . many, many years. Many years,' she repeats.

'Interesting.' I can't help but feel I'm missing a piece of the jigsaw here. I busy myself at the sink, wondering what on earth to do with so many apples. Nellie will know.

'Why do you ask?' queries Charlotte.

'No reason,' I say, keeping my tone light.

'How did you . . .' she frowns '. . . how did you know about the orchard?'

I consider my answer. 'I found it,' I say. Which is true.

'Found it?'

'Yes, I found the door,' I say slowly turning to her, watching her expression change while she strokes the charm on her necklace with her thumb.

'I haven't seen it in years,' she says quietly, looking at me but barely seeing me . . . or maybe she's seeing me for the first time. 'You have his eyes,' she says, and I know she means Grandpa. 'And his spirit.' She smiles fondly, her eyes filling with unshed tears. 'But it won't do any good going into the orchard. It caused a lot of upset when it was closed for good. Some things are best left in the past,' she says, with sadness etched across her face.

I want to ask more but she turns away and the conversation is over. Jason looks at me and shrugs. I swear he's developing a Gallic version already.

'Yes, a huge apple orchard,' I tell Nellie and Lizzie on Zoom that night after a simple supper of omelettes for me and Jason. I'm just pleased he wanted to eat with me, even if he did push it around his plate. Charlotte didn't join us.

'But that's brilliant!' says Lizzie. 'Maybe this is how we can make the château pay its way.'

'How?'

'Sell the apples?' she suggests. 'Or . . . make cider!'

Nellie shakes her head. 'That stuff we had in the restaurant was dreadful.'

'Do either of you know how to make cider?' asks Lizzie.

We shake our heads.

'Could google it,' Jason chips in, not looking up from his phone.

'But Charlotte says opening up the orchard would cause a lot of upset,' I say.

'Why?' my sisters ask.

'I don't know. I'm trying to find out,' I say, feeling as frustrated as they are, being miles away.

'Whatever it is, surely it can't stand in the way of business,' says Lizzie.

I stand up from the kitchen table, walk over to the wood-burner and throw in another log I've brought in from the wood pile. It catches in no time, throwing up flames and heat. I pull around me the blanket I'm wearing as a shawl and feel instantly warmer.

'It's not an immediate answer, though. We need money now. We have to pay Charlotte's monthly allowance or we lose the château. If we miss a payment, the château will revert to the original seller.'

'To Charlotte?'

'Yes.'

'And we end up with nothing?'

'Yes,' I repeat. 'And then there's the tax in January . . .'

'Yes, yes,' Lizzie says impatiently.

'I'd give you money if I had any,' says Nellie. Jason studies her on the screen and I sense he's worried about her.

'I went to see the mayor,' I say, realizing that with Jason's arrival I haven't brought my sisters up to speed, 'to get his blessing to open the château as a B-and-B.'

'That's a great idea!' Lizzie says.

'But he wouldn't give it. He said the town already had an *auberge*.'

'But the owners look ready for retirement!' Lizzie is outraged.

I let out a long breath.

'That's not the only thing. The mayor is Charlotte's grandson, the farmer next door . . . Jacques.'

'*What?*' my sisters exclaim.

'It's Jacques next door,' I confirm.

'And,' says Lizzie slowly, 'if we don't meet our payments the property will revert to the family.'

'To him!' says Nellie.

'Yes,' I say, with a long, slow *phhhffffff*.

'I'll pay this month's allowance on my credit card,' says Lizzie. 'Just to give us some time.'

We all breathe a sigh of relief.

'We really need to find out more about this orchard,' she adds, as I hear her tapping away on the computer, logging into her bank account. 'Oh, and don't tell James about me paying this. He thinks we'd be better off walking away. That's why I can't get away with spending from the joint account. But this'll give us some time to work out what to do with the place. He called it a millstone.'

For a moment, nobody says anything. And, right now, we all know what the others are thinking. He's probably right. But we can't walk away. It's the one thing we all agree on. We can't just hand it back. We may not have been close over the past few years, all with our own lives to lead, but with Grandpa dying, and us finding ourselves with the château, it's the one thing we all have in common and it's a lifeline for Jason. It's a chance for us to have something in the future. We have to find a way to keep it going.

19

It's the noise that alerts me to it, a low moaning. I wonder if Charlotte's reverted to her haunting act. I stop cleaning – I'm working my way through the west wing rooms on the first floor. Downstairs, cleaning included getting up ladders and washing down carved cornices in rooms twice my height, even more. Jason, I decided, was safer holding the ladder than going up it. He doesn't seem very coordinated. He's fallen over two buckets of hot soapy water so far, stepped on a broom, narrowly missing knocking himself out, and tripped over a tall standard lamp, fusing it.

As we work our way around the rooms, I like to think he's loosening up a little with each one. I'm still getting one- or two-word answers, and when I haven't given him a specific task, he's back checking his phone, but at least he's here, not in his room, helping with the chores

I ask him to do, even if it seems he'd rather be anywhere else. In each bedroom, I can see possibilities to add en suites, knock through two into family rooms . . . My mind is whirring.

The moaning gets louder and, having checked in the corridor to make sure it's not Charlotte, I go to the window overlooking the front of the house and the woods beyond. I can hear a low, gut-wrenching moan. Jason has pulled out his phone again.

Tentatively at first, but with a growing sense of urgency, I hurry down the stairs and out of the front door on to the steps. The noise is even louder. It's a desperate sound, and my insides twist in empathy.

I move quickly down the steps. Whoever or whatever is making that noise is in trouble. I'm following the sound and stop outside the door to the orchard. What on earth is going on in there?

'Hey!' I bang on the door. 'Hey!' The moaning keeps up. There's nothing for it. I can't just walk away. The brambles snag and rip at my skin as I reach for the big handle.

I turn it, but the door is stiff, like it was the first time I opened it.

The low moan continues, then stops. What's happened?

'Hey!' I shout again, more urgently, give the door a big shove with my shoulder and fall into the walled apple orchard once more.

I recognize her straight away. Don't ask me how. She looks at me with her big brown eyes and I have no idea what to do. She staggers one way, then lurches back the other, sways and falls to the ground with a thud. I jump back, with a shriek. There's only one thing I can do: find someone who knows her and can help.

20

'Jacques! Hello! Monsieur Mayor! *Allô!*' I try every combination I can think of to alert him and it seems to work. The back door to one side of the farmhouse opens and there is the woman I first saw in the crêperie. Jacques's wife.

'*Pardon!*' I say. '*Je suis . . .*'

She shrugs and tilts her head, even pouts, putting a large bag down beside her feet. 'I know who you are,' she says.

'It's . . .' I try to say it in French but everything just jumbles as it does when I'm trying to read under pressure.

'You are the person here for the château,' she says, with pursed lips.

'Well, I, um . . .' Perhaps I can get on better with her than I do with Jacques. 'Yes, I'm the one from the château,' I say, and smile.

'The one who stole my husband's inheritance!' she snaps at me.

For a moment I'm so shocked by her rudeness that I'm dumbstruck, my face frozen. Then, 'It wasn't like that!' I remind myself this isn't the time for explaining my family's inheritance. I'm here for a reason. 'Look, it's one of the cows, the naughty one, the leader, Flo,' I have no idea why I used my nickname for the cow, 'in the orchard . . .' I continue, trying to get all the information out.

'Cows! It's always about cows! I hate bloody cows!' She tosses up a hand, rolls her eyes, picks up the bag, which I see contains heated hair rollers and a lamp, and goes to shut the front door behind her as she leaves.

'Could you get Jacques? It's really important. One of the cows—'

'It's always about the cows. That's why I left him in the first place.' She tosses her hair and struts off on her high heels.

'Have fun with Papa, *chérie*,' she calls, as a teenage girl appears at the kitchen door. She's beautiful. Long straight hair, nearly to her waist, a crop top under a denim jacket and big scarf, showing off a flat stomach with a diamond piercing in her belly button, scowling after the woman leaving.

'Look, I'm sorry, but could you find Jacques for me? It's really important. One of the cows is in the orchard, hurt.'

'Hurt?'

'Yes. She's on the ground, moaning and groaning. Her head is swinging around . . .'

She doesn't need telling twice, abandoning the school books at the kitchen table, the scowl replaced by concern. 'Papa! Papa!' she shouts, running out of the house, slipping on wellies as she goes. 'Papa!' she shouts, and he appears from a workshop wiping his hands. She talks quickly, pointing to me, then back to the château. He doesn't need telling twice either. He puts down the cloth in his hand and pulls off the white hat he's wearing, not bothering about the apron, and races out of the workshop across the yard and out to the back fields.

'No, the orchard!' I shout, and the words come out in plumes of condensation on the cold autumnal air.

'This way!' he shouts over his shoulder as I stop in my tracks.

'The château orchard!' I shout back.

'I know!' he calls. 'This way – it's quicker!'

I follow him and the girl. He opens a five-bar gate and they rush through it. I stumble as I shut it, then hurry after them until we reach the red-brick wall of the orchard. I have no idea how this could be a quicker way into the orchard than going back into the château grounds but then I see it: a section where the wall has fallen down, with a well-worn path across it into the orchard. Jacques and his daughter climb over the pile of fallen bricks, ducking and dodging beneath the heavily laden branches towards the moaning cow. I'm hoping we've got to her in time.

'*Tant pis!*' I hear him say. Perhaps things are worse than he was expecting.

I watch from a distance as Jacques kneels beside the cow, strokes her head and talks gently to her.

I hear his daughter ask him what's wrong but don't understand the reply. 'What is it?' I ask her.

Her mouth pulls down at the corners. 'The apples,' she explains.

'Ah,' I say, wondering how apples could be the problem. 'Are they bad for cows?'

She shakes her head. 'In moderation, they're fine. They add a little something to the flavour of the milk and the cream and, of course, to the cheese, but not at this time of year.'

'Why not?'

'The apples fall,' she explains patiently.

'Has the cow been injured by falling apples?'

She throws back her head and laughs. 'Papa?' she says. '*Explique!*' pointing to me. I'm confused as to why she's laughing. The cow is obviously sick or hurt.

Jacques looks up at me, his eyes fixed on me. 'Clémentine is right. A little apple in the cow's diet is fine.' He tilts his head from side to side. 'It makes for a unique flavour. But the apples on the ground are starting to ferment.'

I'm still none the wiser.

Jacques sighs, standing up. 'She's drunk!' he says, his hands on his hips.

'Drunk?'

'Yup. We need to get her back to the barn. Ever helped get a drunk cow home?'

I think we can safely say this will be a first.

'There, we did it! *Merci*,' he says, wiping his hands as we watch the cow. She's snuggled into fresh straw in a quiet corner of the big barn, sleeping, and I swear she's snoring too. There is dribble around her mouth. But she's settled. And, Jacques reassures me, she needs to sleep it off.

I feel quite a sense of achievement. I know I only encouraged them all as Jacques put a head collar on his cow and helped his daughter get the animal to her feet. And then, of course, there was moving the pile of bricks away to get her out of the orchard. That wall will have to be mended, I think, making a mental note to put it on my list of jobs to do.

I watch Jacques as he slings his arm around his daughter and they look at the cow with a smile. I feel that pull again, the yearning for something more in my life. Something that was missing between me and Ty.

'If you hadn't got me so quickly, it could have been very different. We needed to get her on her feet and away from the apples. Thank you.'

And this time I don't bat away his thanks.

'*Et toi,*' he says, pulling his daughter close and smiling at her. She smiles back and cuddles into the hug, as content to be there as he is. Again I feel the pull. Is it homesickness? Maybe I should think about going back. Back to how things were. Back to my old room and seeing what work is around. Jacques isn't going to agree to the B-and-B . . .

The young woman whispers to her father. 'Of course,' he says. 'I'm forgetting my manners. This is Clémentine, my stepdaughter.' She rolls her eyes at him. 'And this is Fliss Hope,' he says, as if the words stick in his throat, like tough steak he's trying to swallow.

'*Bonjour,*' says the pretty girl with a beautiful smile, a tiny dimple and beautiful straight, white teeth.

'*Bonjour!*' I reply and add, '*Enchantée,*' just to show I'm trying.

She smiles wider, and whispers something else to Jacques.

'Clémentine is right. Join us, please, for lunch,' says Jacques, very formally, ever the mayor.

'Oh, no, really!' It's time I got back, that I realized there's nothing more we can do here. That I don't belong here. We have this month's allowance on Lizzie's credit card and then, unless we can find a buyer, the château will return to the family, and that will be that. Maybe it's the right thing to do.

I turn to bid farewell to Clémentine. But there is a look of surprise on her face, and she turns to her father.

'I think Clémentine is reminding us to remember our manners,' he says quietly.

And I see straight away what he means. I'm being rude by refusing. 'Of course!' I say, thinking about Jason back at the château, hoping he'll be able to fend for himself. 'Lunch would be lovely!'

I wash thoroughly in the little downstairs bathroom, and Clémentine hands me a fresh towel. I smile and thank her.

'Will your mother be joining us?' I ask. If so, I plan to stay as long as is polite, then make my escape.

'Oh, no. She doesn't live with us. She lives in town, at the crêperie, with Alphonse,' she says matter-of-factly, confirming what Charlotte had told me.

'I'm sorry,' I say. I may just have put my foot in it and my cheeks burn with embarrassment.

'Don't be. It's fine. She can be very high maintenance,' she says, with a wave of the hand, making me smile. She's made me feel more welcome than anyone else has since I've been here.

By the time I come out of the bathroom, the kitchen table is laid. Clémentine is moving around setting out water glasses and ceramic cups.

I wonder what I can do to help.

'Please, sit,' says Jacques, putting a board of sliced baguette on the table.

Clémentine pulls out one of the four mismatched chairs for me, and smiles. I thank her and smile back.

The wood-burner behind me, surrounded by worn, soft sofas is pumping out a glorious heat in the cosy home. But for whom, if what Clémentine says is right? Her and Jacques? Her stepfather? How long ago did Clémentine's 'high maintenance' mother move out? I can't help but admire the girl's acceptance of the situation. But, then, I really have no idea what the situation is, why her mother left. I'm just putting together pieces of the puzzle, probably in the wrong order, as Jacques seems to have done with me, if his ex-wife is to be believed and they really do think I've stolen his inheritance. I look at lovely Clémentine again and feel a pang of guilt.

'Please,' says Clémentine, gesturing to the lunch in front of us as Jacques fills the cups from a jug. From the smell, it's cider and I'm hoping it's not like the one we had at Alphonse's restaurant.

'This looks amazing!' I say, and my stomach lets out a loud rumble. Clémentine puts the back of her hand over her mouth to cover a smile. Jacques politely ignores it. He should try living with Percival the pug.

'Help yourself,' says Clémentine, passing me bread.

Jacques takes a bowl from in front of me and ladles in creamy chicken, smelling of garlic. There are soft, oven-cooked potatoes and green beans, with a melting pool of butter.

'*Merci!*' I say, waiting for his and Clémentine's plates to be filled.

'Chicken Normandy,' Clémentine tells me.

With the plates laden and the delicious aroma of the creamy, herby, garlicky, boozy chicken, my stomach roars again.

'Let's eat,' says Jacques, lifts his cup and takes a sip of the cider. I politely follow, bracing myself for the sharp, vinegary taste, but I'm delighted. It's very nice. Cold, apple taste, smooth and slightly floral. I take another sip, then tuck into the lovely lunch. I've been living off soup from the garden and bread from the shop in the town but it never tastes very fresh, not like this.

I take another sip of the cider. It's just like the one we had the other night when I had the guests to stay. My mind starts clicking, and I'm thinking about the orchard from which we escorted the drunken cow earlier.

'This cider is lovely. Is it from the area?' I ask.

'It is,' Jacques says.

'I had some in the crêperie when I first arrived and it was . . .'

'*Dégoûtant?* Disgusting?' Clémentine helps me out, making me laugh.

'Yes,' I agree.

'Ah, you have to know where to go to find the apples,' says Jacques. 'There is not the same access to the good apples as there used to be in this region.' Again, my thoughts turn to the apple orchard. I wonder if they're good apples or would make disgusting cider.

When we've finished, Clémentine clears the plates and refuses any help from me.

'*Non, non.*' She tuts. 'You are our guest.' And once again I realize I would be insulting her if I insisted.

For dessert, there is tarte Tatin, with cream, and although I'm full, I can't resist the flaky pastry, caramelized edges and soft, sweet fruit with the creamy coating. I wonder who the chef in the house is. 'Did you make this, Clémentine?'

She laughs. 'Papa is the cook in the family!'

And he nods graciously. 'Clémentine is just as good. She just doesn't have the confidence.'

Clémentine blushes and I smile at her. I know that feeling, never enjoying being in the limelight. I try to move the conversation on and away from Clémentine and ask about the cows.

Clémentine seems much happier talking to me about the cows and the farm. 'The herd is all Normandy cows. So the cheese comes from Normandy cows, grazed on grass from here, which is very green, because it rains. And, of course, they have the apples too.'

Then there is coffee. And although I know I'm there against Jacques's real wishes, he is the perfect host and I'm actually enjoying myself.

'So,' I finally say, the cider clearly relaxing my tongue, 'about the hole in the orchard wall. How long has it been there?'

Jacques sits back and I see Clémentine give him a small shy smile, as if he's been caught with his hands in the biscuit tin.

'A tree fell in a storm,' he says.

'And then Pegasus went exploring,' says Clémentine.

'The current owners never repaired it,' Jacques shrugs. I get the feeling he's referring to my grandfather and now me and my sisters.

'So you get free grazing in the château's orchard?' I raise an eyebrow.

'It's the apples that make the cheese so good,' says Clémentine. 'It's why everyone wants to buy it. The apples are like no others around here.'

Jacques regards her with a mixture of pride and scolding.

'*Mais c'est vrai!*' She slips back into French. 'Everyone wants your cheese and they only buy from the other sellers when yours runs out on market day.'

He drops his head and chuckles. '*Oui, c'est vrai,*' he says, giving Clémentine's hand a rub.

'And the cider,' she carries on, and Jacques sighs, unable to stop the truth as it tumbles from her. 'But only enough for the family and the—'

'I'm sure Fliss has the picture,' says Jacques, cutting her off firmly but kindly.

'So . . .' I remember Charlotte's words: *There is more than one way to cook an egg, my dear.* She's telling me to think outside the box to make the château pay for itself. I've been coming up with a big fat zero. This has to be worth a shot.

'Presumably you want to keep grazing the cows in the orchard for as long as you can.'

'It's nearly time to bring them into the barn for winter. The apples, as you've seen, are starting to ferment.'

There is a way I can see this working.

'But if the apple orchard is what makes your cheese so special, perhaps you want to rent it from the château.' I raise my other eyebrow like we're playing a game of draughts. Each making our moves slowly.

He chews his bottom lip. 'No one has been in that orchard for years. Least of all the owner!'

We stare at each other.

'If you mean my grandfather, well, my sisters and I are the owners now,' I say slowly, 'and I could get the wall repaired as part of the château renovations, now I know about it, if that's what you'd like.' This time I tilt my head.

He takes a moment, sips his cider. 'I'm a farmer. If I had money I would offer to buy the château,' he shakes his head, 'but . . .' he gives the Gallic shrug that Jason seems to have adopted '. . . how about . . .' He's clearly taking my suggestion seriously. 'Maybe there could be another way.'

His hand is over his mouth, and he's rubbing at his beard.

Another way? What other way? Some kind of mutual agreement. He couldn't think . . . ! My mind whirrs and goes into overdrive. Is he suggesting what I think he's suggesting? I frown. 'Excuse me?' I say indignantly. I'm wondering if I've heard him right. That may be the French way, but it isn't my way. And, frankly, it's not a suitable suggestion to be making with his stepdaughter present. 'I have a . . . partner. It's . . .'

'*Compliqué?*' finishes Clémentine, and I nod gratefully to her. She has a wise head on those young shoulders.

It feels strange calling Ty my partner because we've never needed such words to describe our relationship. We've always been Ty and Fliss. It's how it's always been in Swn Y Mor.

Jacques holds up a hand and Clémentine laughs. A smile pulls at his lips and then mine as I realize I've totally misunderstood.

'My apologies,' he says, 'what I mean is, your *chambre d'hôte*, the B-and-B. Maybe I was a little hasty in thinking there wasn't room for another business in the town.'

'Well, there clearly is. There's only the one place,' I say, excitement sparking in my stomach.

'And, having given it some thought, maybe you're right. The couple at the *auberge* are quite elderly so perhaps,' he says, tantalizingly slowly, 'we, the mayor's office, should be encouraging new business.'

'And . . . maybe the hole in the orchard wall?' I lift my chin like Charlotte.

'Could remain between friends?' he says. He does his usual shrug and tilts his head at the same time.

'A secret?' I'd hardly call us friends. This may put all my plans back on track and I could find a way for the château to pay for itself.

'Let's just say it could be last on your list of things to do.' He looks at me, and suddenly I feel a warmth flood me as he smiles, his face changing completely. 'I know château owners always have a long list of things to do.'

He's right. My list is ever growing. But this could be exactly what we need to make the place work. And if not, at least I'll have tried. 'Look, I know you don't want me here. And, to be honest, it's not where I planned to be right now.' I think of Swn Y Mor, my home for my entire life. Home, with Grandpa and Ty. I feel a pang of homesickness, a longing to be back in Swn Y Mor, for everything that was there. But everything that made it home isn't there any more. 'But, well, I'm here, whether you or I like it or not.' I can't just walk away. This is Nellie's only chance to get Jason away from whatever trouble he's got himself into. And maybe, just maybe if this place starts to make money, it could give us an income, which Nellie desperately needs, and a home, plus a fresh start for me and Jason. I can't just hand back the château. Not until I've tried everything, and found out why Grandpa bought it. 'We just have to try to get along.'

He nods slowly and I let out a long sigh. Another thought occurs to me: Lizzie's right – the apples must be worth something.

'So, you can have the grazing, but not the apples on the trees,' I add quickly, trying to think on my feet.

'Okay. I agree,' he concedes.

'In that case, the orchard wall', I say, 'will go to the bottom of the list.'

He tops up our cider cups and we lift them. Suddenly something in his face jogs a memory again – more than jogs it: it gives it a shove. That camping holiday here in France and an afternoon spent in a garden, playing in the sunshine, in the pool. It was here! We came here with Grandpa. Just the once! I played with a shy, serious boy, and now I realize it must have been Jacques. He spoke hardly any English and I didn't speak French, but we spent an afternoon swimming while my sisters sunbathed and played hide-and-seek in the woods. I got sunburn and had to stay inside the whole of the next day.

I'm about to remind him of this when he says, 'Though I'd hate to see my family home turned into a theme park.'

'It won't be, I promise,' I say quickly, and we're back to putting up walls between us, although not in the orchard, not yet, as long as he keeps to his side of the bargain.

'To Château des Arbres *chambre d'hôte*,' he finishes, and raises his cup.

'To the B-and-B and successful cheese-making.' I've just become a rookie B-and-B owner.

'However, I cannot be responsible if the business doesn't work, and you fall behind with monthly payments. If that happens . . .'

'I know. The château reverts to the family, to you.'

And our moment of mutual celebration is gone. I decide not to remind him of that summer day when we visited here.

I finish my drink and stand to leave, thanking him and Clémentine. He nods politely, as does Clémentine, and bids me goodbye.

'Oh, please, can you take this to my grandmother?' He hands me a basket with cheese, and a warm pot of the delicious chicken we've just eaten. There's bread and butter, dessert too. 'If you're going that way?'

'Where else would I be going?' I try to laugh but he ignores it.

'I send over meals but I don't think she eats them.'

So this is how Charlotte gets by without going out. Her grandson sends her baskets of food. His face is softer as he hands it to me and I take it. Not such an awful man after all. Even if he and I will never be friends, at least we can be polite.

'Of course,' I say.

As I walk back down the long drive to the château, beside the line of trees and the woods, I pause to drink it in. The sun is low behind it, silhouetting its outline. Perfectly symmetrical with distinctive east and west wings. Tall, pointed roofs on the turrets, and windows like those on an advent calendar waiting to be opened. It's beautiful, breathtakingly beautiful, yet with an air of sadness. Just like Charlotte, I think, as I see her gazing out at the woods, then down at me from her turret room.

When I reach the château kitchen, through the big front door, across the parquet floor, through the arch to the left of the turn in the staircase, a peacock is standing in front of the wood-burner. He's handsome, that's for sure, as if he's in his Sunday best, with blues and greens on his chest, and gold on his back. He's staring at me. The back door is wide open and, under the wrought iron and glass porch, four peahens are peering curiously at me.

'Shoo!' I have no idea where he's come from, but I need to get him out of the kitchen. 'Shoo!' I wave my arms as I put the basket on the table. 'Charlotte?' I call, wondering if she's gone back to her scare tactics – maybe she's not keen on opening this place as a B-and-B after all. Or is this down to Jacques? Can I really trust him when he says he'll let me open the business?

The peacock looks at me, then slowly turns, struts towards the door, as if he's inspected the premises and the new arrival, and strolls back to his ladies, taking in the surroundings as he goes. And just before he does, he poos on the tiled floor by the back door. I swear he turns to wink at me.

'Out!' I say. '*Allez!*' And off he goes, his gaggle of girls fussing around him. I shut the door firmly behind him.

'Oooof!' I clear up the poo with toilet paper and the mop. Then I look around the kitchen. All I need to do is get the château on the internet and take some bookings. I know just the person to help me. 'Jason? Come downstairs and bring your phone!' If he's always going to be on it, he might as well be doing something useful.

21

'I've got one!' I shout at my sisters on Zoom.

'What?' They look terrified.

'A booking! I've got my first booking! We've got our first booking!'

Their faces relax.

'That's brilliant! When are they coming?' Lizzie says.

'Tonight!' I say, frozen with fear.

'Eek!' they shriek.

'Yesterday Jason and I got us on Facebook, Instagram and Twitter. I contacted the family who stayed here overnight and they put up a review on Tripadvisor, and now we've got our first real booking.' My voice is getting higher-pitched by the second. 'For one night.'

'Deep breath. Is it a family or a couple staying over?' asks Lizzie.

'Don't panic,' says Nellie.

'And they want dinner!' I panic.

'You can do it!' Lizzie says calmly.

'I'm no cook!'

'See if the local restaurant will sell you something,' says Nellie, sensibly.

'Okay, I'm on it.' I look around for something to write on. I go to the dresser, open a drawer and pull out a notebook. It's very pretty, with a gold embossed tree on the front. I open it. There are pages missing, but plenty of blank sheets still, with gold trim around the edges. I put 'restaurant/dinner' at the top of my list, in my appalling handwriting. Then:

Clean rooms

Air rooms

Make up beds

Check pillows for firmness

Find spare blankets for end of bed

Towels

Turn on water

Put radiators on

Hot-water bottles in the room

Bottles of water and glasses by the bed

Maybe some greenery in a vase from the garden.
    Or some of the dried hydrangea heads I've seen
    there.

Find vases

Perhaps some chocolates on the pillows?

No. No chocolates, I think, and cross it out.

Biscuits, in case they're hungry and need a snack
Sweep leaves from front door
Bring in wood
Light fires
Check for candles

The list looks as if a spider has danced drunk across the page, but I know what it all says and how much there is to do. I pick up my basket, phone in one hand, and open the back door.

'Okay, I've got to go!' I say to my sisters. The peacock struts back into the kitchen, as if affronted he's been locked out all this time. He heads straight to the wood-burner.

'Why? What's up?'

'Cedric, that's what's up!' I say. 'Speak later.'

'Who's Cedric?' I hear just as I'm ending the call.

'Come on, Cedric! I told you yesterday – I don't know where you're from, but you're not welcome in here.' I have no idea why I've suddenly called him Cedric. But the last thing I need is a big bird making a nuisance of himself when I have guests here.

I make a shopping list for bits and pieces to get when I'm out – bread, milk, flowers – as well as a dish to serve my first guests. I give Jason a list of tasks to do, including sweeping the leaves and cleaning the bathroom by the big master bedroom on the first floor.

'Cleaning the bathroom? Does that mean the loo as well?' He wrinkles his nose.

'Yes, Jason, it does,' I say firmly, expecting to have to do it myself.

He sighs, then goes down to the basement, grabs the cleaning bucket and rolls into action, making me smile.

This is it. If I can pull this off, we may be on our way to saving the château. And just for fun I add 'Mend orchard wall' at the bottom of my list, knowing there's no way I'll get to that any time soon.

22

I return from town, exhausted, frustrated and with angry tears in my eyes. I throw my empty basket on to the table, sit down by the embers in the wood-burner and hold my head in my hands.

'Auntie Fliss? You okay?'

I look up briefly. It's Jason, wearing blue rubber gloves and holding the cleaning bucket. My head drops back into my hands and I let the tears fall. All that effort for nothing.

'Nobody, not one bloody person . . .' I push the heels of my hands harder into my eyes. A sob catches in my throat.

'Not one person, what?' he asks.

I take a deep breath.

'Not one person would sell me what I needed.'

'They wouldn't or couldn't?' he asks gently.

'Wouldn't,' I say firmly. 'As soon as they realized where I was from, who I was, what my surname was, they wouldn't help me. The bread was "all sold out" at the *boulangerie*, even though I could see loaves. He said they were yesterday's and stale!' That didn't stop him selling me stale ones before. 'Rachelle, Jacques's ex-wife, was at the crêperie with Alphonse and said they had nothing they could sell to me when I asked for six portions of the *plat du jour*, mushroom, cheese and spinach crêpes. She said they were not suitable for take-away. I couldn't even get flowers from the florist – she said she was closed early for lunch. And the chocolatier said their desserts were reserved, even though they were in the window with price tags. I may not be from around here, but I know when I'm being talked about, and when I'm being pushed out. It's no good, Jason. I tried. But I can't run a B-and-B if the townspeople freeze me out, even if I do have the mayor's blessing.'

'When things don't work out, it's our job to find a way around them. Remember! There are many ways to cook an egg!'

My head jerks up and Charlotte is standing in the kitchen, Percival under her arm. It's like she springs from nowhere. I don't notice her and then she's there. 'Grandpa used to say that!' A small smile lifts the corners of my mouth, as I feel him close to me, making me sad and happy at the same time. Charlotte's wearing a smile too. But that isn't helping my current predicament.

'No one will help me,' I tell her. 'It's like they all know who I am before I've got to the shop. They ask if I'm on holiday and once I tell them I'm not, they ask my name, and where I'm from, then say they can't help me.'

'This town has a long memory,' she says. 'They blame me as much as they blame you.'

'For what?'

'For . . . everything,' she says, with a flourish of a hand. 'For the orchard being closed down, the town losing its apple supply and its reputation for its cider. For taking away the community spirit. Everything.' She sighs, then claps her hands, making me jump.

'But no good will come of sitting here crying. There is a supermarket in the next town. No one will ask your name there. It is a shame for the town. They are cutting off their noses to spite their faces, as you say. But you will get everything you need at the supermarket . . . if a little inferior in quality,' she says, with downturned mouth. 'But needs must. You can buy ready-prepared meals from a chilled section there. You will get everything you need.'

I sit and stare at her.

'But only if you are quick! Everything will shut at midday. Lunch waits for no one here in France.'

'But I can't get there!' I throw up my hands. There is no way I can walk to the next town. My feet are sore enough already.

'Here, take my car!' she says, and slips a key off one of the chains hanging from the belt around her waist. 'It hasn't been used for many years. Jason, you may need to give it a shove to get it started,' she instructs, and Jason, without slouching or questioning, is already on his way outside.

23

If you've never driven a 2CV before, I'm not sure I can even begin to explain it. It feels like you're inside a washing machine . . . on the stain-removal setting.

As it turned out, I managed to jump-start it into life. Years of practice.

Now I bounce and shudder through the unconventional gearbox all the way back to the château, my shopping strapped safely into the front seat next to me. I've driven so many vehicles in my time, a delivery van for the local butcher, a post-office van one Christmas and even a milk float, when the farmer's old sheepdog would keep me company. But this is a new one on me.

As usual, the drive leading up to the château takes my breath away. I park, locate the handbrake and pull it on tightly. Not like I did in the supermarket car park where the car started rolling backwards as I got out, surprising a few shoppers with their trolleys. I had to jump back in and give the handbrake a good tug.

I run up the steps to the château, calling to Jason, 'I've got the shopping!' as I let myself into the hall. 'They're due this afternoon, at five.' I now have to get the room aired and the beds made. I spot a cobweb I've missed and swipe at it with one hand, kicking the front door shut.

The kitchen is spotless. The fire is stoked and has fresh wood beside it. Upstairs, Jason looks to be making a start on the bedrooms, although his bed-making skills may need a little practice. But his effort is very much appreciated. I smile widely at him. 'Thank you!'

'No worries,' is all he says, but there may be a hint of a smile too. I wonder if he'll tell me what happened eventually to get him excluded from school. But not now. I'm just pleased he seems a little happier and not so withdrawn. Anyway, there's no time for a heart-to-heart right now. We have beds to finish.

It's just before five and I'm ready. Just. There's a big vase of dry hydrangeas from the garden in the hall, which smells of beeswax polish, and I've even run some ivy up the banisters. Jason has lit the fire in the salon, at the back of the house, overlooking the terrace and the old swimming pool. Dinner is prepped and ready to go, thanks to the lady in the supermarket guiding me towards ready-made chicken Normandy. I bought a *tarte aux poires*, pear tart, and will serve it with ice cream.

I have just enough time for a quick wash. I run upstairs and enjoy the hot water I know is costing us a fortune to heat, and only taking as much as I need. I make myself look presentable, then check the bedroom at the front of the house, overlooking the front lawn. It has higher ceilings than the floor above, and I'm assuming this was for special guests. The dining room at the front of the house, under the grand bedroom, is polished and I go down to run my hand over the ornate dark-wood chairs. I'll light the candles once they're ready to eat. I've laid two places at the end of the table and put wine on the sideboard, bread with pale butter cut into chunks and another vase of deep red dried hydrangea heads.

In the salon, we've removed the dust sheets and put them into the basement. I've rearranged the furniture around the fire, put some blankets over the arms and a tray with glasses for drinks. I'm sure they'll want a drink before dinner – I know I would. And that's all I can do, I tell myself, to make their stay as I would like it to be. I just want them to eat well, sleep well and leave here feeling they've enjoyed it. I'll check the fire, I think, and go through the billiard room to open the door into the salon.

It's full of smoke. The fire isn't drawing properly. I throw open the French windows and the smoke starts to dissipate, little flames appearing in the grate. I fetch some more wood from the pile outside the back door and stack it at either side of the grate, just like we used to do in Grandpa's house. I resolve to get a chimney sweep in, open my notebook and run my finger down the remains of the ripped-out pages, wondering what was written there and by whom. Then I add a note to get the chimneys swept next week and look up the word for 'chimney' in French, just in case I ever have to phone the *pompiers*, the fire brigade! Just to be on the safe side.

I close my notebook and leave the French windows ajar. I've bought gin and whisky, just supermarket brands, and some beers. At this rate, I may not make any money from this booking. But, I tell myself, feeling guilty about the money I've spent on Lizzie's credit card, it's a start and if we're to keep this place going, which I think is what Grandpa would have wanted, we have to do this.

It's gone five. I look out at the darkening evening. No sign of them. At six I debate turning off the oven: the ready-prepared meals are in dishes waiting to be warmed through. My stomach rumbles at the sight of them: beautiful chicken thighs in apple brandy and cream. I decide to make myself some pasta and pesto while I'm waiting for the guests to arrive. A little later, my phone pings with a text. It's the guests. They're lost. I put down a bowl of pasta for me and one for Jason and call him.

I find out where they are and, with Jason's help, put a pin in a map on Google and send it to them. Then I turn on the lights down the drive. Some work, others don't. I open my notebook and add it to the list. If only I knew where to get an electrician who wouldn't shun me as soon as he hears where I'm from.

In the salon the fire seems to have settled and is burning merrily. I throw a log on to the cheery flames, turn to shut the French windows and see that Cedric has made his way in again. I shoo him out.

In the kitchen Charlotte has eaten some of the pasta I'd made and seemingly enjoyed it. Jason is with her – clearly, having company has improved their appetites. I sit down at the table and sigh.

'That was lovely, *chérie. Merci*,' Charlotte says, wiping her mouth with a neatly ironed napkin that was meant for a guest, then offers me a glass of wine from the bottle she's opened, which was also meant for the guests. I accept it, take a big gulp and let out another sigh.

Just then, I hear the bell ring and jump up. 'Hi, welcome, you found us,' I say. 'Come in.' I open the big door wide.

The couple look exhausted, with a small overnight bag each. Their eyes are drawn upwards, just like mine were on that first day, to the big window on the stairs, as they take in the hall where I've placed the hydrangeas and the candle next to the vase.

'Wow!' they say in unison. Just like I feel.

'Let me show you your room, Mr and Mrs Pilking-ton,' I say, taking the bag from her.

'Oh, please, Larry and Laura.'

I smile and feel myself relax. 'Now, when you're ready, do come to the salon and have a drink before dinner.'

'Smashing,' they say, evidently in need of refreshment after a long drive up from the South of France. And I breathe a sigh of relief. Looks like I've got this covered.

'Larry, you did mention I was vegetarian, didn't you?'

'Oh, forgot, sorry.' He looks at her and then at me with a downturned mouth.

'He's always doing that,' she says, following me up the stairs, past the big window, the bats darting to and fro outside it like little bombers.

'Vegetarian,' I say. 'Of course, no problem.' I smile. How on earth am I going to work that one out? In this game, I now realize, it pays to be prepared for every eventuality.

24

The next morning, after frozen croissants I've heated in the oven and bread rolls I've cooked from part-baked, served in the dining room with coffee, tea and fruit juice, the best jam I could buy and butter, on Charlotte's instruction, Larry and Laura are packed and ready to leave.

'That was lovely,' she says. 'The pasta with pesto and cheese was delicious. The cheese was amazing!' I'd sent Jason round to Jacques for it, and now send up a little prayer of thanks.

'I'm so glad. And, once again, I'm so sorry about Cedric . . . and the late-night piano playing.' I wince.

'Not at all. Both were charming!' says Larry, and I think I could cry with relief. They pay me, add a big tip and promise a Tripadvisor review. They'll be back as soon as they can, they add.

As I wave them off, I can see Cedric strutting up and down the red-brick wall of the orchard. Looks like even he's making the effort to impress our guests.

Once they've left, I turn off the heating and return to the kitchen, put some of the leftover bread rolls on top of the stove to toast, and some of the oozing cheese on to a plate, like a creamy pond. I pull a blanket around my shoulders and check my emails, then contact the chimney sweep and agree for him to come in a couple of days.

Jason comes in and makes himself toast and chocolate spread. I'm not sure if he's on breakfast or lunch. He says very little and I focus on going through my messages as I bite into the crunchy, buttery bread, topped with creamy cheese. It tastes like heaven. Suddenly I stop, mid-munch. I put down the roll, chew quickly, brush the crumbs from my chest and reread the message quickly. There's another booking enquiry. At first I think it's a joke, a scam or just someone getting a kick from making fake reservations. I check the name of the person applying, then go to the website. It looks real.

'Jason! We've had an enquiry!'

He looks up from his screen. 'Cool.' He nods, sitting opposite me, his head down, one hand on his phone, the other holding his toast. 'When?'

'It's from the organizer of a classic car rally. They want all of the rooms! As many as we can offer! For

171

two nights! And a meal on the first night!' I say in aston-
ishment. 'They say it's the perfect stop-off point on their
annual rally and, if it goes well, they'll use us every
year.' My first big booking! I'm beaming. I'm excited.
We have to say yes. I'm terrified.

'When?'

'In two weeks!'

'You'll have to speak to the mayor again, if you plan
to offer more than five rooms,' says Jason, to my surprise. It's the most he's said since he's been here. 'And
more than five is a hotel, not a *chambre d'hôte*.' Looks
like he's starting to get a grip on life in France. I smile
and then my shoulders drop. He's right. I have to go
back to Jacques and get him to agree.

25

'They're here! Jason, put the broom away!'

Jason throws it into the flowerbed at the bottom of the steps. I can't help but roll my eyes. 'Jason, put it away! Don't just dump it anywhere!'

'Oh, okay, sorry,' he says, and lopes round the front of the building to the back door. November is giving one last show of autumnal glory as the classic cars roll down the drive, as smoothly as I could have hoped for: I've spent days repairing the potholes with a quick-drying filler I ordered on the internet.

'They've made it!' I feel quite emotional. I have no idea why. They're later than I'd expected and I'm learning that that comes with the territory of being a B-and-B owner. But it's happened. Despite all the forms I had to fill in, with Jacques's help, it's actually happening, even when I thought there was no way we could pull it off.

I don't know how to greet them. Should I let them pull up and then open the door to them? But I've swapped so many emails with them that they seem like friends. And I feel quite overwhelmed that these old cars have made it, despite breakdowns, some of them limping along the drive. I find myself clapping and waving enthusiastically from the top of the steps, tears filling my eyes.

As I take in the full spectacle I wish I could share the joy I'm feeling right now. There is something so joyous about those vehicles, celebrating their beauty and elegance, their ability to put on a show, just like the château.

Jason is standing next to me and I give him a quick squeeze. He doesn't seem to mind. Then I see Jacques in the field to one side of the drive, watching as they pass, Clémentine with him, clapping too. He smiles and raises a hand to me, and I wave back, grateful to share this moment. I move down the steps and start directing the cars into parking positions, just like when I was back in Swn Y Mor, working the car parks at weekends. Eventually all the cars are lined up and neatly parked. Everyone turns off their engines, gets out into the chilly evening air and congratulates each other on making it. The atmosphere is one of celebration and excitement.

Just then Charlotte appears at the front door. Once again, it's the furthest she ventures. She takes a glass from the tray that Jason is now holding, ready to hand around. She lifts her glass at me and sips. I think that might be a seal of approval. We've done it! They're here! Hopefully that's the hard part over.

'There's no hot water?' I hear one of the guests in the hall say.

I freeze as I'm about to put the ready-made Normandy stew, bought from the supermarket at great expense, into the oven. I slowly shut the door. No hot water! But I've had the boiler on all day. It can't have run out of hot water already.

Jason comes into the kitchen with his tray of drinks he was handing around outside and opens his mouth to tell me what I already know. I put up a hand. I need a moment to think. What am I going to do? Briefly I wonder what Charlotte would tell me to do. But Charlotte seems to have drifted off into a world of her own. Jason puts down his tray of drinks on the table.

I run and check the boiler. It's not on. I attempt to restart it and it seems to be making some very strange noises, filling the house with eerie groans and moans. But it's working.

'Is everything okay?' asks a woman, wrapped in a towel. She's peering into the laundry room down a few steps from the kitchen. She must be the woman I heard in the hall.

'It's all fine,' I assure her. 'Just Boris!' I tell her.

'Boris?' She laughs.

'The boiler,' I add quickly. 'Yes, old, fat and apparently needs a lot of notice in order to deliver on time. But when he does, the noises promise it will be glorious!'

She laughs again.

'Sorry.' I wish I'd kept my thoughts to myself. 'It was just a bit of fun when I got him first fired up, after I moved in on my own, and it seems to have stuck!'

'Don't worry,' she says, holding up a hand. 'Wow! You moved here on your own? That was brave!'

'Well, I didn't really see it as that at the time. I sort of moved here accidentally.'

'Accidentally?' She smiles, intrigued.

'Here,' I say, 'have another drink.' I take one from the tray Jason was handing around outside and give it to her.

'Well, really I only planned to stay here for a weekend. That seems like a lifetime ago now.' I double-check the boiler and all's well. I breathe a huge sigh of relief.

'And you just stayed?' she asks.

'Well, my sisters and I inherited this place. It was a bit of a surprise. And we've discovered we can't sell it . . . and, well, there's a lot of upkeep, and a sitting tenant, which is very common in France. It's *compliqué*!' I find myself repeating Jacques's words. 'I was the one who was free to stay on. My partner . . .' There's that word again. He never felt like a partner. Partners are there for better or worse, aren't they? I stop myself gabbling. The woman is staring at me, clutching her towel and her drink.

'Give it five minutes.' I top up her glass, and hope she drinks slowly. 'The water should be hot soon enough.' I wonder how much it's all going to cost.

'Well, I think you're very brave,' she says, and takes a sip. 'You did exactly the right thing. This place is beautiful.' She heads back up to her room.

I hadn't thought of it as brave. I just saw it as me being the only one who could stay. The only one who didn't have any commitments. I don't feel brave, just lucky. This room, the kitchen, is my favourite in the house, with the door on to the *potager*, the wood-burner, the steps down to the basement. And I find myself smiling that someone else can see why I love it as much as I do.

Suddenly I hear laughter and commotion from where all the cars are parked.

'The cows are out, on the front drive,' says Jason, out of breath.

'Oh, what next?' My happy moment is gone. I roll my eyes, run to the hall and out of the door.

'Sorry!' says Jason.

'It's not your fault.' I'm touched by his concern.

'I should have seen them. I was photographing the cars and putting them on Facebook.'

'Well, as Jacques is nowhere to be seen we'd better try to round them up ourselves. We don't want any of them going near the cars out there. The last thing we need is for them to do any damage.'

Suddenly there's a whistle. Jacques is at the end of the drive, and my heart lurches for some unknown reason. Clémentine is there too, grinning and waving her hands behind the cows as they start to leave, like a team of unruly kids suddenly being brought back into line by their much-respected coach.

At last I can put the food into the oven and light the candles in the dining room.

'Thanks again, Clémentine. I couldn't have done it without you.' Clémentine has stayed to help serve dinner to the big party, and Jason with the clearing up. The guests are now enjoying a sing-song with Charlotte around the piano.

'I enjoyed it!' She beams.

'You were great,' I tell her sincerely. Even Charlotte had helped, topping up drinks and checking everyone had what they needed. She and Clémentine seemed to have a lovely time together.

'Can I help again?' she asks.

I take a deep breath and wonder how Jacques would feel about it. 'Only if your dad agrees.' I was surprised he'd agreed this time. 'And I'd pay you.'

'No need. It is good for my English. Like English language lessons.'

Just as the group are singing the first Christmas carols I've heard this season, there is a brief knock at the back door. It flings open and there is the furious face of Jacques.

'Clémentine! I have been looking for you everywhere!'

'Sorry, Papa.'

I raise my eyebrows at her.

'Sorry, Fliss.' She stands. 'Goodnight.'

'Night.' Jason waves with a daft smile on his face and I wonder if he may have drunk the dregs of the apple-brandy cocktail we served at the start of the meal. '*Au revoir!*' He beams at Clémentine – the first time I've seen him smile since he got here. Jacques glowers.

Clémentine blushes and dashes out of the door.

'Jacques, I—'

'Next time you want my stepdaughter to work for you, at least have the decency to let me know where she is!' he says.

He doesn't give me the chance to explain any further. He takes a quick look around the kitchen, then turns and marches after Clémentine. Our happy bubble has burst.

'Where is Clémentine?' says Charlotte, returning to the kitchen with the bottle of apple brandy I'd put out to go with the coffee.

'Her father came. She had to leave.'

'Ah,' says Charlotte, putting the bottle on the table. 'Such a shame. I see so little of her. Just when she delivers meals. It was so lovely to be with her in the château. I know Jacques doesn't like her spending time in the place.' She sighs. 'Maybe it's time I went to bed myself,' she adds, looking crestfallen, just as the diners are starting to make their way upstairs.

'Yup . . .' I say, suddenly shattered and realizing I have to be up early to do it all again tomorrow. 'Come on, Jason, let's stack everything by the sink. Leave the washing-up until morning.'

In bed all I can think of is Jacques's angry face. Just when I'd thought I was getting somewhere. I sigh deeply and fall into an exhausted sleep.

The next morning Cedric wakes me with his 'may-awe' cry. I certainly don't need an alarm clock and neither will any of the guests. I throw the covers back. It's freezing. There's frost on the inside of my window. I dress quickly, hat and all, and head downstairs to put the heating on for the guests to wake up to.

Downstairs, in the kitchen, all the washing-up is done.

'Well, I have to be good at something.' Jason is standing by the sink, smiling shyly and I hug him tightly – just as a couple of plates slide from the top of the wet pile. He lunges to catch them, misses and they hit the floor. 'I'll get the broom,' he says, and I watch him sweep up the broken plates, hoping we still have enough for the rest of the weekend. Then my nose twitches.

'What's that smell?' I say, sniffing.

''S not me!' Jason says, holding up his hands.

I lean over the sink and grimace.

I stand up straight as the reality hits home.

'We've got a problem,' I say.

And he slowly nods in agreement.

I look back at the sink. 'Okay, grab me some tea towels,' I say, and sit on the floor. I open the door under the sink and hope I'm not going to surprise a family of mice living there.

I reach in for the U-bend. I've done this a few times but this one is definitely tougher than the ones in Grandpa's cottage and at the public loos. I finally get it off. It's pretty much clear. Which means the problem is somewhere else in the house. A blocked drain. And a houseful of guests. Who will all be getting up and wanting to wash and eat breakfast, very soon.

'Allô! Bonjour!'

A voice cuts across my thoughts and I jump up, hitting my head on the inside of the cupboard. 'Ow!' I shut my eyes tightly, take a deep breath and slowly sit up straight. That's all I need. Jacques! I open my eyes and attempt to smile.

He gazes at me from outside the back door. 'You have a smell,' he says.

'Yes, I know,' I say evenly, my fingers on the back of my head as I try to stand.

'Here.' He holds out a hand and steps into the kitchen. Apart from last night, when was the last time he came into the château?

'I'm fine,' I say firmly. But the hand doesn't move. I look at him and realize it would be churlish to refuse so I take it lightly, not expecting to feel as if I'd been lifted up by an army. I whip away my hand before I begin to like the sensation.

'You have a smell,' he says again, grimacing.

'Yes, I know!' I say again, a little less controlled as I hear movement from upstairs and my guests stirring.

He follows my gaze.

'Blimey, that's a pong!' It's one of the guests, following Jason into the kitchen. Kev with the classic Porsche. 'Brilliant night, love!' he says. 'Particularly the karaoke! Rounded off the evening a treat that piano playing!'

I cringe, knowing Jacques is behind me, and the disapproval that the idea of karaoke will prompt.

'Just a few songs, Christmas carols. That's all,' I say quickly to Jacques, the words *I'd hate to see my family home turned into a theme park* ringing in my ears.

'Thank you,' I say to Kev. 'Um, if you'd like to go through to the dining room, I'll bring you coffee, or perhaps you could grab a jumper and have it on the terrace. It's a lovely morning, even though it's November.' My voice rises. 'Or a walk around the grounds? I'll have breakfast sorted in no time.' I plaster on a smile.

'Not with that pong you won't. It's permeating the house. Turn anyone off their croissants and bread.' He grins.

I'm not sure what there is to smile about.

Then he says, 'Don't worry, I'll have it sorted in a jiffy. Just get my bag from the car. Never travel anywhere without it. Bit like a doctor! You never know when you'll be called on.' He laughs and turns to go out of the front door.

'Kev's a plumber. Well, he owns a large plumbing business,' says Jason. 'I got talking to him last night.'

And I'd kept telling my nephew to carry on serving drinks and stop wasting time! 'Jason, I could kiss you!'

He suddenly beams. 'So I did the right thing, going to get him?'

'You certainly did!'

There's a cough from behind me. 'If you need any help, I could get the plumber from the village,' Jacques says.

'Looks like I'm all sorted, thank you.' I smile.

He bites his lip and nods. 'Well, if you need him, I'm sure if I asked he'd come out.'

'That's great.' I smile again.

Kev reappears with his bag of tools. 'Right, let's get this pong sorted. Old places like this, it always happens. Bit of a blockage and you start getting waste emerging from places you really don't want it emerging! Jason, let's find out where it's pongiest!'

Jason goes off with Kev, passing Charlotte as she arrives in the kitchen with a lace handkerchief over her face, waving it occasionally.

'Oh . . . de smell!' she keeps repeating, and I push open the kitchen window in an effort to clear it. In fact, I should probably open all the windows. 'Jacques?' she says in surprise.

'Oh, sorry, did you want something else?' I ask him.

'Um, no, I just came . . . I can see you're busy.' He's edging back towards the door, having greeted his grand-mother with a kiss on each cheek.

'I am,' I say.

'About yesterday,' he says quickly, and hands me a round of cheese. 'By way of apology.'

'No need.' I smile but take the cheese.

'It's just I was worried. I didn't know where she was. She doesn't usually go out, or not far. She pops over with my grandmother's food, but doesn't stay too long. I was worried, that's all. You know how it is with children.'

And I feel a pang. 'No,' I want to say. But I don't. I bite my bottom lip.

'I can see you're busy,' he says again, and I wonder if there was something else he wanted to tell me. 'It's just her mother didn't turn up again for her visit. I was wor-ried she was disappointed.'

I swallow.

'So, I worry. But thank you for having her here. She had a good time.'

'No problem. I have to go,' I say. 'But thank you for the cheese, and, really, I understand.' I may not have children of my own but I was a child once, and I know how it feels to lose a parent . . . even if Clémentine hasn't lost hers. It must be hard for them all living apart. Sometimes I prayed so hard for my dad to come back. Of course, that wasn't going to happen. But time moved on: Mum was happy again and I had a great relationship with my stepfather, Martin.

He hesitates, and so do I.

'*Au revoir*, then,' he says, and raises a hand. 'Like I say, I could get the plumber to pop by, check on the job. Make sure they know there's work for them. Sometimes one has to learn to swallow one's pride,' he says, and I don't know if he's talking about the townspeople or himself.

'*Au revoir*,' I say. And Charlotte is watching the two of us with interest, I notice.

With the pong gone, breakfast can happen. I race back from the supermarket in the 2CV, wishing I could use the local bakery, but I daren't risk them not selling to me, or palming me off with stale goods. And this morning, I need a lot – Kev is having double portions of everything.

'We'd like to eat out this evening, if possible,' says Terry, the club organizer. 'Can you recommend somewhere?'

'Er, leave it with me,' I say. There's only one place in the town and I have no idea if they will entertain my guests.

26

Later that morning, when the guests are out exploring in their cars, a small van comes bumping and dipping down the drive.

I put down the duster and polish from where I'm running it over the big dining room table. I'd cleared up the breakfast crumbs and fed them to Cedric and his gang, who peck at them in the mid-morning sun, cold but bright. I watch it arrive and park at the side of the château.

A small man with a long moustache covering his lips, wearing a hat he keeps tipping on to the back of his head, gets out of the vehicle.

'*Bonjour*,' I say, hoping he's not looking for a room for the night. I'm fully booked. I smile to myself. Fully booked!

'How can I help you?' I attempt in rusty French, as he approaches and nods in greeting.

'I think it's me who can help you.'

I recognize him now. One of the men from the bar. 'The mayor says you may need a plumber. For ze odour.' He wrinkles his nose and looks around me, into the kitchen, with interest. '*Le plombier.*'

'Ah, that's kind of you to come, Monsieur,' I say. 'But there must be a misunderstanding. The bad smell has gone.'

He's still looking past me into the house. 'Would you like to see for yourself?' I ask. I take a step back, but he doesn't move.

'Please,' I say, and cautiously he steps in, removing his hat and holding it to his chest. He glances around the warm kitchen, walks along the corridor and through the arch into the hall and up the stairs, taking it all in. I say nothing.

Finally he says, 'No smell,' and smiles, his cheeks wrinkling.

'No smell,' I agree.

'My apologies, I should have come sooner.'

'It wasn't a problem. Like I say, I had help. But next time?'

'Next time. Call me. I will come,' he says, and I'm so grateful to hear that. Next time there'll be no Kev around. I thank him and take down his number in my notebook.

He turns to leave but seems reluctant. 'It has been a long time since I've been here. It's been a long time since this place has seen any life at all.' He clears his throat. 'It is good to see,' he says.

Then he bids me farewell and heads out of the château. Like most people I meet who see this place, his eyes are full of admiration for its beauty. As I watch him walk to his van, I see Charlotte staring from her window overlooking the lawn. The plumber turns and nods respectfully to her, and she to him.

Later I get into the 2CV and drive the short distance into town. I haven't been back since that shopping trip where no one would serve me. Well, Charlotte was right. There is more than one way to cook an egg. I found a way to make things happen. I just wish I hadn't had to. I leave the 2CV in the little car park, just like we did on that first day here. The town is so pretty, with its half-timbered houses and cobbled streets. If only it had been as welcoming as it looked.

I lock the car, take a deep breath to settle my nerves and walk slowly up the street to the square and to the restaurant, reminded of the day when everyone turned me away. I push open the door, my heart suddenly pounding.

Monsieur le plombier is sitting at the bar. The owner, Alphonse, also with a big moustache and a huge belly, is wiping glasses. I nod to the plumber and he greets me politely. 'Madame.' He gives a respectful nod, the same as he did for Charlotte.

Alphonse nods to me, too, and suddenly Rachelle, Clémentine's mother, is by his side, clutching his arm, her big red lips like a warning siren to anyone going near her man.

'*Bonjour*,' says Alphonse, with a smile, and I can't help but like him, despite his partner's obvious animosity to me.

'*Bonjour*,' I say.

'You again? The woman living in my husband's château?' she says pointedly.

'*Oui*,' I agree. 'Yes, I'm living in the château.' This time I don't feel quite so on the back foot. She's referring to Jacques as her husband while clinging to another man's arm.

She glares at me. 'My daughter's inheritance!' she snaps.

'The château is . . .' I can't say it belongs to me. It doesn't feel right. I'm not sure a building like that can be owned. Like Charlotte says, we are only custodians of the château for the time we are here.

I decide against arguing. 'I need to book a table for this evening.'

'Impossible! We are full,' says the woman, glaring at me.

I take a deep breath. 'I have a large party staying at the château. They want to eat out. It will be a big booking. And if it works, there will be more,' I say. I look around the empty restaurant and then at Alphonse.

'Plenty more. The château is open to guests now and it could help all of us.'

For a moment he says nothing, then looks down at *Monsieur le plombier*, who gives a gentle nod in agreement with me as he raises his pastis to his moustache.

'At what time?' asks Alphonse, despite his partner's protests. He opens the book and raises his pen.

'Seven?' I say tentatively.

'Seven o'clock.' He shuts the book. Just like that. 'But no tomato ketchup!' he says, and gives a little grin. I smile back and agree. His partner glares at me and storms out. Alphonse barely gives her a second glance – he's clearly used to the door slamming.

That evening, as the classic-car owners leave the cars on the drive and walk into town to enjoy crêpes, I sit down at my iPad and scroll through the pictures of the classic cars Jason has posted on Facebook. Maybe things are starting to go my way.

27

The following morning I hug Jason as I wave the cars off. He's come out of his shell in the past few days. He seems to enjoy being here, helping out, and that might have something to do with Clémentine too. It's colder today, the mist rolling around the château. I shut the door and shiver. I sit down at the table and pull up on the iPad the bank account, which is now much healthier than it was two days ago. And then I hear it: Boris the boiler, apparently giving one big sigh and taking one final breath, then dying with a clunk. Suddenly everything seems much colder.

I watch the little white van dipping and swaying along the drive. Squirrels are charging around the frosty lawn, up and down the trees, gathering their winter store cupboard. And in the distance, by the woods, I see something move. I stand still, hoping to see it again. I catch just the hindquarters but I may have glimpsed a deer.

Monsieur le plombier insists on driving round to the back door. I run back into the hall, through the archway to the kitchen, and let him in. I offer him coffee and he nods, then makes his way to the boiler, seemingly knowing exactly where he's going.

While the coffee brews, I can hear the sucking of air between teeth. I run my finger down the list in my notebook. I have a broken boiler to deal with, wood to collect and rooms to clean, laundry to handle . . .

'*Mais il fait froid!* It's cold!' Charlotte says, coming into the kitchen wrapped in a long fur-trimmed coat.

'I know, but the boiler will be fixed soon,' I say. 'Sit by the fire and have coffee.'

She pulls up a chair and inspects the notebook.

'There's so much to do,' I say. 'I bet when you were growing up here you had staff to do all these jobs. It's such a shame I can't ask Clémentine to help with the rooms but I'm not sure Jacques would approve . . .' I tail off as Charlotte is staring at the notebook, rather than the list, and runs her finger along the torn edges where pages have been removed.

'Yes . . . we had staff,' she says distractedly, running her hand over the cover of the notebook.

'Charlotte, are you okay?' I ask, as I put a cup of coffee in front of her.

She looks up at me, her eyes watery. 'Where did you find this?'

'In the dresser. Was that okay? I needed something to make lists on. I can use something else if it's important.'

She waves a hand. 'It's fine. It was where I always put my important thoughts. Nowadays I have very few important thoughts,' she says sadly.

I hear banging, like a hammer hitting something, clanking, and Boris rumbles into life. My spirits lift, until the boiler dies again, my spirits with it.

'Monsieur!' I say, as the plumber arrives back in the kitchen. I hand him a coffee. 'How's it going? *Ça va?*' I ask urgently.

He accepts the coffee I'm holding out to him.

'Can you save the boiler?' I ask anxiously.

He shrugs. 'I need a part to keep it going for the time being. It is the pump,' he says. 'But one day, I cannot say when, you will need a new boiler.'

'But for now you can save this one?'

'*Peut-être.* Maybe!' He moves his head from side to side and knocks back his coffee.

'Oh, thank goodness! Wait . . .' I rush to the dresser and pull out one of the bottles of apple brandy. '*Merci!*' I hand it to him. 'Thank you for coming out. A gift, *un cadeau*, to say thank you.'

He looks at the bottle and, suddenly, his eyes mist. He looks from the bottle to Charlotte, then back at the bottle he's holding in front of him, in both hands, just as Jacques did. My heart gives a little squeeze at the thought.

'Ah . . . the apple festival,' he says.

I look at Charlotte, who is lost in her own world too. 'Apple festival?' I ask, intrigued.

He nods slowly, then pulls out a corkscrew from his bag of tools, removes the cork from the bottle and holds it to his nose. He inhales, closes his eyes, then opens them and motions to me to bring glasses, three.

I put three glasses on the table. He tuts, goes to the shelf where I'd taken them from and replaces them with a more suitable model, then pours us each a shot. I'm not sure drinking at this hour of the morning is sensible, but when in Château des Arbres . . . If this is what it takes to get the boiler back up and running, so be it.

He lifts the glass to his nose, sniffs and sips. I wonder if the moustache will taste of apple brandy all day. Charlotte lifts her glass, drinks a little, then sips coffee, as if this is the most natural order of events.

I pick up my glass. The brandy smells of the depths of autumn, rich yet fruity, with a hint of winter frost and mist, like today. I sip. Cough. Drink coffee. Burn tongue, then drink again and finish with coffee. *Monsieur le plombier* is staring at the glass, which still has a few drops clinging to the sides. As I watch him, he gives me a wide smile.

'So,' I say, 'can you fix it? The boiler? Can you get the part?'

'If you can bring this place back to life,' he lifts the glass, 'then I can revive the boiler,' he says. I could hug him.

But I'm not sure if he's talking about the château, the orchard or the apple festival.

28

Monsieur le plombier, as I've taken to calling him, not knowing his name, has returned with the part he needs and is working on the boiler. Charlotte has gone back to her apartment. I open my iPad to check my messages. Suddenly my heart not so much leaps, but jolts. There's a message from Ty.

I click on it and read slowly, the words dancing as they always do when I really need to concentrate.

He's seen the pictures on Facebook and thinks it all looks great, which makes me smile. He hopes I'm doing fine and he's putting a friend in touch, he says.

'A blogger, a big one! Wants to come here!' I check out his name and followers, his YouTube channel too. He's American. A surfing friend of Ty's. This could be massive – Mason Grey coming here. Telling everyone about the Château des Arbres *chambre d'hôte*!

I read, reread and triple-check that I've understood Ty's message right. On the one hand, he hopes I'm well, and second, he's handing me this amazing opportunity. My heart and head hurt. Why would he do this? It must mean he still cares about me. Oh, Ty . . . Suddenly my head is in a spin. Here, there is no Ty, no confusion. Just me and the château I've fallen in love with. And I want to make it work. I don't want to go back to Swn Y Mor, I know that for sure now. This is where I want to be. But where does Ty fit into all of that? And this Mason Grey, he may just give us the boost in customers that I need. I check out his YouTube channel again. He has thousands of followers, watching his travels around the world. This is because of Ty.

'Whoop!' I shout. For whatever reason Ty has done this, I'm very, very grateful.

'Jason!' I call up to his room, from the stairwell in the turret. 'Mason Grey is coming!'

His head pokes out of his room.

'Mason Grey? *The* Mason Grey? Coming here?'

'*Yeeees!*' I shout, as he thunders down the servants' stairs.

I show him the message from Ty. Then he beams and hugs me.

Two days later I'm waiting on the steps of the château for my guest to arrive. Everything is ready. Jacques agreed for Clémentine to come round to help once I explained what this blogger could do for us all if he gave it the thumbs-up. Even Jacques couldn't see how this might be bad for the town and agreed that Clémentine could help. She and Jason have been working their way through the jobs I've given them. Every time Jason has spoken to her, he's become tongue-tied. She's blushed and become tongue-tied, too, and it's been lovely watching the two of them working side by side. Jason seems able to work out one end of a broom from the other now and has barely broken any plates during his washing-up.

Jacques has been round to wish me luck, brought a basket of cheese, butter and cream, and told me to let him know how things go.

The town is quivering with expectation, as am I. Everyone has been helpful, urged on by Jacques, their mayor. The baker has insisted I have the bread straight from the oven, and the florist gave me flowers she said weren't up to selling, but I know they were a gift. The only person not looking happy is Jacques's ex-wife, Rachelle, who has sat in the window of her salon, filing her nails and looking at me with disapproval as I pass, but I'm determined to make this work for us all. Once the customers pour in, I'm sure she'll feel less antagonistic.

Claude, the town taxi driver, known as *Claude le taxi*, was dispatched to the station to pick up Mason Grey and now he's coming up the drive. The car stops at the front of the house and, after an exchange of euros, the back door opens. Claude gets the case from the boot, shuts it, shakes his passenger's hand, thanks him for the tip and drives off. No doubt straight back to the bar in the crêperie to report on the important visitor. I'm excited and nervous all at the same time.

'So, you must be Fliss?' He smiles up at me, a brilliant white smile that makes me catch my breath. He has blond hair, expensively cut to look messy, like he's just got out of bed. He's wearing a light blue cashmere scarf that matches his eyes and a light grey woollen coat. Under that, jeans and premium trainers. And the more he smiles, the more the dimple in his right cheek deepens.

'You're Mason!' I state the obvious, then say, 'Welcome to Château des Arbres,' and hold out a shaking hand to the front of the building, letting the château do all the talking for me.

That night, I serve *soupe de poisson*, and Alphonse has insisted on cooking and delivering traditional savoury crêpes for the guest, delivered by a beaming Clémentine.

'How are things?' she says, creeping through the back door with the specially prepared dish.

'*Bonsoir*, Clémentine.' I kiss her on both cheeks as I take it from her. The smell is amazing and I'm desperate to peek inside, but don't want to let out any more of the delicious aroma of cream, apple brandy, chicken and whatever else is in these crêpes. I put it in the oven on low heat and stir the *soupe de poisson*.

'And Papa made a tarte Tatin, with my help . . . and your apples!' She giggles, handing me another dish from the basket over her arm. 'With cream!' She passes me a small pot with a lid.

'Tell him *merci* from me!' I say, with a nod and a smile. Things are definitely on the up.

'Hey!' says Jason, blushing and smiling, and Clémentine kisses him on both cheeks. Then I watch, amused, as she blushes and smiles too. Things, I repeat to myself, are definitely on the up.

'So, what did he do today?' She turns back to me.

'Well, I gave him a tour of the château. Even Charlotte's apartment. It's amazing! You can see everything from the turret in her living room!'

'And he met Grand-mère? How was that?' Clémentine winces.

'Charlotte and Percival were perfectly behaved!' I smile, stirring the soup.

'No pretending to be a ghost? Or playing the piano?'

'Nope!'

'And Cedric?'

'No problems,' I confirm, getting out silver cutlery from the dresser and checking it for fingerprints. I polish it anyway.

'What about the cows and Pegasus?' She giggles.

'Not a peep!' I turn to her.

'So, what did he do?'

'Well, he went around the château, and after the tour, he talked about it into the camera on his phone. Then we went to the woods, and walked the pathways through there and I showed him the orchard. But what he really wants to see is the town, then take a look at one of the beaches near here and check out the surf. *Claude le taxi* will take him tomorrow. He's arranged to hire some equipment from a guy who runs a surf school on the coast.'

'So, all good?' She beams.

'All good!' I beam back and give her a quick hug. 'But right now, I need to get dinner served.'

'I can help,' she says.

'Only if it's okay with your dad,' I check, just to be on the safe side.

'He sent me here, didn't he? With the tarte Tatin and the cream! He must approve if he's done that.'

I wonder if she means approves of our house guest or me. And part of me suddenly hopes it's me.

29

'Come with me!' Mason is standing in the big hall with a small rucksack over his shoulder, smiling that brilliant smile at me.

I'm just clearing up from breakfast and am smiling too: not only did I have wonderful fresh baguettes and croissants this morning, Jean-Pierre, the baker, delivered them to the back door himself, wishing me luck. I've saved the crumbs for Cedric and his gang.

'Oh, I can't. I have so much here to do. A château owner's list is never done!' I laugh.

'I can imagine. This place is truly awesome!' He looks at me and I feel like Clémentine smiling and blushing in front of Jason. 'Come on, when did you last have a day off? And think how much more I'll be able to shout about this place if I've got someone to share the day with. You surf, don't you?'

'Not for a long time,' I reply.

'Yes, go on, Auntie Fliss!' Jason is behind me with my Puffa jacket and beanie hat. 'Charlotte and I can hold the fort here.'

For a moment that worries me. But Mason's right. When did I last have a day off? And it's all for the good of the château, and the town. It's networking. 'Okay, okay, I'll come!' I laugh.

'Great, we'll pick up a picnic!' says Mason, and I'm suddenly very excited about the prospect of a sunny, wintry day at the beach.

'I can organize food,' I say, and dash back into the kitchen and gather bread, butter, cheese into a basket with a blanket. 'We'll take the car,' I say to Jason, who phones *Claude le taxi* and cancels him, with apologies.

'He said it was fine. He'd take his wife out for lunch instead.' Jason is definitely getting to grips with French life and I'm so pleased.

'Go!' he says, after I've checked he'll be fine for the hundredth time.

'Go!' says Charlotte. 'We'll play poker!'

'Don't play poker,' I tell Jason. 'Or drink the brandy.'

He laughs. 'Clémentine can teach me some more French!'

And I see Clémentine is still here, drinking hot chocolate in the kitchen and I know Jason will be fine. It will be lovely for him to have some time off from me and the worries of château life.

'Okay, okay!' I say, as he practically pushes me out of the door. He gives the 2CV its usual bump start, then Mason jumps in.

'To the beach!' he says, and I'm buzzing with excitement. Something I haven't felt in a very long time.

'To the beach!' I repeat, and the 2CV bumps and lurches down the drive. At the end of the drive, I see Pegasus and slow down. Then I realize Jacques is riding him. I'd had no idea he was ridden.

'Wow! That's one big horse!' says Mason.

'A Percheron,' I say, sounding knowledgeable.

Jacques raises a hand as we pass, and part of me wishes I could have stopped, enjoyed a chat and patted Pegasus on this crisp, gloriously sunny morning. But I have to stop thinking like that. Jacques is helping me get the château on its feet for the town, that's all . . . And for his family, I remind myself. And I wonder if, out on Pegasus, he was checking things at the château, seeing how things are going. And then as we pass his farmyard, I feel as if someone has kicked me in the stomach. There, standing at the front door, watching me, is Rachelle, Clémentine's mother. Looks like her visits to Clémentine are back on. Is she watching my progress too? Waiting for me to fail and leave? I don't want to. Not only for Jason's sake but for mine too. I've come to love this place and I can't stop telling Mason about it, all the way to the beach.

30

The wind is blowing, making the long grasses bend, and the waves along the stretch of sand are tumbling over each other like excited puppies. We pick up our boards and wetsuits from the guy with the surf-hire Transit van, there to meet us. Mason pays him, then we take it in turns to change quickly in the back of the van. I'm shivering with cold, excitement and nerves. It's been years since I've done this. I can't really believe I'm going to get back into the water. But something tells me it's time.

'Ready?' Mason says, board under one arm, smiling at me and looking at the waves.

'Ready!' I say. I am. It's time! We race across the sand to greet the bumpy ride ahead of us.

'Whoop!' I shout, catching my first wave in years, then crashing, tumbling and getting back on to the board. This time, I'm not scared. Not like when I took that big hit and never got back on a board. After that I sat on the shore. Today I'll take whatever the waves have to throw at me. I feel invincible. I'm in it for the ride, a bit like life at the château. I'm in it for the ride and I'm not going to let anyone knock me off course.

'Happy?' calls Mason over the wind and surf, the crash of the waves, grinning as we paddle out to sea.

'Very,' I say, and I am. Happier than I've been for a long time.

There's a storm coming. I run around the house securing all the shutters and closing the windows tightly behind them. It's amazing just how long it takes to check each room. My hair is still wet from a quick bath and I'm feeling really alive, like being back in the water. It's different being here. I feel something in me has moved on from Swn Y Mor where I didn't want to get back into the water after my accident, when a big wave took me out, I crashed into Ty and knocked myself out. Here, it feels good. I look up at the darkening sky. The wind picks up and there's a crack of lightning. Thunder makes me jump and laugh. I thought I was only happy when I was back in Swn Y Mor, waiting for Ty to return from working away, or being at competitions. But something has shifted. There's more to life and I want more. Today has made me realize that.

Another roll of thunder, and lightning flashes. I run down the stairs, checking on Charlotte, who has taken to leaving her door unlocked and open for Percival to wander about on his own. She is fast asleep with an eye mask on. I stroke Percival, put down some food for him and he wags his curled tail.

I shut the door on Percival's contented grunting and Charlotte's gentle snoring just as I hear another bang and all the lights go out. I stop at the top of the stairs, hold on to the banister and find my phone, then make my way carefully down to the kitchen.

'It might be tricky serving you dinner in the dining room tonight,' I say, hoping Mason doesn't mind the blackout and it won't put a dampener on his review of the place. Then I stop and catch my breath.

'I found candles. Thought we could eat here, if you'll join me?' His face is lit by candlelight, his hair still shaggy and damp from the sea. He reminds me very much of Ty and I wish he didn't. This place is not about me and Ty. It's about me, on my own, working out what I want for the future, getting back on my feet, like the château.

'That would be lovely,' I say brightly, but feeling slightly unsure. Is this really how I want our review to end up, him eating in the kitchen with the housekeeper when the electricity failed? 'If you're sure? I could always light the candles in the dining room. I don't want you to think this is how I would normally serve dinner in a power cut.'

'Really, this is nice. Cosy,' he says. I hear the pop of a cork, then wine splashing into glasses.

'In that case . . .' I smile, sip and swallow '. . . that would be lovely.'

'It is,' he says, sitting by the wood-burner. I open it and throw in another log. The flames light up the room and his face, watching me.

I put the dish Alphonse has sent with Clémentine into the oven, hoping there'll be enough for two, but if I do a side salad and don't eat much it should be fine. I was going to have an omelette.

Then I realize that the oven is electric. I look at him and we both laugh.

'How does more bread, cheese and salad sound?' I say, hoping this won't mark me down. 'Or I could make an omelette on the wood-burner.'

'That would be glorious! Some of that cheese from lunch would be wonderful.'

I begin whisking eggs. The full extent of my culinary skills. This has to be the best omelette I've ever made! But I'm back in my comfort zone, whisking eggs and heating the butter until it's frothing in the pan on the wood-burner.

'So, what are your plans for this place?' he asks, and I suddenly remember to focus on the real reason he's here. The blog!

'Well, really to get more people to come to the B-and-B, and eventually hold events here,' I say, suddenly very nervous. 'I mean, get the B-and-B up and running first, of course.'

'It's a gorgeous place,' he says. 'And do you see yourself staying and living here? I mean, you own it, right?'

'Well, um, obviously I . . .' How do I say I haven't got a clue what I'm doing, that I'm just winging it? And all the time I'm terrified of getting it wrong. 'You never own a château, you're just its custodian while you're here.' I'm repeating Charlotte again and feeling like I mean it. I've fallen for this place, but I don't feel it's mine, whatever the paperwork may say.

I focus on pouring the egg mixture into the pan and listening to it sizzle in the glorious golden butter. I could have done this at the café when I had the chance to take it over. Why didn't I?

'So, you're here in this big house. What do you do for company?' he asks, sipping his wine, lounging on the pew by the fire.

'Sorry?' I look at him in the flickering light from a candle stuck in a wine bottle on the table, wondering if I've misheard him.

'I said what do you do for company?' He smiles lazily.

'Well, there's Charlotte and Jason,' who is up in his room, probably on his phone, 'and there are the guests, of course . . .' I stumble over my words, not wanting to misread this situation, like I did with Jacques.

'Are you and that guy next door an item?' He nods sideways.

'What? Jacques?' I pick up the pan without a tea towel and burn my hand. I grab an oven glove, pull the omelette off the heat, then run my hand under the cold water tap that groans and moans.

He stands up, comes over to me and takes my hand.

'It's fine.' I try to ignore the stinging in my hand but let the cold water keep running, enjoying the familiarity of the noises it makes.

But Mason doesn't move and I have a strange feeling that he's standing too close for someone concerned about my burnt hand. All the laughter and fun of the day has disappeared.

Suddenly he draws my hand towards him and moves his mouth towards mine. It takes me a second to realize what's going on, the candles, the questions, the slick move. I'm not reading it wrong but I don't want to offend.

'Hey!' I try to laugh it off and step back. I refocus on the omelette, despite my throbbing hand.

'Oh, come on, Fliss. We've had a good day. A good couple of days. Let's round it off properly.'

He moves in closer to me again, his finger stroking the underside of my breast in a well-practised move. Right now, I'd give anything for Jason or Charlotte to come in, even Cedric to cause a distraction. But there's no one.

'I think you'd better stop that.' I try to be polite. I don't want this misjudged action to put paid to his review. I should have been clearer, maybe not so keen to impress him. 'I'm not looking for anyone just now.' I give a little cough as my throat tightens. 'I'm . . .' What am I? In a relationship, coming out of one, confused? '. . . on a break.' I hope that will bring this to an end and we can forget it ever happened.

But instead of stopping he laughs, and carries on caressing me. I tense up.

'Right, let's eat!' I say, stepping away and holding the salad bowl between him and me. I intend to make sure it stays there. Hopefully he'll get the message.

The storm outside rages on.

He stares at me, and suddenly all the excitement and joy of his visit has evaporated.

'Come on, Fliss, let's leave this. I'm hungry for something else.' He nods towards the staircase.

I glare at him. 'I told you. I'm not interested. Ty and I are just . . . taking a break. I'm not looking to be with anyone, right now.' I repeat.

'Come on. Ty told me you and he weren't exclusive. It's fine. He won't mind.'

'I beg your pardon?' I feel like I've been hit by the same wave that brought me down all those years ago in Swn Y Mor.

'When he told me about this place he said you and he had a thing, but you weren't exclusive, just when he was back in whatever that town is called. Said that's when you'd hook up.'

I stand and stare.

He grins.

He steps forward again and this time a low voice comes out of my mouth. 'Don't touch me.' All thoughts of the blog and the advertising it will give this place, the goodwill of the town, disappear. Thunder crashes overhead.

'Look, he doesn't need to know if . . .'

'Out!' I say.

'What?' He laughs, disbelieving.

'Out. I want you out!' I glare at him.

'Oh, come on! Jeez! No need to be so uptight!'

He swigs his drink.

'I said, I want you out!' I repeat and he turns back to me.

'You can't blame a guy for trying. I mean, you're the one showing me around, making me meals, coming surfing with me. What did you expect?!'

'I expected that you would like this place, write us a good review, bring customers to the town, be professional.'

'And I expected you to be a little more "French".' He lifts his glass to his lips. I snatch it, and it slops over our hands.

'Hey!' he says crossly.

'Out!' I point.

'I don't know if you've noticed but there's a power cut. And a storm outside! How do you expect me to leave in this? And, frankly, that is no way to treat your guests! I wouldn't recommend Château des Arbres if it was the last place in France!'

I begin to shake. I've blown it! How did I get it so wrong again? How can I be such a bad judge of character? How could I have believed for all those years that Ty and I were content? I trusted him. I thought we were going to have a future and all the time . . . I swallow . . . I was some kind of booty call. I want to scream, but instead, I say, 'I want you gone in the morning,' a fire burning in my stomach and behind my eyes. He picks up the bottle from the table and turns to march out of the kitchen. All I can think of is Charlotte, talking about the bakery, saying, *Never settle for second best.*

'Out!' I repeat. 'First thing!'

'With pleasure. This place is creepy anyway.'

And with that, he's gone to his room.

I stand in the kitchen and watch the storm rage from the window.

Later, I lie on my bed, holding my phone to my chest, wondering what words there are to say to Ty, having discovered he never considered us 'exclusive'. All those times away, the competitions, the working trips as a surf instructor, the snowboarding jobs. God, I've been such a fool! No wonder his eyes glazed over at the mention of family, children, a future. I don't know who I'm angrier with – him, or me for thinking we had something special: it didn't need changing because I didn't want to mend what wasn't broken. Seems it was broken after all.

I watch the lightning move further across the sky, the thunder petering out. I count the seconds between them, just like I did as a girl with Grandpa, the flashes and crashes moving further and further apart. Because that's where I am now, miles apart from where I was, and I'm not going back. As the storm finally passes, I lift my phone from my chest where it's been lying over my heart as it breaks in two, then look at the screen. I scroll to Ty's name, with hearts and kisses next to it, then move my shaking thumb over it and do what I should have done years ago. Ty was never going to commit. That was never going to change. I know that now. I press block and delete his number.

Then I curl up in a ball and cry myself to sleep. I wish I knew whether it was for Ty and all the years I wasted on him, or for letting the town down and killing the high hopes we all had for this visit.

31

Early the next morning I wake to hear a car on the drive, the slamming of doors and the car leaving again. *Claude le taxi*, I think, listening to the engine fade down the drive. He's gone, with everything I had bragged to Jacques I could make happen. I curl up in a tighter ball and cry all over again.

'I heard a car,' says Charlotte, coming into the kitchen as has become her routine in the mornings now.

'Yes, he's gone,' I say, laying out the breakfast the baker has delivered for Charlotte and Jason.

'Did he not like the château?' she says, with disbelief.

'Let's just say it didn't come with all the extras he was hoping for.' And the words catch in my mouth. My eyes fill with tears. 'And now all the town will know.'

She shakes her head. 'Believe me, I know what it is to be the talk of the town . . . a scandal! I have spent too many years hiding away. What other people think doesn't matter. If I had my time again, I would hold my head high and look people in the eye, not feel ashamed.' And before I can ask any more I hear water dripping.

'Ze guttering,' Charlotte says, with disdain. 'It's the leaves. They blow,' she swirls around a hand, 'with ze storm. They fill the guttering and the water has nowhere to go, other than places it shouldn't.' She tuts.

I rush out of the back door and take deep breaths. There's a nip in the air, mixed with the smell of woodsmoke from the fire. But there's cleanliness too, as if the storm has brought in clean fresh air for us to breathe. She's right: the water isn't going down the drainpipes. It's overflowing, creating puddles, creeping in under the door frames and through the window panes in the kitchen. I sigh.

Pegasus pushes his head through the fence and I realize I missed seeing him there yesterday. I missed Cedric too, strutting around the place, trying to move into the château where he believes he belongs. I missed Charlotte's late-night piano playing and Percival the pug, all tucked away and on their best behaviour to impress Mason Grey. It's Mason Grey who should have learnt how to behave, I think angrily. But here and now, the guttering is blocked and there is only one thing I can do.

'Show me how to get to it, Charlotte,' I say.

Up in the attic, in one of the storage rooms, I open the skylight window, and take a huge breath of the cold, crisp air. 'Just don't look down,' I tell myself, pulling a chair towards me.

'Hang on, I'm coming with you!' says Jason, appearing behind Charlotte in the old attic room – it could make another bedroom some day, I find myself thinking, probably to distract myself: I'm about to go out on to the roof of a château in winter, with a rope around my waist.

'No, no, you stay here. Just hang on to that rope,' I say, having wrapped the other end around my stomach. I climb on to the chair, hoist myself up and swing my feet out on to the roof and the ledge there. I step out and don't look down. The only thing I can do is keep looking where I'm going. Forwards. My heart is thumping. I feel like I'm wing-walking on an aeroplane. Not on my bucket list of things to do. I reach the blocked drainpipe, water spilling over the top, and kneel down, grateful it wasn't that hard to find. I hear Cedric and glance at the ground. My head swims and I scrunch my eyes tight shut. Focus, I tell myself. Keep going.

'You can do it!' says Jason, from the window.

'Yes, you can!' I hear Charlotte, and think it's probably been a long time since she's been in these store-rooms. Hand shaking, I reach down and pull the leaves from the drainpipe, then pick up the broom I've brought with me and dislodge the blockage that's gathered there. Suddenly it shifts and Jason passes me out the kettle, full of cold water. I go back to the drain, tentatively, my back to the outside edge and pour the water into the drain-pipe. It runs down it. Job done! Then I replace the chicken-wire cap, presumably there to keep the leaves out, that had blown off. Now all I have to do is get back to safety in one piece. I stand and turn back to the open window, my heart still thudding. I reach Jason and Char-lotte's outstretched hands and practically throw myself inside it, almost crying with relief.

'I did it!'

'You did it!' says Jason.

And if I can do that, I can do anything. Despite Mason Grey and his visit, I am going to make this place work, I think determinedly. I just have to work out how.

I hear banging and look out of the window from the safety of the attic room. It's the door to the apple orchard, swinging on its hinges in the now gentle breeze. Must be the cows again. They're a part of this place, as are Pegasus and Cedric. But I'll never be able to make this place pay by the end of the year if I don't come up with some-thing. A few guests here and there are not going to fill the bank account that has just been emptied for repairing the boiler and putting on the best for Mason Grey. The memory of his visit makes me shudder.

I'm glad he's gone, and I'm glad I've seen Ty and our relationship for what they were. I thought I was so lucky – he was so good-looking, so easy to be with – when actually he may have been the worst thing that happened to me. I go back downstairs and outside, a quick glance at the roof where I've just walked, happy to be on terra firma now, and set off towards the orchard door where a branch has come down, damaging the hinge.

I pull at it hard. It doesn't budge. I pull harder, putting all my anger into it. Eventually it shifts and I'm out of breath but feeling a whole lot better. The door, though, swings in and out and falls into the orchard. The leaves have all blown from the branches, but there is still fruit on them and on the ground. There are no cows in sight and I wonder if they've finally gone into the barn for the winter. I miss them already. The air is cold: I pull my coat tightly around me and my hat over my ears, like a shell I'm retreating into, protecting me from everything I don't want to face right now. But I have to face this. Jacques will want to know how the visit went. Lots of people went to lots of trouble to help me. I've let the town down, promising big things and huge publicity. I thought it was going to be perfect. But nothing's perfect, I think, as I bend down and pick up a windfall apple. I turn it in my hand. I bite into it. It's so fresh. Not too sweet, but not too sharp either. It's subtle.

I pick up a few more and carry them in the front of my big jumper. I've no idea what I'm going to do with them.

I WhatsApp Nellie with a picture of them in my jumper.

'Apple sauce?' she replies.

'That's a lot of apple sauce.' I show her pictures of all the windfalls on the ground and the cold lunchtime air nips at my nose, making me sniff. I make a video call to Nellie and show her a picture of them in my jumper.

'What about apple chutney as well as apple sauce?' she says, and I see her scanning her selection of old cookbooks.

'Well, I could. Maybe I could find something online.'

'I have a perfect recipe for apple chutney,' she says, and I know she's on a mission. 'It's perfect for using up apples. Apple jelly too!' Nellie has always known how to make the most of the food she has to hand and never wastes anything.

'You really should become a chef. You know that, don't you?' I tell her.

'Phfff!' She waves a hand. 'Right now, I'd settle for being able to pay the rent, since my hours at the super-market have been cut.'

'Oh, no!' I wish I could help her but there's no money in the kitty. Maybe the chutney will help a bit.

'How are the twins?' I ask.

'Okay. Missing their brother. Never off the phone to him.' So that's who Jason's been messaging all this time. 'But Jason's okay, is he?' she asks, and I know she must be missing him and worrying about him.

'He's fine.' I smile. 'Really happy.'

'Not getting in the way?'

'He's doing brilliantly. Really helping me. Great at washing-up! Hardly breaks anything, these days!'

'Ah, at least I've taught him something!'

'And for helping me get the right people to fix things when I needed them.' I smile, thinking of Kev and 'the pong', but am then reminded of the new boiler I'll need to buy, after paying Charlotte's allowance and the tax bill. I need to get some guests in. Or some other form of income.

I get a flashback to Mason Grey bellowing at me before he grabbed the bottle and disappeared to the room. The best room in the château that Jason and I, even Charlotte, had worked so hard to get ready for him. I'm so angry on their behalf, and for the towns-people who helped me.

'I'll send you over the recipe.' Nellie brings me back to the here and now. 'Fliss?'

'Hm?' I say, shaking him from my thoughts.

'Do you think we'll be able to keep the château going?' she asks. 'Do you think you could find a buyer for the apples?'

Suddenly we seem to have switched roles, like I'm the eldest trying to reassure the others. But I'm the one who's here. I'm also the one who sent our blogger packing, with our chance of getting winter bookings.

I sigh. 'I don't know, Nellie. I really don't know. But I hope so. I just need an idea.' There must be something we can do with the apples.

I walk back to the house and put the apples into a bowl, racking my brains for a way to put things right with the town.

Cedric has followed me in and I shoo him out of the back door.

Jason arrives in the kitchen, followed by Clémentine, who still blushes when he talks to her, but this time they're laughing.

'Hey, you two, I could do with a hand picking up windfalls in the orchard if you'd like to help.'

'Okay,' Jason says.

'I can help too,' Clémentine adds. 'I promise I've checked with Papa!' She kisses Charlotte on both cheeks.

Charlotte smiles at her, then peers at the apples in the bowl. 'You've been in there again?' she says, suddenly looking like she's seen a ghost, just as she did when she realized I'd discovered the orchard.

'Yes,' I say. 'Would you like one?' I hold out the bowl to her and she lifts a shaking hand.

'Are you okay, Grand-mère? Would you like me to get Papa?'

She shakes her head. 'I'm fine really,' she says, with a crack in her voice as she reaches out and takes one of the imperfect apples in her frail hand, which is covered with paper-thin skin. We all watch her as, slowly, she lifts it to her nose and closes her eyes. Then she opens them slowly and looks at me.

She rubs the apple with her thumb, as if it were a baby's cheek, finding comfort and joy there. 'You went back?' she asks quietly.

'A branch fell on the door,' I say, deciding to say nothing about Jacques using the orchard for the cows.

'And how is the orchard?' she asks, as if it is an old friend.

'Well, the birds are singing still in there. The leaves have blown from the branches. But there are apples on the branches, as well as the ground.' I see delight on her face as I describe it, as if she's drinking in the memory.

'Would you like to see it,' I ask tentatively, 'for yourself?'

Clémentine and Jason seem to hold their breath.

'I would,' she says, barely audible.

This is a woman who is about to go outside for the first time in years and I'm as nervous as if I'm taking a young colt out for the first time, terrified that he'll bolt.

32

'Ready?' I ask. We have found a shawl to wrap around Charlotte and a hat, in the attic where I love rummaging and finding clothing that's been tucked away. She's unhappy that the hat doesn't go with her outfit. Her arm is linked through mine and I'm holding her hand tightly. Or it may be her holding mine tightly. Clémentine has found her a pair of boots at Jacques's house and finally, timidly, Charlotte pokes her head out of the door. She hesitates and I stop, convinced she's not going to do it, but she lifts her head and smells the air, as if getting a scent of home . . .

'It's just there.' I point to where the cows trampled the brambles and now the doorway is wide open, offering a glimpse of the trees beyond.

And slowly, very slowly, Charlotte puts a booted foot over the threshold of the back door, and on to the stone step. As the other foot follows she seems to waver, and Clémentine steps in to hold her other arm and hand. Jason brings up the rear, like a well-behaved pageboy. All of us are hesitant as we approach the orchard.

She holds out her hands, letting go of mine and Clémentine's as we reach the doorway into the apple orchard, and holds the wooden frame. I'm hoping she won't just bolt back. But she doesn't. She stares as if she's standing at the entrance to Heaven and it appears to be everything it promised. Her face is lit as if she's standing in bright, brilliant sunlight. She's drinking it in, as if she's in need of refreshment after a long journey.

Eventually, without looking at any of us, she walks into the orchard, like a foal taking its first tentative steps, growing bolder and steadier with each one. She stretches out her fingers to the branches as if greeting old friends she hasn't seen in years. She is focused on the trees as if she's seeing stories between the branches where the early-morning mist gathered and swirled.

'Did you used to come here, Grand-mère?' asks Clémentine.

'Grand-mère,' Charlotte says, considering the name. 'I'm a *grand-mère*, a great-*grand-mère*!' she calls to the trees, making Clémentine giggle. 'And, yes, I came here all the time when I was young,' she says, tears sparkling like crystals in her eyes.

Charlotte seems in no hurry to leave, although the day is getting colder by the minute.

'Why don't we pick up the windfalls while we're here?' I say cheerily to the others, leaving Charlotte to her thoughts for now as she continues to explore, but I'm worried as she's venturing further from home.

'I'll look for boxes in that building over there,' says Jason, tripping as he sets off. 'I'm fine, I'm fine!' he says, and Clémentine giggles again. At least it's a step on from blushing, I think.

I start to pick up apples from the damp grass, droplets of water clinging to them. Clémentine does the same. I try to keep an eye on Charlotte, the hem of her long dress getting damp on the grass.

'Auntie Fliss!' I hear Jason call. He's holding up two wooden boxes. 'There's loads up here!'

'Keep an eye on your grandmother, Clémentine,' I say, and run to meet Jason at what looks to be the gardener's cottage, with a large potting shed. Although I came in here when we helped the drunk cow home, I didn't notice much. But this is an actual little cottage. There is ivy growing round the window frames and the wooden door is covered with brambles. But the potting-shed door is open and I step in to see a pile of wooden boxes stacked like a Jenga tower, possibly left in a hurry.

Jason is walking back through the orchard towards Clémentine, swinging the boxes. I reach in to grab another couple and they topple. I reach to catch them, and eventually I step back as they fall at my feet, dust flying up. A shaft of light appears through the branches to illuminate the wall behind the boxes. There is writing on it, handwritten messages . . . I stretch out my hand to the pencil markings, drawings, notes and sketches. And pinned to the wall are pages from a notebook . . . the notebook I've been using. And on them I find letters, poems, declarations 'to my one true love' signed with a C and a kiss. And on the walls, in pencil, a drawing of hearts, with the names Charlotte and Dafydd inside them. Charlotte and Dafydd, my grandfather. I slowly reach up to them and start to trace the words with my finger, feeling suddenly close to Grandpa, when a voice makes me jump. 'Clémentine?'

I turn back to the shed door.

'Clémentine! What are you doing here? Your mother is waiting in the house for you!'

Jacques is walking through the orchard and he doesn't look happy. Oh, not again!

'Jacques!' I try to stop him before he gives Charlotte a fright.

'Why is it that whenever I need to find Clémentine she seems to be with you? No doubt here to see the famous blogger!'

'Sorry, Jacques,' I say, trying to get him to keep his voice down. 'And, the blogger has gone,' I add quietly, but he doesn't hear. He clearly has other things on his mind.

'I – I just don't want to get her hopes up, to think that our family is a part of this place any more. You understand, don't you?' he says.

'I know, I'm sorry. But, honestly, she doesn't think that. She and Jason have become such good friends. Charlotte and she are really quite close too.' And I point.

He follows my finger, his eyes widening as he sees Charlotte walking through the branches talking gently to herself and smiling.

'Grand-mère?' he says, and stares in total disbelief.

33

'So, you came here a lot then, Charlotte?' I walk over to join her. Jacques keeps his distance, presumably not wanting to disturb the extraordinary scene and pop the happy bubble that Charlotte seems to be in.

'Oh, yes!' She smiles. 'They were happy times. Not just for me. This place, it was the heart of the town,' she says. Jacques's face softens as he stands and listens to his grandmother. 'Every year about this time we would have the apple festival. All the villagers would come and pick the apples and help press them up in the barn,' she gestures to it, 'and the cider would be ready for May, when the blossom comes. It was wonderful. Everyone would get their share of cider. The town was known for it. It's the apples. Late developers. They can last until Christmas. We always had apples at Christmas.' She picks one from the tree and holds it to her nose, reminding me of the red apple decorations we put on the tree each year. Jacques, too, seems to be remembering a happier time but was it before his wife moved out, or when he was a child and life was more carefree?

'So this place was pretty fruitful!' I wonder why it's not a cider-producing orchard any more and hope for some answers now.

'Oh, yes! People came from all over to buy our cider. The town was known for it.'

She's actually skipping! And the questions are scratching away at the back of my mind. Could this be the answer to the château's future? I mean, how hard is it to produce cider? That could be how we make the château pay for itself.

We continue to pick up the windfalls and put them into boxes. I decide to stick to windfall chutney to start with.

'So . . . what happened, Charlotte? Why was this place locked? Why isn't the cider being made?'

She turns to me, tears filling her eyes. She tries to speak but closes her mouth again, all the time rubbing the charm on her necklace as if it reminds her of happier times. I'm willing her to tell me what is clearly swirling through her mind, like the early-morning mist that always lifts.

'One winter, the last before the orchard was closed, we had freezing rain that coated the apples on the trees, making perfect ice sculptures. The apples eventually rotted and slid away to nothing, leaving just the icy shell. Ghost apples, they call them. Perfectly formed on the outside, empty within,' she says.

I wonder if it's the apples she's talking about, or herself.

'And the orchard here?' I say carefully, and I know Jacques is watching me and Charlotte from a distance.

She opens her mouth, but no words come out.

Then there's a shout: 'Auntie Fliss! Auntie Fliss! Phone! Your phone!' Jason's calling.

I don't know whether to leave Charlotte now and turn my attention to him or ignore him. I look at Jacques, who is clearly as frustrated by the interruption as I am.

'Auntie Fliss!' he calls more urgently. I look back at Jason. 'I just went in to get my phone to take some pictures,' he says, coming up to me, 'and yours was ringing. You need to speak to these people. I said you'd ring straight back.'

'Perhaps,' says Charlotte looking from Jason to me, 'we have enough apples for one day.' And the chink in the door that nearly opened to me is shut again.

She drops the apple into the wooden box under the tree and links her arm through mine.

'We have to go,' says Jacques, quietly. 'Clémentine's mother is waiting to see her.'

'How come she's suddenly visiting so much?' asks Clémentine, echoing what I was thinking. 'She never used to come so often.' Clémentine doesn't look happy about it.

'*Oui, je sais,*' says Jacques, putting his arm around her and walking with her. They may be stepdaughter and stepfather, but to me and anyone else looking on, they are just father and daughter, reminding me of Martin, my own stepfather, who was there throughout my growing up, and all the tears and tantrums of the teenage years.

'Grand-mère? Are you okay to get back inside?' Jacques asks.

'I am,' she says. 'And I'm ravenous! What is there to eat?'

And we all laugh.

'I will send Clémentine with something when her mother leaves. Enough for everyone.' He smiles, and I find I'm smiling too. There's some kind of happiness in this orchard and I want to bottle it.

'*Au revoir.*' He nods to me, and holds my gaze, as I do his, and I feel something I haven't felt in a very long time. A feeling of— Oh, no, it can't be! I can't let this happen. I cannot fall for this man! He is the last person I need to find attractive, caring, attentive for so many reasons. For a start he's a Cadieux. And married – though, according to Clémentine, he and his wife separated at least a year ago. Besides, I definitely do not want another relationship right now. Definitely not. The only thing I want to pour my love into is this glorious house. And if I don't, it will be Jacques who will benefit. He'd never feel the same about me.

'*Au revoir*,' I say, finding it hard to turn away. Clémentine looks up at him, then back at me. '*Au revoir*, Clémentine,' I say.

She waves. 'Thank you for a lovely time,' she says.

'You're always welcome, as you know.' I'm not sure I should have said that, whether Jacques will be cross.

But he says, 'Thank you,' and then they turn to leave the orchard by the far side.

Charlotte and I turn to walk the other way to the gate. I don't rush her: whoever was on the phone can wait. This is a special time, I think, as we walk slowly back through the orchard, the light beginning to fade, the cold air nipping our noses and ears, frosty tips forming on the grass. For a moment my thoughts are with Jacques and Clémentine going back to their warm kitchen in the farmhouse, and the look on Charlotte's face as we stood in the orchard at the end of a lovely day, thinking about the drawings and messages on the wall, Charlotte and Dafydd and the heart, and the words 'hope' and 'for ever' in curly writing. Jason is still waving the phone at me as he jogs towards us in the orchard.

I'm holding Charlotte when Jason, as if it's the most natural thing in the world, arrives on her other side and the three of us walk to the back door.

'They've gone, but I said you'd ring straight back,' says Jason.

'Who was it?' I say, hoping it was neither Mason Grey nor Ty. I don't want to speak to either of them. There's nothing left to say.

He gabbles something so fast that I know I must have misheard him.

'A what?' I ask him.

'A wedding!'

I finally grasp what Jason is saying.

The evening air is suddenly very chilly but the warmth in the kitchen from the wood-burner is lovely as we step inside. Jason has added wood to the fire – I'm so proud that he's thinking for himself.

As Charlotte steps back inside, she is seemingly back to her normal self, quieter, the laughter gone with the twinkle in her eye. The young woman who walked through the apple orchard has disappeared.

'It was a woman on the phone, the couple who came here for the classic-car rally. The woman you spoke to when the boiler needed restarting. She said she loved the place. Loved what you were doing here. They want you to organize their wedding party.'

'Here? At the château?' My head spins. A wedding!

'Yes! All the rooms, a weekend of meals, and the blessing here,' says Jason. 'They said if anyone could sort out their tricky family, it was you! Oh, actually, they told me not to tell you that bit. Sorry!' He holds out the phone to me.

'When?' I ask, excited and terrified.

'Ah, that's the other tricky bit. The wedding venue for their party has had to cancel. They won't be open again until after the new year and she doesn't want to wait.'

'What? New year?'

'Uh-huh,' he says. 'They have their registry office booked to do the official bit in the UK and they don't want to change it. But they want a festive blessing and wedding party on New Year's Eve at the château!' He beams widely.

'A wedding at the château,' Charlotte says softly, as she moves slowly through the kitchen pulling off her hat and patting her piled-up hair.

I look at her, then at Jason, in sudden horror. 'But that's only a month away. I'd never be able to do it!'

'Then, what *are* you going to do? Turn it down?' Charlotte says sternly, eyebrow raised.

'I—'

'Sometimes in life we have to take the risk,' she says. 'And from what I've seen of all you've done here so far I can think of no one better to organize a wedding.'

'I agree.' I spin round. Jacques is stepping over the threshold through the back door, holding a large pot between two oven mitts and a baguette under his arm. 'Clémentine is with her mother,' he says, 'so I said I would bring over dinner for the hungry chatelaine!' I hear the smile in his voice.

He walks into the middle of the room, probably the furthest he's ventured into the château in years, and places the big pot on the table. I know he's trying to protect Clémentine and not wanting her to think that their family is part of the château any more, but it seems so wrong he's cut himself off from it altogether. This is progress indeed.

A day of firsts. His first back in the heart of the kitchen and Charlotte's outside it! My stomach flips.

'Me? Organize a wedding party? Here?' I look at them all as if they're crazy.

'It's just what the place needs – always has done!' says Charlotte. 'Now it's time!'

34

'So you want . . .' I press the phone to my ear, pen in my other hand poised over my notebook. I run the tip of my finger down the jagged edges of the torn-out pages and think again of the poems and notes I found on the wall in the potting shed. Notes from Charlotte to her 'one true love'. Drawings on the wall from Dafydd Hope, my grandfather. Pictures of hearts, with initials and the date, when my grandfather would have been twenty, a young man. But why here? What I do know is that those two people were clearly very much in love, but that's all.

I turn the pages of the notebook and there, at the back, is the list I started making: the cost of the new boiler and the tax bill. And I remind myself of what this wedding could mean for the future of the château.

Charlotte is sitting by the fire. I can still see the smile on her lips from her walk in the orchard and at the prospect of a wedding at the château. This could mean everything.

'So, let's start again.' I take a deep breath to settle my jangling nerves and focus really hard on writing down everything the bride-to-be tells me.

'Well,' I say, finishing on the phone and turning to Jason, Charlotte and Jacques, who has put a delicious casserole in the oven to keep warm, the smell of the slow-cooked beef and herbs making me hungry. 'Looks like we've got a New Year's Eve wedding to plan for!'

'Whoop!' shouts Jason, and hugs Charlotte, who hugs him back. Then, at a nod from her, he goes to the dresser, opens the cupboard door and offers me a bottle of apple brandy. A huge smile breaks across my face. Who needs Mason Grey? This is it. This is the start of Château des Arbres as a wedding venue! Now all I have to do is arrange it. Which may be easier said than done with the townspeople after the fiasco with Mason Grey. I'm quite sure *Claude le taxi* will be passing on the news that Mason Grey will not be featuring the château in his travel vlogs.

'So, Mason Grey has gone.'

Seems Jacques heard me after all in the orchard. I nod and drop my head.

'And I take it that it didn't go well.'

I shake my head, willing myself not to cry. 'He wanted more than was on offer during his stay,' I say, my cheeks burning. I swallow. 'Everyone in the town must know by now. They'll hate me all over again. And I don't blame them.' I'd promised them so much and delivered nothing.

'The town will survive,' says Jacques. 'They have before.'

'But I can't put on a wedding party in the château without their help and cooperation. I need them if I'm to pull it off. All of them!' I make a list in my head, which includes the local florist, the baker, the *auberge*, the crêperie and, of course, the hairdresser, Rachelle, Clémentine's mother.

I'm so busy with my mental list that I don't notice Jacques guide me to a chair and gently insist I sit.

Jason pours the amber liquid into small glasses and puts one in front of me.

'To moving forward,' says Jacques, surprising me and raising a glass.

'There is more than one way to cook an egg,' says Charlotte.

'Good riddance,' says Jason.

We sip. It's a taste I'm getting accustomed to and to enjoy. A taste of here, of the new Fliss, who's not going back but moving on.

'Well, I may not know what I'm doing, so I'll just keep muddling through!' I smile, feeling a huge wave of relief.

'Sometimes we just have to go with what feels right at the time,' says Charlotte again, and I don't know if she's talking about me organizing the wedding, or the memories the apple orchard brought back today. Maybe, in time, I'll find out a little more.

'Is Clémentine joining us?' she asks brightly.

'She's having an evening with her mother,' says Jacques, looking quite at home in the kitchen, the furthest he's been into the château for years, always sending Clémentine with meals for his grandmother, only checking on her from the threshold. Today has been a big day for them both.

'Your dinner is ready,' he says, wiping his hands on a tea towel.

'You're welcome to stay and join us,' I say, laying the table with the tarnished silver cutlery that lives in the wooden drawer in the dresser.

'Oh, yes, that would be lovely,' says Charlotte, smiling.

He hesitates.

'You did make it, after all!' I laugh.

He still hesitates, and I know he doesn't want to get too used to spending time at the château, a château that will never be in his family again.

'I'll lay an extra place,' says Jason, and does just that, taking the decision out of Jacques's hands. 'I'll serve,' he adds. Again, I love seeing the change in this boy!

It's been a good day for all of us, and we raise a glass to good health and happiness. Once again I catch Jacques's eye, and wish his knee wasn't quite so close to mine under the table, and that it didn't make me feel quite as excited as it does.

'*Joue de boeuf*,' Jacques explains, when we all have a plateful.

'My favourite,' says Charlotte, picking up her fork and tucking in as if she's always had such an appetite.

We smile at her enthusiasm as if watching a fussy child eat properly for the first time and ask for more.

'Slow-cooked beef cheeks with apples.' Jacques raises his eyebrows and laughs a little. And I like his laugh. 'Cider, carrots, onions, spices and seasoning.' He picks up his fork and takes a piece of bread from the basket Jason has put on the table.

I put a forkful of the beef into my mouth, where it melts and slides down my throat, making me sigh with delight at the flavours. The sweet flavours of the apples, cider, carrots and spices. I have no idea when I last felt so content.

'It's Clémentine's favourite too. I make it in big batches and freeze it,' he says.

'Why do you refer to yourself as her stepfather?' I ask, feeling bold in the warm, relaxed atmosphere.

'Because that's what I am,' he says. 'When her mother and I met, Clémentine was very young. She was part of her mother. But I never wanted her to feel she had to call me "Papa". I wanted her to make that choice for herself. I didn't want it imposed on her.'

'Looks to me like she's made that choice. A long time ago!' I smile. 'It's just you who needs to know what a great job you're doing.' I chew another mouthful of the delicious casserole, and I don't know if it's the warmth of the kitchen, the company, the food or the wine, but I find myself suddenly wanting to talk.

'After my father died and Mum married Martin, it was Grandpa I looked to as my dad. It's not what you call them that's important, it's what they mean to you. Grandpa was so much more than my grandfather. He was my dad, my best friend, my mentor. He was just always there . . . He was more important to me than anyone . . .' I trail off.

I look at Jacques across the table, the candle in the bottle flickering, and I think he may have blushed.

'*Merci*,' he says, and for a moment, it feels like it's just him and me.

'Yeah, let's be honest. She lucked out with you as a dad! Mine was a right twat!' says Jason. 'But I did okay with Mum and a couple of great aunties!' We all laugh.

'It is good to hold on to love when you find it,' says Charlotte. 'Hold on to it tightly.' We fall silent as we eat and, once again, I can't help but think about the drawings and letters in the potting shed. Until Percival snores loudly, exhausted by his journey to the apple orchard, making us laugh all over again.

35

I'm up early, in woolly jumper and two scarves I've found in the drawers up in the attic: treasures that have been left untouched for so long. Jason is up without me having to hassle him out of bed and is feeding the fire in the wood-burner.

'Coffee's on,' he says, and I smile.

'Okay, I'm going to get those apples in and make them into chutney. Your mum's sent me a recipe. Perhaps we could use some at the wedding party . . .' My mind starts whirring on wedding plans. But, first, I need details on how all this works. I'm going to have to talk to the mayor, check he's happy about the number of guests. This is now an event. I'll have to go and see him . . . and that thought, for the first time, makes me smile.

*

I pull on my trainers, which look decidedly less smart than they did when I arrived and now have a dozen stories to tell, what with overflowing guttering, the vegetable garden, the cows . . . They've been through a lot but they're still holding up. A bit like me. I stand up to see Charlotte with a shawl around her and the same hat she wore yesterday.

'Charlotte?' I ask, surprised to see her up so early, with little pink flushes in her cheeks.

'You are going to the orchard.' It's a question and a statement at the same time.

'I am.'

'Then I would like to return with you.'

'Okay.' I open the back door. Cedric is there, spreading his splendid tail, showing off all the colours in his feathers. I throw out the breadcrumbs from yesterday's loaf to him and his gang.

Charlotte watches with interest. 'Ah, the peacocks. I've seen them from my window. I didn't know we still had peacocks. We always used to have them.'

We set off for the orchard. 'Um, we don't. Not really,' I say. 'They just arrived, a little while after I did.' Pegasus is there leaning over the fence and Charlotte jumps. 'Jacques's horse, Pegasus,' I tell her.

'Ah, yes,' she says. 'There was always a horse to help at harvest.'

In the orchard the birds are still singing and a pair of red squirrels swing from tree to tree.

We begin collecting the windfalls again.

'The apple festivals were the highlight of the year,' she says, her face young and alive again as she repeats the story she told me yesterday. But I wonder if this time she'll tell me about my grandfather and how he ended up owning this place.

'Tell me about them,' I say, not looking at her but picking up apples.

'Oh, they were wonderful! All the town would come and pick and then there would be a bonfire, over there.' She points to a stone circle in a clearing. 'There would be a big pot of stew, or a hog roast, and warm spiced apple juice from the fruit they had pressed earlier in the day, and the last of the previous year's cider. And fireworks. We always had fireworks. People set off guns or fireworks in the orchards in winter to wake the spirits and hope for a good new year ahead.'

'Why did it end, Charlotte?' I stop what I'm doing and turn to her. 'Why was the orchard closed?'

She takes a deep breath and this time I'm praying Jason won't interrupt.

'My father was a very proud man. He was the château owner. He had standing in the community.'

I carry on picking up apples and say nothing.

'I was young and very much in love. Your grandfather was just a few years older than me. He was the gardener here.'

'Here! This is where my grandfather lived and worked?' To think I never knew.

'In there.' She points at the gardener's cottage.

I think of the pictures in the potting shed, his handwriting, his declarations of love. Hers too. I feel him here, with us. I can't believe I didn't know about this.

'We were very much in love,' she says again, with a deep sadness.

'I always thought he and my grandmother were childhood sweethearts.'

'After he left here, he moved back to Britain and married your grandmother. That was where he stayed, loyal to her. I married and stayed loyal to my husband, and had a son. Jacques's father. But he and his wife are both dead. It's just me and Jacques . . . and Clémentine,' she adds, with a smile.

My brain is racing, little things my grandfather would say. That camping trip was near here. 'Did we come here once, to visit?'

'Yes.' She laughs. 'You and Jacques played in the woods, where the deer graze. It was after my husband's death. Dafydd came to check on me. My father never knew of that visit, of course. It was very carefully planned, just a meeting between friends. Nothing else.'

I *knew* I'd met Jacques before! I knew it! I blush at the memory of my childhood attempts to speak English to him and him not interested in speaking back. He was more interested in my sisters, who ignored him, compared suntans and left him to walk with me into town.

'Why was he here?' I say, as I reach for another apple. 'I mean, how did he come to be here in the first place?'

'He came to see the Normandy beaches. It was 1960. He was eighteen. I was just sixteen. He was born during the Second World War. He had an older brother, who died on D-Day at the same age he was, eighteen.' She shakes her head. 'I think he felt he wanted to be nearby for a while so he got a job here tending the grounds.'

Grandpa always liked to be outside. He was never happier than when he was tending his small, neat garden.

'And was he happy here?'

'Very happy,' she says. 'He stayed, for nearly two years.' Then I see Charlotte pull out a cloth from a bag she's carrying over her shoulder, laying out a muslin sheet and putting apples into it.

'And why did he leave?' I ask.

She doesn't answer. Instead she says, 'We store apples in the cellar, wrapped in newspaper, or here, hanging them from the trees. They keep well into winter this way.'

I watch her tie the muslin sheet into a bag and hang it from a branch. 'Keeps them safe,' she says, looking like a young woman again. It's as if she's keeping her memories safe, here in the apple orchard.

'Did you meet here, with Grandpa?'

She giggles. 'It seems so strange you calling him that. He is still a young man in my mind.' She's smiling. 'Yes, we met here.' And it seems the door isn't totally shut on the conversation.

We continue to pick and hang the apples from the trees.

'There's so many here,' I say. 'There's no way I'll be able to use them all in chutney, unless I go into business with it. There's enough apples here to keep the whole village in cider, and a few bottles of apple brandy too!'

She's staring at me. 'I think your grandpa would be very proud of what you're doing here,' she says. It's as if she's seeing him in me.

'I don't know if I can do it, Charlotte, a wedding. I've managed to get away with a few B-and-B customers so far, but that was by the skin of my teeth. I can't mess up someone's big day for them. I'm scared. What if I can't do it? What if I end up a laughing stock just for having thought I could?'

'You are a very capable young woman.' I wish I felt it. 'You will do it.'

I take a deep breath. 'Will you help me, Charlotte? Organize the wedding?'

'It would be an honour,' she says, and dips her head.

'In that case, I'll give it my very best shot.'

36

'Grand-mère! What are you doing out here again? You'll catch your death of cold.'

It's Jacques.

'Helping gather apples,' she says. And the door she opened on her memories has slammed shut once more.

'And what do you plan to do with them all? I know a cider-maker if you want to sell them,' he tells me.

'You do?' I take a deep breath. 'Actually, I don't think these apples belong to me, or the château,' I say.

Jacques frowns. 'We agreed I would use the land to graze the cows, but not take the apples.' He rolls his head from side to side. 'Other than the odd one or two for a pie.'

'I need to make this wedding work,' I say, looking up at the branches.

'I know, and . . .' Jacques hesitates '. . . you have my full backing. While I may have wanted or hoped that the château may come back into our family at some time, I realize now that I couldn't keep it going. Not like you have done, breathing new life into it. I couldn't do what you're planning now with this wedding. The château is in good hands.'

I'm slowly processing what he's just said. 'This place could be amazing as an events space but I can't do it on my own.'

'As I say, you have my backing. I'll help all I can.'

'Thank you. But for this to work, I need the trust of the town again. And I have a feeling I know how to build it. If it works, we may just be able to pull off this wedding.'

'Go on,' he says.

'Bring back the apple festival,' I say.

'The apple festival? I thought you were organizing a wedding. Haven't you got enough to do?' He laughs.

'Why don't we just let the villagers back in to make cider?'

'Let them back in?' Jacques tilts his head.

'Help clear the orchard of the apples. I can't use them all and maybe, if we let them come back to make cider, they might be less suspicious of me. Let them have the cider apples and perhaps when I need them to help with this wedding they'll be there for me. I can't do this by nipping to the neighbouring supermarket. I need the town on board. I need them to forgive me for Mason Grey and the visit that came to nothing.'

'She's right,' says Charlotte. 'And you do not need to apologize for Mason Grey. He was never going to understand this place. But it takes a community to put on a wedding. This town hasn't been a proper community for a long time. Not since my father closed the gates to them and forbade anyone to come near them.'

'Why did he shut the orchard, Charlotte?'

'This is where he found us together, me and Dafydd. As I said, we were very much in love, but he was so angry. He sent Dafydd away, closed the orchard and locked it to make sure nothing like that ever happened again. And, I think, to try to erase Dafydd from our lives. The orchard was never opened again. Our love meant that everybody else had to suffer the consequences of our actions. That was my fault, mine and your grandfather's. It's time to lay the ghosts to rest,' says Charlotte. 'Put on the apple festival, Fliss!'

Jacques looks between us. 'It could bring back a lot of memories,' he says worriedly, to his grandmother. 'The town remembers being shut out of the orchard, told it would never reopen, because he had found you there with a foreigner. He was angry and you must have been embarrassed. Are you sure this is something you're happy with?'

'Some memories shouldn't be shut away. They should be enjoyed.' She smiles. 'Among the bad, there are still good ones that should be celebrated.'

Jacques seems unsure. Charlotte wanders off to the gardener's cottage. 'It seems that lots of things change when you're around, Fliss,' he says.

'Look, I don't want to make your grandmother unhappy. Far from it. But you can see how happy she is in the orchard. She likes being here. She likes being outside. If we bring the locals back, maybe they'll be there when we need them. And if we're going to do this wedding, we'll need them.'

'Look, I'll try, but I can't guarantee that the locals will be on board. It won't be easy to regain their trust after the years they've been shut out from here. But I'll do all I can. Are you sure you want to do this?'

'Yes,' I say firmly, but inside I'm shaking. 'If this comes off, I can pay the tax bill and buy a new boiler. And if we can do more, it will keep up Charlotte's allowance. Who knows? We may even start to make money. The place may not fall down around our ears!'

'And do you think you can do it? The apple festival and the wedding party?'

'I'll need a lot of help. But we have to try. Otherwise the house reverts to you, and you and Charlotte will be in the same boat, trying to find the money for the new boiler and the tax bill. None of us really owns this château. We're just looking after it for the time we're here.'

He nods slowly. 'I think you're right. Let me know how I can help. Only you can save this place. You have the skills.'

'No.' I laugh. 'I've just got a little bit of lots of skills but maybe I've found somewhere to put them to good use.' All this time, while I thought I was drifting along without a plan, I was actually learning lots of different things. Suddenly I feel quite proud of myself: I'm exactly where I should be and every little job I've had in the past has led me here.

He smiles at me, and again I have that falling feeling, like Alice in Wonderland, falling down the rabbit hole, unable to do anything about it.

'First of all, let's get the villagers back into the château grounds – we'll plan the apple festival and hope they come,' I say. Butterflies ricochet around my stomach as he smiles.

37

For the next few days, as December rolls in with an icy blast, we gather in the château kitchen and have lunch together, setting out all the jobs that need to be done for the apple festival at the weekend, including sending out word that everyone is welcome at the château to pick apples and make cider. We plan drinks – aperitifs, Clémentine corrects me – and small appetizers. As we plan who will do what, Jason on bramble-clearing and tidying in the apple orchard, Jacques on appetizers with Clémentine, and me on, well, everything else, Charlotte sits by the fire talking about how the apple festivals used to be. I write down buzzwords to help me remember how she described it and hope we can make it just as it was. I hope they'll come, because if they don't, I have no hope of organizing a wedding in around four weeks' time.

On Saturday lunchtime, the first weekend in December, after a morning of cleaning, checking there's no pong in the château, draping bunting and fairy lights around the trees in the apple orchard and laying a big bonfire for lighting later, with all the brambles Jason has cleared, I think we may be ready. The frosted tips on the grass have thawed, and the afternoon is bright and light and cold. I'm as nervous as a child on their first day in school. Jason looks as if he's had a fight with a gang of alley cats: he's covered with scratches from the brambles and the bonfire building.

'I'm fine! *Pas de problème,*' he tells Clémentine, when she asks.

We all go out on to the front steps, and Jason walks down the drive to open the gates, now back on their hinges and freshly painted. I wanted to create a good first impression. Charlotte has hurried across the lawn to open the newly repaired door into the orchard, my skill with a drill is better than I remembered. The brambles have gone and the fallen tree has been logged and stacked, firewood for next year. Every part of me aches. My hands are red and raw from painting and pruning in the cold December air and I just hope it will all be worthwhile. For once this week it isn't drizzling or raining.

The archway into the orchard is free of brambles. We've cleared away the weeds around the gardener's cottage and the potting shed and piled them into the bonfire pit. Jacques has been in the barn and tested the apple press. I've left all of that to him and am really grateful he's got stuck in. As mayor, he's also spoken to everyone, and invited them to be part of the apple pick, and to bring containers to make cider. Some were delighted, others, apparently, a little unsure.

The winter sunshine is slipping through the bare branches of the trees, so bright that I have to shield my eyes with a hand. I want to send up a message of thanks to whoever is in charge of weather today. The red squirrels are still busy chasing through the trees, the frost all but burnt off the lawn, and the day feels full of promise. Charlotte is wearing an unusual selection from her winter wardrobe: a large hat, with a scarf tied over it, a long dress and coat. She might have stepped out of a sepia photograph. She has finished the look with a brightly knitted scarf Clémentine has given her and is wearing it with delight.

So, here we stand. It feels like the longest wait of my life. If no one comes, I will have no choice but to turn down the wedding. There is no way I can do it without the town's help. If I can't pull off the wedding, I can't pay the tax bill, and the château will return to the Cadieux family, to Jacques. Jacques has no way of raising the money to replace the boiler or the time to run the place as a *chambre d'hôte*. The château will be left to decay.

Jacques catches my eye and my stomach flips. 'Jacques, what if no one comes?' I say.

'It'll be okay,' he says, takes my hand and gives it a gentle squeeze. Clémentine grips the other and smiles at me. Then Jacques gives me a little wink and I feel more alive than I've ever felt.

'Listen!' he says, his eyes sparkling, like the sunshine through the trees. Jason drops the tray of welcoming drinks he's carrying with a clatter.

'Sorry, sorry!' He holds up both hands and Clémentine rushes to help him clear up the cups of cider he's dropped, with surprisingly few breakages.

Then, I hear it – the first throaty sounds of a belching Renault undulating down the drive where Jason has been cutting back the undergrowth.

I can hear the church bell in the distance, and as it finishes chiming, the first of the villagers parks in front of the château and steps out. It's *Monsieur le plombier*, with two more vehicles behind him: the butcher and baker and their families. They came! And more are following.

'They came!' I exclaim to Jacques. 'Thank you!' I hug him, which he wasn't expecting. After the initial shock, we cling to each other for a moment, and I slowly slide my arms away from him, feeling awkward. 'Sorry!'

'No, my pleasure!' he says, with charm.

I run down the steps and attempt to direct the cars into an orderly line, but it doesn't have the same impact on the locals as it did on the classic-car owners, and they abandon their vehicles in the area I've suggested.

Alphonse gets out and hoicks his trousers over his belly, the legs tucked into wellington boots. Jacques goes down to meet him and thanks him for coming, which I find surprising, considering Alphonse is living with Jacques's wife. Jacques introduces me formally, as if we've never met before and as if they have no idea who I am. I go along with the polite introductions even though I know exactly who everyone is. Then, with Clémentine by her side, Charlotte descends the steps from the château, head high, a chatelaine to the last. Everyone turns to watch the woman who has stayed inside for all these years. And when she makes it to the bottom of the steps, she greets them with a smile. They say how good it is to see her out.

Out of Alphonse's car steps Rachelle, Clémentine's mother, apparently attempting the same grace as Charlotte, but no one pays her any attention, which I think annoys her. '*Bonjour!*' I say, and go over to greet her. She takes my outstretched hand by the very tips of her fingers and gives it a cursory shake. 'Thank you for coming,' I add, but she doesn't look happy to be here. She scans the outside of the château and gives an approving nod, then looks towards the orchard with disdain.

'I'm hoping we'll be able to work together, Rachelle. I'm organizing a wedding here at the château and I'd very much like to offer a hairdressing and beauty service.'

She looks me up and down. Then she smiles. 'I am very much looking forward to spending more time here at the château. Especially now my husband has started to take an interest.' She looks at Jacques, who is greeting arrivals. 'I mean, what could you know about châteaux or château life? I think you have very little hope of making this business idea work. Like today. The locals will never buy into your plan, bribed by a few jugs of cider. It will be a disaster. But I will be here and I will be happy to help bring a little glamour to the bride's day.' Her smile doesn't reach her eyes and I feel once again as if I've been doused in cold custard.

But she'll be on board for the wedding. Hopefully there will be many more afterwards and that's what counts today. More cars pull up behind the others and on to verges. People get out, greet the mayor and look at the château with interest and awe. No one has been here in years.

Jacques beckons the party towards the orchard. '*Allons!*' he says, and everyone, carrying containers from their cars, follows, an excited chatter filling the air as we walk to a place that used to be full of fun and laughter and has lain silent for years. Now the anticipation of laughter returning is almost palpable. We arrive at the gate and step into the orchard. Everybody is looking up and around, and any earlier suspicions about their invitation to the château are gone. An afternoon of picking and pressing lies ahead, then a bonfire will be lit and aperitifs will be served. I look around as the working groups, generations coupling up, like Charlotte and Clémentine, find a tree and begin picking. The orchard fills with laughter once more. Charlotte could not have looked happier. Even Pegasus seems to be enjoying the day from his place overlooking the fallen wall.

38

As the sun starts to go down and the chill sets in, Jacques and Jason light the bonfire.

The air of anticipation is back as everyone gathers around the open-sided barn to the side of the potting shed. The smell of woodsmoke fills the air and we light tealights in jam jars, the ones I'd planned to make chutney in, and hang them from the trees with gardening string. In the barn, the atmosphere is crackling as much as the electric lights.

Many of the men attempt to push round the large stone apple press, laughing at how heavy it is. I look about for Jacques but can't see him. But I hear excitement in the orchard and even cheers. I move out of the barn to see Jacques leading Pegasus, harnessed, into the orchard. He looks beautiful and very happy – they both do! And tears spring to my eyes. They both do, I repeat to myself.

As much as I've tried not to feel anything for this man, as much as I came here to heal my broken heart, nothing has stopped me falling for this grumpy, frustrating, sardonic, kind, helpful, caring and very beautiful man.

And then, as Pegasus is harnessed to the heavy arm of the press, the first of the apples are tipped into the top. Jacques needs to offer very little encouragement for Pegasus to move on and around the stone circle of the crusher. Everyone holds their breath as the old press rumbles and shakes into life. When the apples have been crushed, they are scooped out and put into the press, in layers, wrapped in cloths. The screw is tightened and everyone waits until a trickle of brown, muddy-looking juice runs out and everyone cheers! The press is tightened further and more juice appears. The smell of the newly pressed apples in the barn is sweet, fruity and fresh. It makes my mouth water.

The group celebrate some more and I'm thinking it's time to hand round the drinks.

Jason tends the fire while Clémentine and I hand round glasses of red wine or *crémant*, and plates of fabulous hors d'oeuvres Jacques has prepared. Wooden boards with slices of hard cheese, baguette and sun-dried tomatoes that explode with flavour when you bite into them, then cold meats, thinly sliced, with tart little cornichons, and finally rounds of soft cheese, rubbed with garlic and baked, then served with more baguette to dip into the warm, creamy, gooey centre.

As the last of the apples for today are tipped into the crusher and prodded down, the press is loaded again. Plastic containers are filled and put into car boots. The group gathers around the bonfire and I top up glasses while Jason and Clémentine hand round cheese and meat, and I take more cheese rounds from the embers of the fire and serve them, with more slices of baguette. I've cut it on a table to one side of the fire by the light of a large lantern Jacques has placed there.

As I move around with more drinks, pouring red wine into glasses, or *crémant*, the fire glows and the jam jars in the trees twinkle. Someone starts to sing and everyone joins in. Jason and I watch, smiles plastered on our faces. Even Jacques is joining in, Charlotte too. Clémentine stands with me and sings quietly. The place is full of happiness.

'If I had a wedding, I'd want it just like this,' I hear myself saying out loud.

'Then that's what you should do,' says Charlotte, and I turn to her. She has a point. If everyone was smiling like this, it would be the perfect wedding.

But one face is not. Rachelle is looking at me, then at Jacques, and her face is ever more thunderous. She's clearly unhappy that the day has passed without a hitch and is such a success, judging by the townspeople's faces.

39

The guests leave, thanking me for a wonderful evening, their cars heavy with apple juice ready for cider-making. Their boots heavy with mud from the orchard, they kiss me on each cheek and shake Jacques firmly by the hand.

'*Merci*,' they all say.

'So good to be back.'

'Welcome!' they say to me.

'Let us know how we can help in the future.'

'*Merci!*'

And as the cars drive back to the town Jacques and I stand on the steps, wave and smile.

'We did it!' I say.

'You did it,' he corrects.

'No, Jacques. We all did it.' I'm thinking of Charlotte, Jason and Clémentine.

As the final vehicle leaves, beeping and waving, Jacques and I walk down the drive slowly and shut the gates. On the way back to the château we gaze at it and smile. There are lights on, there is a real chill in the air, the stars are overhead, like thousands of tealights in jam jars. We walk back into the orchard, check that all the candles are out and douse the fire. Pegasus is in his field with a warm rug on and extra hay, seemingly as happy as everyone else to be back in the orchard in the middle of all the fun.

Slowly we breathe in the scent of woodsmoke, freshly pressed apples and cold, frosty air. I take a final deep breath, as does Jacques, and then, as if it's the most natural thing in the world, I turn to him, as he does to me, and I can't not do what I've wanted to do all day. As the stars shine brightly, and the cold nips our noses, I reach forward, as he does, and for one moment it seems my lips will find his. And for one moment, I wonder if I should stop. But I don't. I do exactly what my heart is telling me to and lean into the kiss.

Back in the kitchen, Clémentine's mother, Rachelle, is sitting in Charlotte's chair, taking me by surprise. I find myself blushing.

'Oh, hello,' I say to her. 'Have you come for Clémentine? She's in the basement helping Jason in the lower kitchen.' We've put all the glasses and washing-up there.

'No.' She taps her long nails on the wooden kitchen table and smiles at me. Again, I don't feel any warmth there. 'I 'ave come to talk with my 'usband.'

Suddenly the air in the room seems frosty. I bend to open the wood-burner and load on more logs, hoping to hang on to the happy atmosphere of the apple orchard for just a little longer.

'The château has had quite a transformation,' she says to me. I feel I'm being damned with faint praise. 'A bit like my 'usband.' She gives Jacques a soft smile as he steps into the kitchen behind me. He looks down and may also be blushing.

'Excuse me, I'm going to check on my grandmother. She's had a busy day,' he says, and the happy atmosphere is gone.

'Fine, *chéri*! I will wait and walk back to the farm-house with you.'

Clearly she's not intending to return to Alphonse at the restaurant tonight.

Jacques's earlier happy face hardens. He nods, then goes out of the kitchen into the hall and up the stairs.

Clémentine's mother stands and pulls herself up tall. She wants him back. It's not hard to read. And, if I'm not mistaken, it's not just her husband she wants but this place too.

'*Bonsoir!*' She nods. 'It was a . . .' she hesitates '. . . jolly night.' I feel thoroughly patronized. My cheeks flush. 'It helped make things so much clearer,' she says.

'Let me know when your bridal party is arriving. I will make sure they get the very best service I can offer. But make no mistake,' she lowers her voice and I'm straining to hear her, even though I don't want to, 'you will have no chance of making this plan of yours work. As I say, you know nothing of château life. You have no hope of making this place pay for itself on your own. And when it fails, when you mess it up, I will be waiting and I intend to be back where I belong, as chatelaine here. You will no longer own this place.' She smiles at me in triumph, and my cheeks burn even more.

But hope is exactly what I have.

40

Over the next three weeks, I throw myself into getting everything ready for the wedding. I have a list as long as my arm, with daily emails from the bride, the bride's mother, the groom's mother, and I'm making sure I have a list of all their needs, dietary and otherwise.

Clémentine and Jason have been an incredible help, always happy to get stuck in with whatever I ask, as has Jacques. In fact, after the apple festival, the whole town is gearing up for the wedding party and I just hope I don't let them down, like last time with Mason Grey. The only dark cloud on the horizon is Rachelle, Clémentine's mother, who seems to be 'popping in' to the farmhouse more and more frequently, much to Clémentine's annoyance.

'Why can't she just stay at Alphonse's? Why does she keep coming here? She never used to. We just stuck to the agreed monthly weekend visits, and even then, she didn't always remember. And when she did turn up, she couldn't wait until they were over! She's never been very maternal. She doesn't like the farm. She's only here to spy on what's going on at the château. She wants this wedding to fail. She wants the château back in the family. She thinks she could do this better. She didn't love my papa, just the idea of the château. But not the work. She wants to be a chatelaine, but she doesn't understand the work involved. She has never liked getting her hands dirty. It might damage her nails!' she says, as she helps me polish the silver cutlery in the dining room where I'm working on the seating arrangements for the wedding lunch. It's a squeeze but I think I can do it by adding a couple of extra tables in the corners. And I still need to finalize the menu and decide who is going to cook. I am wondering if Alphonse might be persuaded to come here and act as chef, but then I'd have to navigate Clémentine's mother to visit and ask him. I put it on my list of things to do.

Right now, I let Clémentine talk. I know I mustn't say anything about her mother planning to come back and reclaim her position as wife to the heir of the château: if this wedding is a failure, she will get her wish. And it has to be perfect: it's these two people's special day that they'll remember for ever. In any case, I can't bear to think of leaving this place, or the people I have come to love. My thoughts turn to Jacques.

Charlotte joins us in the dining room. Percival is at her feet, trotting behind her. 'Can I help?' she asks.

'Of course,' I say, grateful.

Charlotte reaches across for a teaspoon, and as she does, the silver charm on the long necklace she always wears clanks against the edge of the table. She picks up the teaspoon and a cloth. With her other hand she holds the charm on her necklace. And I recognize it. 'It's a ring!' I say.

'Yes,' she says. 'Too big for me to wear, these days, but I always keep it close.' She wraps her fingers around it. Clémentine looks up from polishing the knives and peers at Charlotte's hand.

Charlotte smiles, as the sun shines in through the now very clean windows, thanks to Jason's hard work. Charlotte opens her hand and holds the ring out to us in her palm. The teaspoon is in her other hand, next to it.

'It's made from a teaspoon!' Clémentine giggles, as does Charlotte.

'Not just any teaspoon,' says Charlotte.

'A silver one,' I add.

'Look again,' says Charlotte, taking the ring off the long chain and handing it to me.

'The pattern is exactly the same as the pattern on the silver cutlery here,' I say. I pass the ring to Clémentine to look at.

She studies it, then picks up a silver teaspoon. 'Was it made from one of these?' she asks.

'Uh-huh.' Charlotte nods. 'It was very common in big houses for someone to steal a teaspoon and make it into a ring for the one they loved.' Her eyes sparkle softly and naughtily. 'Like an eternity ring or an engagement ring. It would take ages to soften the spoon enough to make it into a ring. Often done at night when no one would know.' She takes the ring back. 'And you could tell which house or château the ring came from by the design of their cutlery. This one is from Château des Arbres.' She nods at the cutlery laid out on the long shiny table.

'Made for you by someone special?' I say hesitantly.

She nods. 'Very special.'

I know she's talking about my grandfather again.

Then she picks up a spoon, sits next to Charlotte and begins polishing.

'How old were you when you first fell in love?' Clémentine asks, and I smile watching the pair of them polishing and Charlotte telling Clémentine about when she was seventeen. 'The same age as I am,' says Clémentine, hanging on her words.

'But things are done so differently now,' says Charlotte, tutting and shaking her head.

'Not really. People still fall in love. Fall in love with people they shouldn't. They still have families to contend with,' says Clémentine, sagely, and they focus on polishing the cutlery. The two have developed such a lovely friendship and bond over the past few weeks, I think, now that Clémentine spends more time inside the château and Charlotte outside in the orchard. Before that they barely had a chance to know each other, with Clémentine dropping off food, not coming into the château, and Charlotte never going out. I hope, whatever happens, that it will continue, and think of the bond I had with my grandfather. The days when he would talk and I would listen, but also the days when I would explain to him how social media worked and set him up with his own Twitter account – he posted pictures of his garden on it. Charlotte and Clémentine have something to learn from each other.

'If you two are happy, I'm just going to check on Jason in the orchard,' I say, and I swear Clémentine's cheeks go a little pink at the mention of his name.

'Tell him I'll be out to help him when I've finished here,' says Clémentine. It's a big step from being tongue-tied when she was around him and constantly blushing.

'I will.' I leave them to it, discussing life and love and polishing the cutlery in the big, beautiful *salle à manger*.

'Hello? Jason!' I call, but I can't see him. 'Jason?' What was frost this morning has left the grass wet, and droplets of water on my trainers, like diamonds, remind me of Shirley Bassey's wellingtons, the year she sang at Glastonbury, studded with diamanté. Suddenly I wonder if we could have a music festival at the château, with bands playing in the orchard, camping on the field where Pegasus is and the cows were. My mind starts whirring with ideas until I remind myself that I still have to pull off my first wedding before I can think of any more events. And it needs to be perfect. As the orchard is! In fact, I'm not really sure why Jason's in here tidying. It's not like we're going to be using the orchard. He said he wanted to make sure it was at its best in case anyone popped their head in. And I suppose he's right. The more of the château and its grounds that are looking their best, the more people might want to make bookings. And we can put photographs on the website and Facebook page. But still I can't see Jason.

'Jason?' I shout. Where can he be? I look around the orchard, remembering our night here, the bonfire, the scent of apple juice in the air, and the smell of the burnt cinders, which still lingers. And I remember the kiss between me and Jacques. Nothing has been said. Nothing since Clémentine's mother was waiting for us in the kitchen and I don't think anything else will be. Like a guilty secret I can think about only when I let myself, like tasting forbidden fruit. He was never mine to have, I think, letting the memory back in for just a moment.

'Hey!'

I jump and turn. Jason is there, tapping me on the shoulder, a little out of breath.

The lid slams shut on the memory of the cider-making night, which is shoved to the back of my memory once more, alongside the laughter at school when I tried and failed to read aloud. I push the lid shut tighter on that one too and give Jason all my attention. That and the wedding.

'Where did you come from? I've been looking for you!'

'Oh, just checking the boundaries for the wedding. I've stacked more stones in the hole at the end, just temporary, so Pegasus doesn't get through.'

I smile. 'I bet he'd love to be part of a wedding!' Jason agrees.

'Okay, well, I need to go and see if I can sort out catering. It's no good having a glorious house if I haven't got anything for the guests to eat,' I say, 'or anyone to cook it.' My mind turns back to that problem. 'Maybe an outside caterer would be best for the job. I'd better write a list of all the meals I need catering. And a list for the baker and the florist.' I sigh. 'And for Clémentine's mother of who needs their hair doing and when.' I open my book, which I'm never without, and make a new list.

'Mend the wall,' is still at the very end of the book and I wonder when that'll happen. I wander back towards the château, caterers at the forefront of my mind.

'Okay!' Jason waves, and I can't help feeling he's up to something.

'Are you okay, Jason?'

'Yes, fine.'

Suddenly the worries we all had when he first came here start to bubble up inside me again. Has he been in touch with 'old friends', the group he was mixing with at school? I walk back towards him.

'You'd tell me if you were in some kind of trouble, wouldn't you?'

He stares at me and his eyes go dead, as if he's back in a place he doesn't want to be. 'I didn't want to do it,' he says. 'I . . . was persuaded to.' He picks an apple from the tree and rubs its skin with his thumb. 'They set me up. Planted some weed in my bag. Said if I didn't sell it they'd say I stole it. It had my fingerprints all over it, they said. But I didn't want to. I said I'd sell just the one bag. I thought the money would help Mum. She works so hard.' He brushes away tears from his eyes with the sleeve of his jumper and I don't know whether to hug him there and then or let him finish. 'Anyway, once the bag had gone, they said I had to sell more, or they'd grass me up . . . S'cuse the pun.' He attempts a smile. 'I was stuck. If I didn't make the payments to them, they'd find a way of making sure I did. I was in debt to them. All I could think of was the twins. I didn't want them hurt in any way. I had to do it. I just didn't expect to get caught. Getting excluded was the best thing that happened to me. They didn't have access to me every day at the school gates. And when you suggested me coming here, it was such a relief. Although I was embarrassed that you had to get involved. But I feel guilty leaving Mum and I worry about the twins. I speak to them all the time, but I don't want them caught up in this. It would kill Mum.' He dissolves into proper tears and this time I do reach around him and hug him hard.

'We'll think of something,' I tell him. 'We will. Your mum is an amazing woman.'

'I don't want to worry her any more. I've put her through enough. I just don't want the twins ending up in the same position I was,' he says.

I feel his pain and am so proud of the mature young man he's become. I know we have to think of something. I brush away my own tears.

'I promise you, I won't be getting mixed up in anything like that again,' he says, with a weak smile.

'We'll work something out,' I tell him, and slowly let him go. All this time he's had all this on his mind. I see him stand up straight and breathe deeply, like he's shared the problem and a weight has lifted.

'I love being here, Auntie Fliss. Thank you.'

And he looks so relaxed in the orchard. At least something good came out of all of this.

'Clémentine says she'll be out to help you in a while,' I tell him, and he smiles properly this time.

'Great,' he says, and takes a big bite of the apple in his hand.

'And don't forget to check all the outside lights are working,' I tell him. 'You and Clémentine.'

'I won't,' he says, as I start to walk away.

He's happy here. Happier than I've ever known him, here in the apple orchard. Maybe he'll be a gardener, like his great-grandfather. I return to the warmth of the kitchen, putting another log on the fire and pulling a blanket around my shoulders against the cold, crisp air. I open my iPad to look for local caterers, and add them to my list to contact. But Nellie and the twins keep nudging into my thoughts. There must be a way to help her out of there.

I'm jolted out of my list-making by a knock at the door. My heart leaps and swoops and I know it shouldn't and wish it wouldn't. We just have to go back to how we were. Friends, neighbours. We were getting on fine, and now everything has changed. I have to take it back to how it was.

'Hi,' I try to say casually, but it comes out as anything but. 'Come in.' He does so without question.

'The house is looking amazing!' he says, and I wonder if he's trying to take things back to just before the apple festival, just before the kiss, when things were going fine.

'Thank you,' I say. 'That's down to everyone, though, not just me. Even Charlotte's been polishing silver this morning with Clémentine! They've been having a lovely time.' I'm on safer ground now.

'It's Clémentine I'm looking for. She's not answering. Never does.' He holds up his phone.

'Maybe we should get walkie-talkies for the château.'

'For the next event. It's a good idea,' he says.

'Let's hope there is a next one,' I say, and sigh. I haven't forgotten Rachelle's warning that I'm bound to mess up. 'I need a caterer to do the food for the wedding. I'd ask Alphonse but I'm not sure he'd come here. Besides, he has his own business to run.'

Jacques nods. 'There is a woman in the next village. She does home catering. I can text you her number.'

'Great!' I say.

'Tell her I sent you.'

'Brilliant!' I breathe a sigh of relief. 'Now, let's find Clémentine.' I lead him out of the kitchen.

'Her mother's here again.'

'Again?' I say, not looking at him.

'She wants to see Clémentine and persuade her to help with a client's hair or something. Shame she's never been so interested before now,' he says quietly. I don't turn to look at him. 'But she is her mother and . . .' He trails off and looks around the shiny cleaned hallway.

'Wow! This is terrific!' he says, as if seeing it for the first time. 'You've worked wonders.'

'Well, it was always here, just needed a good clean. Some love and attention.' The big window at the top of the staircase reminds me I need to check that the chicken-wire cap is still over the drain on the roof. There are so many things to worry about with a château! Ha! And my sisters and I thought this place was our winning lottery ticket!

We walk through to the dining room where Charlotte is still polishing the last of the cutlery and singing to herself.

'Hello, Grand-mère!' says Jacques, clearly happy to see her up and about, enjoying herself. He kisses her lightly on both cheeks.

'We're looking for Clémentine,' I tell her.

'She's gone to join Dafydd, I mean Jason, in the orchard,' she corrects herself. 'She's been thinking about Grandpa.'

'Okay, we'll go and find them,' I say.

Jacques knows the way to the orchard perfectly well but I don't seem able to leave him to it. I pull the blanket I'm wearing, like a shawl, around me, breathing in the chilly air as we leave by the front door and walk down the steps to the raked-over gravel drive and across the lawn to the orchard gate, lost in our own thoughts as we revisit the orchard together.

41

'Jason!' I call, as I open the door and step back into the orchard.

'Clémentine!' calls Jacques.

'So, how are things?' we say at the same time as we walk through the trees still hung with bunting and jam jars that I'm loath to take down just yet.

'Good, good,' we reply at the same time, and laugh.

'You first, how are plans for the wedding?'

'Fine, I think. Especially if your catering lady can do the food. That will be a big tick on the list!'

'I'm glad,' he says. 'It's great to see the place come back to life.'

'And you?' I ask tentatively.

'Yes, thank you. Clémentine is seeing much more of her mother. It's so-so,' he says, rocking his head to and fro. I can just imagine how it is if Clémentine's face is anything to go by when she's called back to the farmhouse.

We stand and stare at each other for just a moment, and for the whole of that moment I wish I could kiss him again, like I did the other night, but I know I can't.

'We should probably . . .' he says awkwardly.

'Yes, of course,' I say, just as awkwardly, and I wonder if he was feeling the same, or maybe now that Clémentine's mother seems to be back on the scene, all thoughts of that kiss are gone.

We march on through the orchard. Suddenly I have nothing to say to him. It looks like that kiss changed everything, like we've gone one step forward and two back. I swallow uncomfortably, cross with myself. Especially because I was the sister who wanted to stay here because there would be nothing to distract me and Ty would have time to work out whether or not he wanted a future with me. And now there's Jacques, whose estranged wife is back. Once again, I feel like a fool. And I'm angry, angry at the years I've wasted. I didn't come here to fall in love. I came here to make this château work and that is what I'm going to do. Then, louder than I imagined it would come out, I shout, '*Jason!*'

Surprised, Jacques also calls, his hands cupped around his mouth. But his mouth is the last thing I want to think about. I'm never going to think about his mouth again.

'Clémentine!'

Suddenly they appear, again as if from nowhere. But it's not nowhere. It's the old gardener's cottage . . .

No one moves. Jason and Clémentine look at us guiltily. And there was I thinking life was on the up and things were settling down.

Slowly I turn to Jacques. 'I'm sure—'

'What? That this isn't what it looks like?' he says, clearly controlling his growing fury as he takes in the situation in front of him.

'No, she's right, it's not!' says Jason, panicked. 'I can explain.'

'Don't!' he says angrily, his fists tight. 'Clémentine, your mother is waiting for you. Please go now.'

'Look, Jacques, let them explain. I'm sure—'

'From where I'm standing, this looks like history repeating itself. Seems that the men in your family have a habit of making assignations with the women in mine in this orchard! We must go,' says Jacques.

Suddenly all my frustration and fury bubbles up. 'Jacques! You can't just punish these two for what happened in the past. They were just being young people.'

'No, you don't understand,' says Jacques. 'But you're not a parent!' he says, and stalks off.

'No, but I was young once!' I call angrily. 'I remember what it felt like to fall for someone.'

'Your mother is waiting, Clémentine!' Jacques calls.

Now Clémentine turns on her father. 'Clearly you wouldn't recognize love if it was right under your nose!

You chose completely the wrong woman to be with, but that's okay! How come I can't make my own choices? I can see things far more clearly than you!'

I'm furious but so is Clémentine. She and Jacques need to sort this themselves. Like Jacques says, I'm not even a parent. I storm off towards the château in the opposite direction, vaguely wondering if Jacques will make it over the pile of stones Jason has used to build up the hole in the wall.

42

'I really would prefer en suite!'

'Is it cold? What should I bring? I've heard châteaux can be very damp.'

'Is there a vegan option on the menu? I do occasionally eat chicken, though, if it's been properly looked after . . .'

'Can I bring my dog?'

'Can I bring my cat?'

'Is there a supermarket nearby? Where can I get my hair done?'

I run my hands through my hair. The list of emails goes on, and this is a small wedding. Imagine what a big one would be like. I could never do it.

I sigh loudly and start to reply.

'I can organize hair appointments,' I say, and make a list to take to Rachelle for a group booking, but trying to get all the guests that want their hair done to agree to a time is like trying to herd cats. Talking of cats . . .

'Sorry, no cats or dogs,' I reply, imagining the chaos with Percival and Cedric. That's one disaster I can avert.

'You're working early,' says Charlotte coming into the kitchen, wrapped in a shawl, her hair up and in place. 'Have you even gone to bed? Do you know it's Christmas Eve?' She's transfixed by the debris in the kitchen.

I sigh and accept the refill of coffee she offers me. 'If I'd known it would be this hard . . .'

'Come on now,' says Charlotte.

'The mother of the groom is refusing to come if she thinks the weather may be bad.'

'But it's winter!'

'Or if she hasn't got an en suite. And she's insisting on bringing her own vicar to bless the marriage!'

'Well, at least you don't have to find a celebrant. Although you could always ask Jacques to be master of ceremonies. She'd probably like it if the mayor was doing that.'

I add it to my list: ask Jacques to be master of ceremonies. Not that we've spoken since we found Jason and Clémentine in the apple orchard. Jason has been quiet, getting on with his chores and retreating back into his shell, I think sadly. Although clearly I'm not delighted to have found him and Clémentine in the gardener's cottage.

'It wasn't what it looked like,' is all he's said. 'I thought you'd believe me.'

'I want to, I really do. But you must realize what it looked like to Jacques. And he's very protective of Clémentine.' I give Jason his list every morning and he goes about his tasks without complaint, but the spring in his step has gone.

I look at today's list for me. It's a different list from the one that contains immediate things I have to do in the house. Like getting the chimneys swept, beds made up, floors mopped. I've done all those, nearly. And different again from the long-term list of things that can wait, like repairing the swimming pool, replacing the boiler and, at the bottom still, 'fix orchard wall', although, as I said, we've done a makeshift job on that already. I run my finger over the words, thinking again of Jacques and the deal we made.

'It's agreed, then,' says Charlotte.

'Sorry, Charlotte, what's agreed?'

'I will move into the bedroom that was meant for the mother-in-law and she can have my suite. Just for the wedding,' she adds, with a raised finger.

'You – you'll move out of your suite?'

'Just for the wedding. Because if the mother-in-law is happy, everyone else will be allowed to be happy. I know. I had one.'

'Your mother-in-law? Didn't you get on?'

She shakes her head, her mouth turned down. 'I think he loved her more than me. In fact, I know so. My wedding day was more about her than it was about me.'

'And what about your husband? Did you love him?'

She sighs deeply. 'It seemed the right thing to do, to try to repair things. But she never really accepted me. She didn't think I was good enough for her son ... but she liked the idea of being part of the château. But after my husband died and my father ran out of money, she wasn't so keen to be associated with it any more.' She gives a wry smile. 'And you? Was there never a wedding on the cards for you?' she asks me, and I'm stopped in my tracks.

'There was someone,' I say. 'But we didn't think we needed a wedding. We were happy as we were. Or so I thought ...' Mason Grey's words sting me all over again. 'I came here to get away. I wanted him to miss me, to realize he wanted a future with me. I think I thought if I stayed here long enough he might follow. But I was wrong. He didn't want that. Actions speak louder than words. He wouldn't follow me to the ends of the earth ... It wasn't the perfect relationship.' I swallow. 'It was the convenient one.' Tears spring to my eyes but they don't fall.

'And now?'

I consider the question again. 'It's over. I've moved on.' I smile. 'I love being here. I don't want to be any- where else. I just want this to work . . .' I trail off.

'Never settle for second best,' Charlotte reminds me, and I think of those early days when the bread I was sold was yesterday's. 'Send the email to the mother-in- law and then join me in the hall.'

'In the hall?'

But she's wandered out, singing to herself.

I turn to the keyboard and type an email to the bride and the bride's mother-in-law-to-be, telling her I have a suite with a turret and its own bathroom. I press send and it whooshes off. Then I close the lid and go to find Charlotte in the hall.

'Huh!' I catch my breath. 'It's beautiful!' I say, as I stare at the huge Christmas tree, with Jacques, Jason and Clémentine all out of breath.

'My way of saying sorry,' says Jacques.

And I'm not sure what I'm more surprised by – the tree, everyone together or Jacques saying sorry. I look at the tree again. I was thinking of doing ivy and cuttings from the garden in a big vase on the table here. But this? This is just perfect.

'Jason came to speak to me,' Jacques continues, his head slightly lowered. 'And I understand now . . . that I overreacted.' He gulps.

I couldn't be more proud of Jason than I am right now, as he lifts his head and pushes back his long fringe to show off his lovely face, with its high cheekbones.

'A lot of memories have been brought back by opening the apple orchard. A lot of things from the past that have led us here. My head was in the past, not in the future. And . . .' he takes a deep breath '. . . I hope you and Jason will stay a part of our future.'

The smell of fresh pine fills the hallway, making me feel quite light-headed. A part of the future, a future for us all here at Château des Arbres, and I couldn't feel any happier than I do now. Happy tears fill my eyes as I hug Jason, hard.

'Ow!' He laughs.

'Now all we have to do is decorate it!' Charlotte claps her hands together, the lace at her wrists falling this way and that.

'I have some ideas,' says Clémentine, excitedly.

Jacques looks at her fondly and Jason smiles widely, brushing his hair off his face again, as if the boy has grown into a young man overnight.

'I made some red apples for decorations with red baubles and gold bows. Grand-mère said apples always featured in the Christmas decorations here,' Clémentine adds.

Charlotte nods. 'The apples and the orchard were always at the heart of this château,' she says. 'I thought we could put some from the orchard in bowls and in garlands around the fire, with the gold bows.'

'I'll go and find some greenery to weave up the staircase and around the fireplaces. Jason, can you come with me?' I ask, really keen for the hall to be dressed as it should be. *Never settle for second best* . . . I hear the words again.

'Sure,' says Jason. He's miles away from the silent, bumbling lad who arrived here.

We all go about our jobs, and for a few hours I forget any emails that still need answering and focus on dressing the hall, the staircase, the salon and the dining room with dark green ivy and shiny holly with bright red berries. And with Jacques here, apologizing, us all together again, I couldn't feel happier.

Finally, when I'm standing back and gazing at our work with a satisfied smile, Jacques calls us into the hall. 'Everyone ready?' he asks, with a twinkle in his eye. And, beaming, he reaches down and switches on the Christmas-tree lights. They flicker on and off, then stay on and we all cheer.

'We're very nearly ready,' I say, this time not bothering to pull out my list. The house is decorated and the caterer briefed and booked. The rooms are made up. Ahead of the wedding party arriving on the thirtieth, in just six days' time, everything is in place. As the lights on the tree twinkle I don't think I could be any happier or more excited.

'Now all we need to do is cook our Christmas meal for tonight,' says Jacques.

My face drops. 'Oh, God! I forgot you eat on Christmas Eve!'

'And you? Do you have anything for tomorrow?' he asks.

I grimace. 'I've been so busy thinking about the wedding, I hadn't really thought about cooking for us.' I feel so stupid. Christmas has completely passed me by.

Jo Thomas

Suddenly, there is a knock at the door and a ring on the bell.

'Who's that?' It can't be any guests arriving early. They were still emailing me just a few hours ago.

Jason grins, glancing at Clémentine and then Jacques, who smiles back. 'You may not have organized Christmas dinner, but I have,' he says.

'What is this? Dial-a-dinner?' My heart is thumping.

'Open the door!' he insists, and I know it can't be a Tesco delivery out here. What on earth can he have arranged?

I put my hand to the big wooden door, twist and open to a blast of 'Good King Wenceslas' coming from behind a large poinsettia and a box of groceries. The poinsettia and groceries move to one side to reveal the smiling carol singers. And tears roll freely down my cheeks. It's my sisters – and the twins!

'Happy Christmas!' They throw open their spare arms and beam.

'What? But what are you doing here?' My hand is over my mouth in utter shock.

'We brought Christmas dinner,' says Lizzie, my middle sister.

'And I'm going to cook it!' says Nellie, who leans in for a huge hug with her son. 'You've grown!' she exclaims and hugs him again, giving in to tears. When she finally releases him, the twins hug him, shorter and stockier than Jason, as happy to see him as he is them.

His eyes screw tightly shut with relief that they're here and safe.

'Come in, come in!' I wave everyone inside, hugging them hard and suddenly realizing how much I've missed them, as I make introductions and ask Clémentine and Jason to pour some drinks. My sisters put down their bags and the poinsettia, which is dwarfed by the Christmas tree. My sisters and the boys stare at the tree.

'Wow!' they all say.

'Jacques got it from the woods,' I say, pointing out of the front door. 'So it didn't cost us anything!' We all laugh.

'This place is amazing!' Lizzie says spinning around, taking in the hallway, so different from the last time we were here.

'You've done a fantastic job,' Nellie says, spinning the other way.

'She has,' Jacques agrees, and I can't help but beam, blush and well up all at the same time.

'*Absolument!*' says Charlotte.

Clémentine and Jason come into the hall carrying trays with glasses and a bottle of *crémant*, lemon syrup and sparkling water for the youngsters.

I catch my breath and my hand flies to my mouth again. 'How long are you here for? Say you're not going until after the new year! And what about James?'

'He's spending it with his parents. He knew how important it was for me to see you,' Lizzie says.

'But what . . . Wait! Where are you going to stay? The wedding guests will be here in six days! I don't have any spare rooms!'

My sisters are crestfallen and the twins look worried.

Jason sighs dramatically. 'That's what I've been trying to tell you. Clémentine and I . . . That's why we were in the orchard.' He turns to Jacques. 'We were in the gardener's cottage, cleaning it up. It has two bedrooms, a small kitchen. I know what you thought, but please come and see,' he says to me. 'I wanted it to be a surprise, to say thank you for bringing me here. Clémentine has been helping me. It's small, but cosy and warm. Come on!'

We all follow him, including Charlotte, to the orchard. Jason goes into the little gardener's cottage and we all catch our breath, but Charlotte's gasp is the loudest, and I catch her arm, hoping she's not going to faint again, like when we first met.

43

Charlotte doesn't hesitate to step into the cottage and run her hand over its faded walls. It's been shut up for years, but is now as clean, comfortable and welcoming as it ever was.

'We just made use of what was here and did it as best we could,' says Jason.

'Looks like he takes after you, Fliss!' says Nellie.

'A bit of both of us! Your frugality and my love affair with anything old that shouldn't be thrown away,' I say, pulling around me the little jacket I found in the attic room, in one of the chests. Those clothes must once have belonged to someone who lived in the house and, somehow, my things from home just don't seem to fit here.

Charlotte sits down on one of the beds. 'This place is wonderful!' she says.

'We thought it was a shame it wasn't being used and that it might be useful for extra guests,' says Clémentine.

'Or I could move in,' says Jason.

My eldest sister looks at him with a mix of happiness and sadness all at one time. 'Does that mean you're not coming home?' There's a catch in her voice.

'I meant move out of my room in the château. But . . . yes, if it's okay with you, I'd like to stay. I could look for a college here maybe. Clémentine could help me.'

'I can see you're happy here . . .' She looks at Clémentine, who reverts to blushing. And then, without words, Nellie and Jason hug each other.

'We'll be fine here in the cottage,' says Lizzie, as we watch the twins bouncing on the beds. 'It'll be fun!' I blink. I can't remember the last time Lizzie talked about having fun. In fact, I'm not sure she's ever been up for 'fun'.

'Right! Come on, let's eat!' says Nellie, sniffing, as she pulls away from Jason and he leads us back to the kitchen in the château, where the oven is switched on. Jason puts Christmas songs on his phone and we take it in turns between French and English ones – Clémentine insists on controlling the music.

Charlotte is at the table making swans with napkins, while Jacques and I are sent to lay the table in the dining room for us all to have Christmas Eve dinner. He lights the fire and the candles. I set the places between the greenery I've laid down the table. It looks like a Christmas card, I think, as I stand back and attempt to photograph it for our social-media pages, but my eyes are all blurry.

'You have to believe you did this,' said Jacques, coming to stand beside me. 'You made all this happen.'

I feel as lit up as the Christmas tree.

'If you hadn't come along, I don't know what would have happened to this place, so *merci*,' he says softly. And once again a frisson ricochets between us. 'I want you to know that I think you are a very special person indeed. You have been wonderful with Clémentine. I'm sorry for any problems I gave you. I just . . . I wanted to protect her, after me and her mother . . . after she left. I was scared of her getting hurt.'

'And are you still scared?' I look at him.

'Petrified!' He laughs and so do I, and I feel our bodies move a little closer to each other, as if they're being drawn together, and want that kiss on my lips all over again.

Suddenly the door flies open.

'Papa!' It's Clémentine. 'Papa!' she repeats urgently and we jump apart. Immediately I start to rearrange the ivy down the middle of the table. Clémentine is at the door, holding it ajar, but then it's pushed open and there, staring at us, is Rachelle, her red lips and nails letting me know she means business before she even speaks.

'Well, this all looks very cosy!' she says, and I have no idea if she's talking about the room, or Jacques and me.

She speaks then quickly in French, just to Jacques, and I try to keep up.

He clears his throat and reverts to English. 'Of course,' he says politely. 'Clémentine's mother was saying she has presents to deliver for us and is looking forward to having dinner with us.' His eyes are wide as if he's at a loss. This is his wife, Clémentine's mother. He can't turn her away, I can see that.

'Perhaps we should leave and have dinner at home. Clémentine?'

'No! Papa!' she throws up her hands. 'We nearly have everything ready here.'

Clémentine's mother looks around. 'I'd be happy to stay here,' she says, with a smile, as she peels off her coat. 'It has quite a welcoming feel now.'

'Come,' says Clémentine, scowling. 'You can help in the kitchen!' She grips her mother's sleeve.

'But I could stay here and help with the table. Add some touches,' she says. 'I'm sure Fliss knows her way around the kitchen better than I do. And I've just had new nails!' She waggles them.

'The dining room is finished,' says Clémentine, firmly.

'Really?' says her mother.

'You can help in the kitchen,' repeats Clémentine, hustling her mother out of the room.

A smile springs to Jacques's lips. 'A chatelaine in the making.' His face lights up, soft and gentle as he talks about his daughter. Then he seems nervous, unusually for him. Neither of us knows where we are now and we try to read each other's faces for some sort of guidance.

'I'd better get a little more greenery in. Don't want Rachelle to think I haven't finished the room.' I try to smile.

'It is perfect as it is,' he says, stopping me dashing outside to gather more holly.

'And I'd better change,' I say, feeling shabby in my work clothes compared to Rachelle's smart Christmas outfit.

'The room looks beautiful, just as it is,' he says, looking at me directly, 'as do you.' And I tingle with excitement all over again.

44

Dinner is long, drawn-out and filled with laughter despite Rachelle's disapproving presence, but no one is paying her any attention. I think it's the relief. Everything is in place for the wedding. By the end of the year, we'll have done it! And I have my family here, eating our favourite Christmas Eve meal, made in the UK and brought all the way to France: a delicious fish pie, with crunchy golden mashed potato, creamy sauce and flaking fish. I look around the table. Everyone I care about is here. My sisters, Jason, the twins. Charlotte is beaming broadly, as is Jacques, and Clémentine laughing with Jason. It's just Rachelle who doesn't seem to be enjoying herself.

'We never have anything like this on Christmas Eve,' says Clémentine, in delight. Jacques is smiling too.

'I was hoping for oysters,' Rachelle says. 'That is what we usually have at Christmas, don't we, Jacques?' She prods her food with a fork and, at a look from Jacques, attempts the fish pie tentatively, as if being asked to eat cat food.

'Sometimes it's good to ring the changes,' says Charlotte, from the head of the table. She's wearing a paper hat as stylishly as only Charlotte can, determined to keep it on for the whole of Christmas by the look of it. And it suits her! I raise a glass to her and she returns the gesture with a smile.

The fire burns brightly as more and more logs are added to it, no one showing any sign of leaving the table early. I decide to clear away the first course and bring out the trifle Nellie has made and the cheese-board Jacques has brought. I'll put them on the table together to save any concerns over which comes next. Everyone can just help themselves, cheese, trifle or both.

'Here, let me,' says Rachelle, as I stand to clear the plates from the main course.

'No, it's fine, really,' I say, in a warm happy bubble. Even her disapproval of my being here can't burst that. 'You're a guest and it's good practice for me.'

'Oh,' she says, 'I'm really not,' and suddenly my bubble is squeezed of a little air as she follows me to the kitchen with a pile of plates.

'Just put them by the sink,' I say, feeling weirdly uncomfortable in this kitchen I have come to love. I throw another log into the wood-burner.

Suddenly Rachelle is standing very close to me. I can smell her sickly floral perfume, which seems out of place in the warm kitchen, with the scent of pine and beeswax from the main hall, which fills every room that leads off it.

'You have done a good job on this old place,' she says.

'Thank you,' I say, putting more bread into a basket to go with the cheese.

'But I wouldn't get too comfortable here. Now I've seen what can be done with this place, how the English have a taste for these older houses, I can see there is money to be made here. As I told you, I plan to take back my rightful place, here, as chatelaine just as soon as you understand that you have no hope of running a place like this with just your nephew for help. You know nothing about our ways in France. Your idea will fail,' she says, without a hint of humour or a smile. 'Soon!' she adds.

I stand stock still. Jacques's words come back to me. He was talking about Clémentine as 'a chatelaine in the making'. Is that what he's hoping for? For them to take back this place still?

45

I carry the cheeseboard into the dining room, my hands shaking, but no matter how much Rachelle has unsettled me, walking back into the dining room is like walking into a great big hug, the laughter, the warmth, the love. As I enter the room Jacques catches my eye. We hold each other's gaze and smile, even though I'm trying not to. His is not a look that says he wants me out. In fact, if I'm not mistaken, it's very much the opposite, and I find myself returning it. And, once again, I have no idea what's going on. I'm definitely feeling something for Jacques that was never there before, something deeper than I've ever felt, a connection that is both thrilling and feels like it fits, but he's not free to be with me, and I won't settle for second best. Not this time.

I smile around the table and notice Rachelle is missing. I breathe a sigh of relief and hope she's gone home. Even Clémentine is smiling wider.

'Papa? Are we going to church later for midnight mass?'

'Of course, *chérie*,' he responds. 'To give thanks for what we have.'

The door opens and a draught blows out the candle flames on the table. I shiver.

'You were all so busy laughing, you didn't hear the front door, so I did the honours,' says Rachelle, coming back into the room. 'I hope nobody minds,' she says. 'It's just my natural instinct to be the hostess here.' She smiles again and opens the door wider and we all crane to see the visitor. I get up and grab cutlery for whoever is to join us at the table.

'*Bonsoir, bienvenue,* come in,' I say, wondering if it's more weary, lost guests and wondering where I'll put them to sleep, and how to explain they have to leave before the wedding guests arrive on the thirtieth.

'Hi,' says the voice, and I look up from the cutlery I've set next to mine and stare. 'Wow! This is some place you've got here!' he says.

'*Merci*,' says Rachelle, without a flinch.

'Hey, Fliss!' He gives me the familiar lazy smile.

'A friend of yours,' announces Rachelle. 'Come all the way from the UK!'

'Ty!' I finally manage to say as the warm air disappears from the room and a cold blast blows in.

46

We finish the dessert and cheese, and Ty makes a great effort to compliment everyone on their contribution to the table, particularly Jacques, asking about the cheese and the history of the place. Jacques answers politely, but the happy, relaxed Jacques who put up the tree and laid the table with me is gone.

My sisters look at each other and then at me, wondering what's going on and why I didn't know he was coming.

Ty spots their confusion. 'Thought I'd surprise you,' he says to me. 'Besides, I had trouble getting through to you. Like you blocked me or something.'

'You certainly did surprise me!' I smile tightly. It's Ty. He's here. But something doesn't feel right, even though he's made the effort to get here for Christmas.

'I travelled for hours. This place isn't easy to find,' he says.

I fill the glasses at the table. Apple brandy for Ty and Jacques, Nellie and Charlotte. I'm having cider from the barrel Jacques brought over. It slipped down so easily with the fish pie and now the cheese.

'A friend of yours?' says Jacques, quietly. 'Or a lover?'

Only Jacques could make Ty's and my relationship sound far more exciting than, in hindsight, it was.

'It's . . . *compliqué*,' I tell him.

While Rachelle is trying to make small talk with Ty, and establishing we were together, Ty is charming Charlotte and the evening picks up again. This is how it is meant to be, isn't it? But the look on Jacques's face seems to say otherwise.

'Okay, who is for church?' says Jacques, standing, checking the big clock and wobbling, much to Clémentine's amusement, and mine.

Rachelle tuts.

'I should stay here and clear up,' I say, much as I'd like to see the church.

'Dad could stay with you!' says Clémentine, quickly.

'Your father needs to be at church, Clémentine,' says her mother. 'And I'm sure you and your boyfriend would like some time together, Fliss.'

He's not my boyfriend. It was always just Ty and Fliss . . . no boyfriend references. Maybe it would have been different if we'd had labels. I have no idea what he was to me actually, now I think about it. Charlotte described him as 'a friend'. Is that what he is, or was? A very good friend? It was comfortable, easy. Was I just deluding myself all these years that we were more than that? But he's here now. And I have no idea why. Weeks ago this is exactly what I had hoped would happen, that he would turn up here. But now? says a voice in my head as Jacques looks at me again.

I take more plates to the kitchen and am followed by Rachelle.

'I'll leave these here for you and Ty to sort out. It will be good to have some time alone with Jacques. There is something I need to talk to him about, to ask him. A personal thing, between husband and wife, you understand?' she says, shoving me out of the picture, hard. And then she looks at Ty coming into the kitchen laughing with Lizzie. 'Or maybe you don't.' She raises her pencilled eyebrows. Maybe she's right. Maybe I didn't know the closeness of a couple, who have taken vows to stick by each other through thick and thin, as she drops the plates into the sink, splashing me.

Jacques comes into the kitchen. 'All this can wait. You should come to church,' he says to me.

'It's fine. You go! It'll be better to get this done now.' I wave a hand at the piles of washing-up and suddenly feel shattered.

'You're part of this community. You should be there,' Jacques insists.

'It's fine,' says Ty. 'I'm sure Fliss is cool with it. Be good to catch up,' he says, picking up the bottle of apple brandy that Jacques has just put down. He finds glasses and pours just two.

Jacques looks at Ty and the apple brandy he's pouring. Then back at me. 'I understand,' he says, and I'm not sure he does. I'm not sure I do.

'You go,' I say.

'No, stay!' Clémentine tells Jacques.

'Go!' I wish it was Jacques and me staying here in the silence of my happy place, in the kitchen at the heart of this beautiful house.

As hats and gloves are pulled on and everyone is talking and checking I'm happy to stay behind, finally the group, including Charlotte, Nellie, Lizzie and the twins, delighted to be staying up so late, leave through the big front door and I shut it behind them. The house falls silent. The Christmas lights on the tree flicker but stay on.

I take a deep breath. Ty is here, I tell myself, and turn back to the kitchen. But something has changed. Is it being here in the château? Do I want him back? Why else would he be here? What's changed? If only I knew what it was.

47

'So, how have you been?' He grins, handing me a glass. Suddenly we're not the same old Fliss and Ty: we're different, like old friends, even strangers, meeting after a long time. I know what's changed. It's me.

The lights flicker off and this time stay off.

'Is this place haunted?' he asks.

I sigh. 'No. It happens.' I can hear the pitter-patter of rain starting to fall and think of the group walking into town to church, picturing Jacques, with Rachelle, her arm tucked through his, Clémentine and Charlotte, wrapped up warm, Charlotte enjoying life outside the château for the first time in years, Clémentine seeing her parents back together. I wonder how she's feeling. My sisters are here too, and I'm so pleased. I look back at Ty, his face lit by the burning applewood logs in the wood-burner. It's such an attractive face, I think. So familiar, and yet completely different. It comes closer to mine and all I can think of is Mason Grey. I pull away.

'Hey, what's up? Aren't you pleased to see me? I've come all this way!' he says, half-joking. 'At Christmas!'

He's right. It's Ty and he's here. At Christmas. Is this it, him finally committing to us? Isn't this what I wanted? A future together?

'I know. Thank you.'

'Brought the board. Thought I'd check out some of the waves on the coast while I'm here.'

And suddenly I'm irritated. Is he here to see me or check out the surfing? But I brush away my irritation. He's here. Of course he'd want to surf. And if the surf's good he'll want to stay.

'So, what do you think of the place?' I ask, feeling proud of the château.

'Bit hard to see in the dark.'

Suddenly the lights come back on.

'Oh, there we are. No need to get the broom out and stand on the stool,' I say, his face suddenly harsher in the light.

'So, Mason was here. Said the place wasn't for him.' He laughs.

'He said you told him we weren't "exclusive", Ty,' I say, feeling a strange strength rising in me. I don't know if it's the apple brandy or that I ran away without really telling Ty how I felt.

'Well, we've never been totally exclusive, have we? Y'know, what with me travelling, and you being back in Swn Y Mor, on your own.'

I look at him hard. I remember him saving me from the sea that time and feeling so grateful he was there. And if he hadn't been? Maybe I would have got out on my own after all. Maybe I would have been able to run the beachside café. Just because I loved him for all those years doesn't mean I can't live without him. I can. I have.

'I was, Ty,' I say, and he looks agitated. 'I was,' I repeat.

'Look, Fliss, I've been thinking . . . If you want all that stuff, marriage, kids,' it's like I'm hearing these words from another room, like in some kind of dream, 'maybe we could do it, make it work. This place is pretty awesome and maybe I could set up a surf school here, finally stay in one place. We'd make a great team,' he says, as if he's told me I've just won the top prize on *Who Wants to Be a Millionaire?*. For a moment everything I wanted to hear from him before I left for France is coming out of his mouth. The scenario I dreamt about when I first got here, that Ty would come and tell me he'd thought things through, that he wanted exactly what I wanted. A future. And now Ty is here and, in his own way, that may have been a proposal, an offer of a future, moving forwards together. I look at his familiar face in the dark shadows of the wet and windy night. His high cheekbones, his shaggy blond hair, which is more of a mess than sexy shaggy tonight. The tiredness is beginning to show around his eyes.

'Let me get this right.' I take a deep breath to control my nerves. 'You – you want to ask me to marry you and for us to have a family, a future together.'

He smiles the big wide smile that always made my stomach flip with excitement. He steps forward and takes my hand. 'It's always been Ty and Fliss,' he says quietly, and kisses the tips of my fingers. And this is the bit where I would smile, melt and relish the way he makes me feel.

Made me feel.

'Has it, Ty?'

He looks as if he's been put off his stride and takes a moment to find it again. 'If it's about what Mason said, about us not being exclusive, that was y'know, then. I'm talking about now. We were still young before, finding our way. Making sure.'

'When I thought we were together, Ty and Fliss. When I told everyone we didn't need to be engaged to show the world we were a couple because that's what I thought we were. "Don't mend what isn't broken" we used to tell people who asked when we were finally going to go official.'

'Okay, I've made mistakes. And I get it, for better or worse. That's in the past. Let's move forward. Make a life here, you and me. Like I say, if you want the marriage bit, the babies, let's do it. If it makes you happy,

I'm happy. If it's what you want, I'm in!' He kisses the tips of my fingers again.

I look at him, then around the kitchen. I did make this work, I think. On my own. And I think of Jacques's words: *You made all this happen.* When I needed Ty, he wasn't here. He never was, not for me. If I wasn't enough for him then, why would I be enough for him now? Finally I know exactly what I need to say.

'No, Ty, it's not about if I want all that "stuff". I needed you to want it too. I needed you to want me enough to be with me exclusively.'

He stands up straighter, dumbfounded. 'Fliss, come on, give me a break, I've just said we'll do all that. Settle down, have kids. Be a full-time couple.' He slides his arm around my waist and I slip out of it. 'What's going on here Fliss?'

I glance up at the clock. It's nearly midnight. 'Us. Ty . . . Well, what I thought was us.'

'That's what I'm talking about too!'

'No, you're talking about getting married, doing what all your friends are doing, having children, because you think that's what you should be doing, what I want. I needed you to want to commit to me, Ty. I was committed.'

He lets out a long sigh.

'I didn't need a wedding. But I did need to feel you were as committed as I was . . . and that one day, in the future, there would be a family because you wanted it as much as I did.'

He's lost for words.

'But you don't, Ty. Not deep down. And no amount of wedding bells will make you feel that, or promise to be exclusive.' God, I hate that word! 'Us was about trust and loyalty . . . We clearly have neither. I was wrong. Without that, there's no us.'

'I came all this way! Surely that shows how committed I am.' He grabs at straws.

'No, Ty, that's not commitment. That's wanting a soft landing. Your career looks to be coming to an end and you're looking for get-out without crashing out. Well, I'm sorry you came all this way but I'm not your soft landing . . . and I have a wedding to organize. Not yours and mine, but for a couple who are very much in love. And I plan to make it the best I possibly can. The day they'll remember because they made a commitment to each other and started the next phase of their lives together.'

For a moment he stands staring at me, then storms out of the kitchen. It feels much warmer for him leaving, and me being here alone. I don't cry. I've cried all my tears over Ty. Instead I pour an apple brandy and think of Charlotte's words: *Never settle for second best.* I won't, whether it be a baguette or a relationship. I will never accept second best again.

I hear Ty's VW camper van drive off down the lane, and I sit in the silence until the church-goers come home.

'Are you okay?' Jacques walks into the kitchen, pulling off his scarf and his hat. 'Where's your friend? Ty?'

'Gone,' I say.

I look at his face, which is full of concern. Why didn't Ty ever look at me like that?

'Are you okay?' he asks.

'I will be,' I say. And I know I will. I can do this on my own. With the people I have around me. My sisters appear, pulling off coats and smelling of the cold night air, their hair covered with raindrops, followed by Charlotte.

'Ty's gone,' I say, wanting to get it out of the way quickly. They come straight to me and hug me. No words needed. Even my sisters and I have grown closer since the château came into our lives.

'As it is said, "Don't cry because it's ended, smile because it happened",' says Charlotte, from the doorway.

Just for a second all the happy memories flood back to me and I nearly cave in, either run after him or buckle and descend into a sobbing heap. But the moment passes. I will remember the good times when I'm ready. I feel like I've already moved on.

'Come, my dear. A chatelaine must keep the ship afloat. You have a wedding to organize and a team of people waiting for your instruction.'

I manage a smile. 'Indeed,' I agree, and take a deep breath. 'I have a wedding to pull off!' I lift my chest and look at Charlotte, then Jacques, and smile. 'It's Christmas

Day,' I say. 'Let's get out some more *crémant* and toast new beginnings.'

'*Une bonne idée!*' says Jacques, and immediately falls into step, helping with glasses and wine from the fridge. I must remember to account for it when I'm totting up the bottles drunk at the wedding and paying the wine merchant. I gaze at Jacques, happily singing to himself, full of Christmas spirit. He stops and smiles at me and I smile back, and there's a fizzing in my stomach, just like the *crémant* he's just opened, fizzing out of the bottle. For a man who didn't like to set foot in this place, he certainly seems at home, I think, and beam at him working his way around the kitchen.

Just as we reach the tray of glasses and bottles to take into the salon, the lights flick off again.

We stand and gaze at each other, something drawing me to him. I'm wondering if it would be wrong to wish him happy Christmas and maybe ... My lips seem drawn to his and his to mine, and I'm wondering if he's feeling the same thing. And the fizzing in my stomach is about to bubble over, like the bottle.

'Come on, it's Christmas!' Clémentine runs into the kitchen and stops. We jump away from each other – it's becoming a habit – both snatching at the tray, glasses wobbling and falling. Then we turn to Clémentine and see her smiling, and we laugh and follow her to the salon where everyone is waiting.

Pop! goes another *crémant* cork, and the wine is poured into glasses. Clémentine looks so happy she could burst, the room lit by candles and the fire. Jason too!

Jacques hands round the glasses, and Clémentine pours lemon syrup for the twins topped up with sparkling water, then proposes a toast to a '*Joyeux Noël*'. We raise our glasses and sip. As we do, Rachelle clears her throat and walks over to stand by Jacques, slips her arm through his and says, 'Jacques and I were talking on our way to church.'

When I was here talking to Ty. I try to shake off the discomfort of the kitchen conversation and replace it with the warmth and excitement I felt as Jacques and I prepared the *crémant*. But the warmth and excitement seem to disappear as she slips her arm through his. Clémentine's smile slips too, when she spots her mother's arm through Jacques's.

'I was telling Jacques how lovely it was to be back here at the château, how much I've missed it. He was telling me that I was missed, too.'

I see Jacques open his mouth to say something. But she silences him with a finger to his lips.

'And I've decided it's time. I've made a mistake. I'm coming home. I'm coming back to live with Jacques, to be here and a part of this place in the future. I'm sure Fliss will see how much I have to offer the place and how I can help make this a real French experience.

After all, people are coming for a bit of France,' she laughs, 'not little Britain.' And I presume she's referring to the meal tonight, which makes me so cross. 'I've missed it,' she continues. 'And Clémentine, my daughter, too. Leaving the farm was a moment of madness, I see that now. I'm over it. I'm back and I intend to make myself as useful as possible around here!' She beams and the room once again feels icy cold.

For a moment no one says anything, not even Jacques, who is standing stock still. Rachelle raises her glass. Clémentine runs from the room and out of the front door, letting it slam behind her. The atmosphere turns as damp as the weather outside.

48

It has rained for days. I was hoping it would miss us, but the wind picked up and the dark clouds rolled in. Even the Christmas lights on the tree can't lift the dark gloom.

I go around all the rooms, check the radiators, running my hand over their chunky rectangular ribbed tops. I also take the time to let the warmth seep up through my bottom as I rest on each one in turn. Not like the rooms on my side of the house where the wood-burning stove from the kitchen heats a few radiators, but not many and not very well.

I look out at the dark skies, then down the lawn towards the woods and see the deer there, grazing among the trees. I double-check the hydrangea heads, still dried and beautiful, combined with other foliage from the grounds in vases, the bottles of water, and tug at the thick duvets for which I've maxed out Lizzie's credit card. I double-check the bathrooms for hot water, running my finger under the taps. All working. I make my way downstairs to the salon and the dining room, laid up for this evening's meal. Rows of tables, a bit snug, but we managed it. If only this was a summer wedding, we would have held it on the lawn. Maybe next year, I think, and surprise myself. Am I really thinking we could pull this off and still be here next year?! If Rachelle has her way, there'll be weddings here, but I won't be organizing them.

Jason is outside putting more fairy lights into the trees alongside the drive and next year I'd like there to be even more fairy lights, if I'm here. I just have to focus on getting this wedding right and paying the tax. I'm not going to let Clémentine's mother distract me from the property we own and how to make it work. I'm not going to be driven out. Neither am I going to play second best. Christmas Day and Boxing Day passed quietly after the excitement of Christmas Eve. Why didn't Jacques tell me that was what they were discussing? My mood is as black as the clouds in the sky. But all we need is for the weather to clear for the weekend and a bright start to the new year. Without Jacques or Rachelle in it? I worry about Clémentine. I hope she'll still visit and spend time here.

I look out of the window again as fat raindrops hit the panes and slide down the newly cleaned windows.

I check the time on my phone. The guests are late. All I can do is wait. The rain falls heavier. And as I wait, all I can think about is Jacques, with Clémentine's mother, in the farmhouse next door. Her practically celebrating already that the château will be back in her hands by the new year when I realize I can't do this. I'm not a wedding organizer. I'm just someone who's done a lot of jobs back in the UK.

What was that look between Jacques and me in the kitchen, as we poured the *crémant*? Do I just misread signals? Is he like Ty's blogger friend, Mason, thinking that just because I'm not in a full-time relationship I'm happy to accept any crumbs thrown my way? Or, like Ty, happy not to be 'exclusive'? Well, I'm not! If they're not free to love just me, I'm not interested. I think of Jacques once more and a part of my heart where a crack has appeared cracks a little more.

I'm standing in the rain, in the middle of the road, waving my arms as if I'm in a Zumba class. Hours after they should have been here, I can see a small convoy of cars, with British number plates, slowing down in front of me.

'Down the drive and park to the left,' I say, over the sound of driving rain, from under the big hood of Charlotte's waterproof poncho, waving a hand to the right, down the drive, and getting more rain thrown in my face.

Once the cars have all parked, away from the front of the château, the weary travellers get out and make a run for the front door, delayed, tired and avoiding the rain, with no chance to take in the outside of the château. I point them in the direction of the hall and tell them to leave their luggage. Jason starts carrying in their bags. The wedding party is taking in the high ceilings, the Christmas tree and the fire lit there.

'Imagine having to clear the cobwebs in this place!' says one of the older women in the party. I'm assuming she's an aunt as I start to put names to faces, judging them from their emails.

'And the heating bill!' says another.

'It's beautiful!' says the bride-to-be, her face lit up. 'Just like I thought it would be!'

'It's lovely to see you back here,' I say, recognizing her straight away as the woman who stood in a towel in the kitchen when Boris the boiler was playing up.

'It's lovely to be back! Thank you so much.'

'I'm dying for the loo!'

'I'm dying for a drink!' says the father of the bride.

'Everybody!' I clap my hands from the first step of the stairs. 'Welcome, *bienvenus*, to Château des Arbres,' I say nervously. 'Let us get you to your rooms, then please do join us in the salon for a drink before dinner.'

I lead them upstairs and see Charlotte nod her approval at me.

When I get down to the kitchen, there is panic. 'What's the matter?' I say, looking at the stricken faces.

'The caterer can't get through. The rain has flooded the road,' says Jason. Having delivered all the cases to the right bedrooms, he's now just off the phone.

I stare at him in horror. 'So I can't feed all these people? Noooo! It can't be happening!'

Charlotte joins us. 'Don't panic,' she says smoothly. 'Think.'

But all I can think about is Rachelle. She was right. I can't do this. She'll be here doing this much better than me next year. I've blown it already. Why didn't I get the caterer to come earlier?

'Think,' Charlotte repeats.

For once, Lizzie has no suggestions. She looks as much at sea as I am. I walk around in circles, my fists to my throbbing temples.

'I am thinking . . . and all I can think is that I have a houseful of guests I can't feed!' There's no way I can ask Jacques. I can't let him or his wife know I've fallen at the first hurdle. Suddenly it's all crashing down around my ears.

Nellie is rolling up her sleeves.

'Of course! Nellie's here. She can cook!' I say to Charlotte, who slowly smiles and nods. I kiss Nellie firmly on the cheek. 'We need three courses. Just something simple, but filling,' I tell her, and Charlotte sits by the fire and watches the sudden activity in the kitchen, enjoying every moment of it.

'It's what I do! Let's see what you've got.' A smile spreads across Nellie's face.

'Jason, take round drinks as soon as they come downstairs and keep the glasses topped up. Lizzie, you'll be needed to chop,' I instruct. 'Jason, keep the guests talking.'

'On it,' he says with a smile.

'Well, dried pasta and fridge leftovers it is!' Nellie says, having rummaged through the cupboards. 'My speciality!'

Jason hugs her hard, then goes to serve drinks, as if he's been doing it all his life. 'With Angel Delight for dessert. Stuck a few packets in my case – butterscotch. Jason used to love it.'

In next to no time a three-course meal is waiting to be served.

There are baked cheese rounds, like we had at the apple festival, for starters. Cheese I had for the wedding day, but I'll deal with that tomorrow. Then there is pasta in rich tomato sauce, for vegetarians, with olives, from a jar, roasted peppers, courgettes and aubergines from the *potager* that I picked when I first arrived and froze when I had too many. For the meat eaters, there is pancetta, which always seems to be in my fridge and is great with omelettes, chorizo, roasted peppers and onions. It'll go down a treat with the red wine the wine merchant has sent for the weekend.

And dessert, Angel Delight, with curls of chocolate from Nellie's handbag, her travelling snack.

The diners are delighted and finally retire, exhausted, to bed. The vicar, who came with the wedding party, looks especially jolly as he makes his way to his bedroom on the second floor, bouncing off the staircase wall. The bride and groom's families have retired to bed. The mother-in-law is delighted with the chatelaine's suite. Bridesmaids and best man have been dispatched upstairs, the couple's friends too. All the rooms are full and it feels wonderfully warm. The tree lights still glow in the hall.

We gather in the kitchen, with bowls of pasta for ourselves and a glass of red wine each. Lizzie is on her phone, or her calculator more like. 'You know, by catering this yourself you could have earned much more in the way of profit. Look at what you would have paid for tonight's meal, compared to what something homemade could have cost.' She shows me the figures on her phone.

'Wow!'

She's right.

'A pasta supper, or risotto,' Nellie suggests.

'With local cheese, or pasta with a cream sauce.'

'Something substantial and welcoming.'

We all look at each other. But I have to get through this wedding. There may not be another. Tomorrow is New Year's Eve, the wedding party.

'Jacques just rang,' says Jason, returning to the kitchen from the basement where all the plates and pans have been piled for washing up.

'He did?' My stomach and heart leap to attention. 'Did he ask for me?'

He shakes his head. 'He said the road is flooded in the other direction now, into the town. He says hopefully it'll clear soon. And to let him know if we need any help.'

My spirits collapse to the floor again. 'The flowers are due in the morning. If the caterer couldn't get through from the next town, the flowers won't make it through either. We'll have to go out early in the morning and see what we've got,' I say, almost defeated but not quite dead in the water. 'Oh! The cake! The croquembouche!'

'Always wanted to have a go at one of those,' says my sister.

'Really?'

'I've watched them make them on *Bake Off*. Always wanted to have a go. If not, there's always apple cake.'

A smile begins to spread across my face. Maybe, just maybe, we could get this together.

49

'What's that smell?' I say. It's not apple cake, that's for sure! 'Oh, no, not again!'

The bride is getting ready for her big day and there's a smell. I run down the stairs in the turret, through the curved and padded door along the passage and into the kitchen.

'Jason, ring *Monsieur le plombier*, and tell him it's urgent!'

'But he can't get through. The road is flooded,' Jason reminds me.

I swallow.

A good chatelaine asks for help. I remember Charlotte's words and now I know exactly what she meant.

'Wait there!'

I pull on the poncho and boots, run to the back door and down the drive.

*

My heart is hammering as hard as my pounding on the door.

'Fliss!' Clémentine's face lights up as she sees me. 'Do you need my help?' she asks.

Her mother appears behind her and stands in front of her. '*Oui*, Madame? How can I help?'

'Um, it's Jacques, actually. I need his help. The road is blocked and I need the plumber to come.'

'Tut . . . A shame. My husband is out right now. I'm sorry.'

'Well, could you tell him? When he gets back? I really need his help!'

'Of course.' She shuts the door. Something tells me she has no intention of doing any such thing.

I stand with the door shut in my face. I can hear arguing from behind it. I don't want to get Clémentine into trouble.

I turn and run back to the château.

'Jason, tell everyone we need them to gather in the salon . . . for photographs. It's a before-and-after shot. And use your phone camera.'

'But I thought the groom wasn't supposed to see the bride!'

'You're right! Groom's family in the library in the turret and bride's in the salon. Tell them it's a tradition!'

As the parties start to descend the stairs I can hear some mumbling.

'Never heard of this before.'

'Maybe a French thing,' says the aunt.

'Lovely staircase. Must be hell to polish . . .' says another.

'Make sure they have Kir Royale! *Crémant* with a drop of crème de cassis in the bottom of the glass,' I instruct Lizzie, then run to the bedrooms, trying to find the source of the smell.

I'm in one of the guest bathrooms with my hand halfway down the U-bend, just as Kev did, but it's no good: I can't fix it. I could cry!

Suddenly the bedroom door opens and in comes *Monsieur le plombier* and sets to work. Jacques is behind him. 'You came!' I say gratefully.

'I brought your plumber on the tractor.' He puts out a hand to help me up. I wave him away – I need to wash!

'I didn't think you'd get the message.'

'Clémentine came and found me. Look, I need to talk to you.'

I nod sadly.

'Maybe later,' I say, not keen to hear what he wants to talk about, but knowing I can't put off hearing about him and Clémentine's mother for ever. Right now, though, I have a wedding to get ready.

'What else can I do?' Jacques asks.

'Speak to my sister in the kitchen? See if we can get some of the food from the caterer?'

'It'll take too long on the tractor.' He shakes his head. 'I have an idea . . .' He goes off to find my sisters.

With the blockage sorted, the facial wipes removed from the pipework, I go downstairs followed by *Monsieur le plombier*. I thank him profusely, then tell him to go to the kitchen and my sister will give him something to drink.

I let the gathered groups go back to their rooms, the women first, then the men, making sure they don't meet. I point out that nothing must go down the toilets other than what's meant to.

I breathe a sigh of relief.

Outside the rain is heavier and the lights are flickering.

And then they go out altogether. It may be the middle of the day, but it's so dark outside that the château is really gloomy.

I rush around with candles, the bride's room first.

Then into the orangery at the back of the house, where the blessing is due to take place. It's so dark. Suddenly Jacques and Clémentine are with me, lighting candles, tealights in jars, just as we did in the orchard. When they're all burning, we stand back and look. 'It's beautiful,' I say.

'It is,' says Jacques. And Clémentine is smiling once more.

'Where's the vicar?' I say, as we're nearly ready to start.

'In the salon,' says Jason.

The smell from the kitchen is fantastic and I have no idea how my sister has managed to rustle up this menu, but I have a feeling Jacques was involved.

I head into the salon where I can see the top of the vicar's head. He's snoring.

'Mr Williams? Clive?' When I get no reply, I step in front of the chair in which he's sitting.

Head lolling, Mr Williams's hand is placed firmly around his glass, and the bottle of *crémant* beside him is empty. In his other hand he's clutching a typed sheet of paper.

'Oh, no . . .'

'Mr Williams?' I shake him, but there's no stirring him. The pre-wedding drinks have taken their toll. I throw up my hands and run into the kitchen.

'The vicar giving the blessing is drunk!' I say, throwing up my hands again. It seems to help. 'He's passed out!'

'You'll have to do it,' says Lizzie.

'What? I can't. I'm not a vicar.'

'Not give a blessing exactly but make the speech, or whatever it's called.'

'I can barely get the words right at the best of times!' I say, holding the piece of paper I took from Mr Williams and peering down at it. The words jumble on the page as they usually do when I have to read something important.

'It's the only way!' Lizzie says.

'Where's Jacques? He's the mayor – he should do it.'

'Gone back to the farm with Nellie to sort out the rest of the meal. It's down to you, Fliss,' she says, and I shudder.

My worst nightmare is about to come true. I'm going to ruin their wedding day.

I read and reread the text on the vicar's sheet of paper and attempt to memorize it as the groom's family start to gather in the hall, and where we've lit candles down the staircase. I've reminded them to blow out their candles upstairs before they come to the orangery. There, they gasp at the room lit by candles.

'Do you think they did the power cut on purpose?' asks an aunt.

'I don't know, but it looks beautiful!'

In the kitchen, the wood-burner is stoked up and the pot of *joue de boeuf* – Jacques has brought it from his freezer, Clémentine's favourite that he cooks in batches – is placed on top to keep cooking and jacket potatoes are baking inside. Jacques is now nowhere to be seen. Neither is Jason.

And at two o'clock, I have no choice. The bride has arrived in the hall, and I walk into the orangery to await her. There's no music without electricity. But suddenly I hear the unmistakable voice of Edith Piaf singing from what sounds like the antique wind-up gramophone in the salon. That's what Jason and Jacques must have been doing. As the bride walks down the aisle in the orangery, which is decorated with holly, ivy and golden bows, to meet her groom, my eyes fill with tears. So much so, that as I try to read the words on the page, they dance around even more than usual. My hands are shaking and I have no idea how to make this happen.

'*Bonjour*, welcome,' I say, but can't see a word that's written on the page.

'We're here today to celebrate a wedding, to celebrate love,' I say, hoping my eyes will start to focus but they don't. I pause. It's a long pause. I feel a cold sweat coming on. The guests shuffle in their seats. I look up and around in panic. I see Charlotte: *A good chatelaine asks for help.*

'Um . . .' I fold the typed sheet, which is useless to me. Once again I feel exactly like I did at school, standing in front of the class and trying to read to them all. I feel as sick now as I did then. And then I become aware of the orangery, how beautiful it is, how beautiful this whole place is. Not because it's perfect, but because parts of it are imperfect and I love that about it. This may not be perfect, but I can only follow Charlotte's words. Her advice hasn't let me down so far.

I clear my throat and raise my voice above the mutterings of 'Where's the vicar?' and 'What's she doing?'

'As I say, we're here to celebrate love. Does anyone here have anything they'd like to say about love, and the couple we've come to celebrate with?' I look around, smiling, and when no one puts up a hand, a little more desperately. Then, there is movement from the back of the room, and footsteps.

'Yes, I do.' My heart does an excited flip.

50

'This is Jacques Cadieux, Jacques is a farmer here and the local mayor. He's also the grandson of Madame Charlotte Cadieux, the chatelaine. He grew up in the château.' I introduce him as the aunts ask each other again what's going on.

'I did grow up in this house. The château. And for many years I've thought it was the house I missed when I left and knew I wouldn't return. I thought it was the house I was jealous about when the new owners took over. But it wasn't the house, it was the love I felt in the house as a child. Love is . . . a journey. And sometimes on that journey, we take the wrong path. But love will find you and put you back on the right path to where you are meant to be and who you should be with. Trust in the love. It doesn't leave you even if you lose sight of it for a while. When you find the person you really love, you know it. You don't need to ask anyone else if it's right. And you must do whatever you can to hold on to it and not let it go.'

I can barely breathe. If only someone was saying those words about me . . . and I wish I didn't feel they were. Because it can't be true.

The bride and groom are beaming at him.

'Now, who would like to come and speak about our bride and groom?' he asks, and slowly, one by one, the guests get up to say a few words. There are tears, laughter and even applause.

When the last person has spoken and the bride and groom have declared their love for each other in front of their family and friends, he says, 'In my official capacity as mayor, I think we can well and truly pronounce our couple husband and wife.'

As we head towards the salon behind the bride and groom for photographs and more *crémant*, I look out and see that it has stopped raining. We may even get a few pictures at the front of the château, I think.

I open the doors on to the terrace. The sun is pushing its way back through the trees, low and bright. 'How about some photographs outside?'

Everyone agrees.

The bride looks lovely, wrapped up in a fake-fur-lined cape with hood. A real winter wedding scene.

And when everyone has their glasses charged again, I check that they're all present. Someone is missing. 'Where's the mother of the groom?'

'She went in to get her lipstick.'

I'll fetch her and check she's warm enough. I grab a pile of thick blankets I got in the market for anyone who'd like one round their shoulders. And then think, what's that smell?

Oh, no, not again!

But this time, it's not the plumbing. It's smoke.

51

I wrench open the door to the hall. Smoke is drifting down the stairs. I cough as it catches me in the throat. I put my face into the crook of my elbow and cough again.

'Call the fire service!'

Jason does exactly as he's told, and I hear him telling them, in clear French, the address. His time spent with Clémentine is clearly paying off.

I run up the stairs.

The smoke is coming from under the door of Charlotte's apartment where the bride's mother-in-law is staying.

'Hello! Hello!' I bang on the door. Then try the handle. It's locked. I bang again, then turn and run down the stairs. 'Charlotte, I need the key to your apartment!'

She frowns but doesn't argue. She undoes the chain from around her waist and hands me the whole thing.

I run back upstairs. From the terrace I can hear chatter, laughter, and then 'Can anyone smell smoke?'

'Yes! I can.' It's the aunts again.

'Hope it's not dinner!' Someone laughs and others join in.

They haven't realized. And I'm thinking that's a good thing.

My fingers are shaking as I find the big key, put it into the lock and open the door. Smoke hits my chest, making me cough, and stings my eyes. There are flames licking up the curtains beside a candle – clearly where the fire started – and the bride's mother-in-law is lying on the bed, eyes shut.

'Wake up! Wake up! Fire!' I shake her and she comes round, coughing and spluttering.

'I just thought I'd have forty winks.' She coughs. 'Lovely ceremony!'

I pull her to her feet, my eyes running, the smoke making it hard to breathe.

Suddenly I'm gripped with fear. What if I can't get us out of this? She's no light weight.

And then there's a loud hissing sound and the flames die down. Through the smoke I can see a figure. I'd know it anywhere. It's Jacques, with the fire extinguisher. And when the flames have gone out he says, 'Here,' and takes the other side of the groom's mother. We support and half carry her downstairs and out of the front door to find that the *pompiers* have arrived.

'*Bonjour*, Monsieur Mayor. Madame!' they say politely, as they run past and up the stairs.

'Thank you,' I finally say to Jacques. Our guest is taking deep breaths of clear air and drinking apple brandy, mixed with water, for her nerves.

'No problem,' he says.

'You always seem to be there when I need you,' I say quietly.

'Maybe it's because you're always on my mind,' he says, just as quietly. 'Thinking of you, in that fire, made me realize how much time I spend thinking about you.' But I know, no matter how much I want to tell him he's on my mind too, that it can't be. I think of him at the wedding ceremony, the words, the way he looked at me, making me feel it was me and only me. But he's back with his wife now, Clémentine's mother, and I have to step away. He's forbidden fruit. Just like Charlotte and my grandfather. When they couldn't be together they learnt to smile because they had to. I walk out to the patio, wondering how I'm going to tell the bride and groom that the house is full of smoke and their wedding dinner is ruined.

But as I return to the terrace, no one's there. They've all gone.

52

I can hear voices. Laughter even. I just can't see them! Then I realize the voices are coming from the orchard.

'I thought it might be a good safe place to be,' says Jason, and I feel another surge of pride in my lovely, grown-up, responsible nephew.

'It is,' I say, looking around. 'It is!'

'I lit the fire,' he points.

The bunting is still hanging from the trees, and he and Clémentine are busy relighting the candles in the jam jars on the trees.

Jacques joins Jason with a smile and a pat on his shoulder and they walk together to the lit bonfire. My sister has brought out the pots of *joue de boeuf* from the kitchen and is putting jacket potatoes around the fire as the initial flames die down to a warm glow.

I invite the *pompiers* into the orchard to join us for a thank-you drink, once they are happy that the fire in the east wing is completely dead. Then I hear a tractor arrive. It's Alphonse, bringing the townspeople – business owners, *Monsieur le plombier*, the florist, the couple from the *auberge*, the baker – with food and bottles of cider. He heard about the caterer being unable to get through from *Monsieur le plombier*.

Nellie makes warm spiced apple juice for those who don't drink.

Cedric and his gang have joined up in the orchard – he even puts up his tail feathers to the delight of the guests: the last of the day's sun shines off his green and brilliant blue plumage and he struts around as if he's at a royal garden party.

And then, as if the sight couldn't get any more perfect, Jacques leads Pegasus into the orchard with the bride and groom on his back. Everyone cheers. As he helps them down, I notice the boots the bride is wearing: wellingtons, not the dainty ones she had on earlier. The hem of her dress is tinged with wet from the grass but she doesn't seem to mind, judging by her huge smile. Jacques smiles at me, then calls to Jason, takes a tray of drinks from him and slowly walks around the orchard offering glasses of wine while Pegasus is stroked and patted.

'He never did like being left out of a party!' He offers me the tray and I take a drink with a grateful smile.

Then, with drinks handed round, beef stew served in bowls with the potatoes and bread, *Monsieur le plombier* sits on an apple tree stump, opens a black case and pulls out an accordion that he begins to play. The baker is a saxophonist and the chocolatier a guitarist and they join in. The aunts, fuelled by *crémant* and apple brandy, begin to dance, as do the bride and groom and the bride's mother.

'It's perfect! Thank you for the most perfect wedding ever!' says the bride with her groom, eyes sparkling in the firelight.

'I'm so sorry about the apartment, I really am. I thought I'd just have a snooze before dinner and I left the candle burning,' says the mother-in-law, as I hand round Alphonse's crêpes, cooked on the open fire.

I notice Rachelle is standing beside him laughing, flirting as he cooks, and I wonder how Jacques feels about that.

The villagers are all there in the orchard, where they should be.

My sisters stand with me and raise their glasses. 'You did it!'

'*We* did it!' I say, and raise my glass to them. 'All of us!' And I wonder where Jacques is.

'Well, maybe it could be your wedding next?' Nellie says to Lizzie, smiling.

Lizzie looks down at her glass and shakes her head.

'There isn't going to be a wedding. James and I split up. He said he thought I loved my work more than him.' She takes a sip of her drink. 'He was probably right.'

A strange sense of relief seems to wash over her and she gives a little laugh and we join in.

'But seriously,' I say, looking into the fire, 'what are you going to do now?'

'Well,' she takes a deep breath, 'I certainly need to think about that.' She scans the wedding party, the tealights in the trees, the happy faces. 'You did so well here, you know,' she says.

'Well, I've realized you can't do it all on your own,' I say, dreading the thought of trying to. 'It's okay to ask for help. But also never to accept second best! Oh, and to think outside the box. There's always a solution. Charlotte taught me all that. Although maybe in my heart I knew it. I just needed to do it.'

The twins are now taking turns to have rides on Pegasus, who is happy to oblige with Jacques holding the reins. My heart couldn't be any more full of love for him, even though I know he's not mine to have. But I will always remember this.

'Imagine if we all stayed and helped you run it,' Nellie says almost absent-mindedly. 'I could cook, and Lizzie could do the books.'

'Really? That would be perfect!' I say, louder than I meant to.

Lizzie laughs. 'Together we're stronger . . . a team!' she says firmly, and the words change from fun to a mad but real idea. 'You'd still run the place, but we'd be your back-up team. Wouldn't we, Nellie?'

Nellie is watching Jason, happy in the firelight, chatting with Clémentine, acting the fool. 'This is the perfect place to be,' she says. 'But where would we all stay? You need the rooms for B-and-B guests. And Charlotte's apartment will have to be redecorated.'

Charlotte is standing next to me. 'Don't worry.' She waves a hand. 'It's time that apartment was freshened up. It's been stuck in the past for years. Just like me!'

'Thank you. It has been the most wonderful day,' says the mother of the bride. She hugs me tightly, then goes off to dance, with Jean-Pierre from the bakery, in the barn where we crushed the apples.

'It'll take a little time to sort out the apartment, but I'll get on to it straight away,' I say, starting a new list in my head.

'I think,' says Charlotte, thoughtfully, 'that it's time I moved out of the château.'

'What?' I'm shocked.

'I'm taking up far too much room in the east wing. A family should be living there.' She looks at Jason and Nellie. 'Plenty of room for you all on that side of the house. And if I'm not in the château, it will make it easier if you do decide to sell.'

I catch my breath. 'Where will you go?'

She glances around, then says quietly, 'There was a child you know. A girl.' Her eyes fill with tears. Tears that have been locked up for a very long time.

'You and my grandfather?'

She nods. 'She didn't survive.' She shakes her head. 'He never saw her, but I named her Florence. No one other than my parents knew. She was a secret. An embarrassment. But to me she was a gift from Dafydd. Here, I can imagine how she would have been if she had survived. I can hear her laughter in the trees.'

I swallow hard.

'I think of how she would have looked like him so I would always have had a piece of him here.' She turns to me. 'But you are just like him. You remind me of him so much. Nothing was ever too much trouble.'

'So how did he end up owning this place?' I ask finally.

'Because I asked him to buy it. My father fell on hard times. The whole village did, once my father shut the orchard after he found Dafydd and me here. We'd fallen asleep together. I can remember his arms around me to this day. My father was furious. People stopped coming to the town for its cider. Neighbours stopped looking out for each other. You have brought them back here. My father was about to sell the château and I contacted your grandfather. He told me if ever I needed him I should get in touch. He wouldn't contact me. I did. He made an offer on the château. Used his savings as a down payment, then paid the monthly allowance so that I could stay here until I died. My father was furious when he found out where the offer had come from, but it was that or lose the roof over our heads. Your grandfather didn't buy the château to spite my father and his family, as my father believed. He thought it was an act of revenge all those years later for sending him away, but your grandfather bought it to save me and my family.'

Tears are rolling down my cheeks. He had stayed true to his word. Stayed loyal to his family, but never stopped caring for his first love. He was always there for her. It was love.

'But still where will you stay, if you're not in the château?'

She turns towards the gardener's cottage. 'I will be quite happy here, in the orchard, in the little gîte. Just me and my memories in the orchard.' She smiles, and I swear I hear the sound of a little girl's laughter in the trees.

'Oh, I nearly forgot, your keys,' I say, handing her back her belt.

She wraps her hand over mine and gently pushes the belt back towards me. 'You have proved yourself to be the perfect chatelaine. It is your turn now to run this place. You are the custodian of the château and should have the keys.'

There's a lump in my throat when I try to say 'Merci' as she hands over the mantle, one chatelaine to another.

'Now, with me out of the way, all you have to decide is whether to sell up and leave . . . or stay,' she says. And my eyes immediately turn to Jacques, who is watching Clémentine's mother as she flirts with the restaurant owner.

'Now I will find Jason for a drop more apple brandy before bed,' Charlotte says, and drifts away.

My sisters look at me and at each other.

'Well,' I say, 'what are we going to do?'

I'm standing in the dark now, gazing into the orange glow of the bonfire. It's much colder, but there's a stillness in the air too, a feeling of expectation. My nose tickles with the chill. A blanket is placed around my shoulders breaking into my thoughts.

Some of the wedding guests are making their way inside now. The rooms don't seem to have been too badly affected by the smoke on the other side of the château. Some are in the library and I can hear music drifting through the rooms. Others are still enjoying the warmth of the fire outside, with the locals.

Jacques is standing beside me.

'Thank you,' I say, pulling the blanket around me. 'I should go in, check on everyone.'

'Wait,' he says, and we both look into the fire. I can see his warm breath in the freezing night air, and wonder if he can hear the thumping of my heart.

'So, you have done it. You have pulled off the wedding. You will be able to pay the tax tomorrow?' he says.

'Yes.' I let out a long sigh. We've done it.

'And now what?'

I let out another long sigh. 'Charlotte is going to move out of the château, into the gardener's cottage, here in the orchard, so we can sell the château if we want.' I swallow.

'She told me earlier,' he says. Then adds tentatively, 'And what did you decide, you and your sisters?'

I take a deep breath. 'We're going to stay, Jacques. It's right for all of us. We want to make a real go of the château as a wedding venue . . . without the pong and the fire. And then there's Boris the boiler!' I try to laugh.

He does too and I love to hear it.

'I hope Rachelle won't mind too much,' I say, trying to keep my tone light, but clearly failing.

'I hadn't asked her back, you know, when she announced it on Christmas Eve. I said I thought Clémentine was pleased to see her. I want her to be involved in Clémentine's life. But when she announced it, I didn't know what to do for the best, for Clémentine's sake.'

'You're a great dad, Jacques,' I say. 'Clémentine doesn't want a stepdad. She wants you, her papa, her dad. Like my grandpa was everything I needed in a dad. You've done a wonderful job bringing her up. A lovely father.'

He nods. 'No more stepfather . . . just a dad.'

'Just a dad!' I echo.

'And I hope I will be again one day.' I feel him turn to look at me, but I can't look at him. Is he telling me they're having a baby?

'Sometimes in life and love, you take the wrong path, but love will eventually put you back on the right one,' he says, echoing what he said in the wedding ceremony. 'Rachelle and I are not back together. I have talked to Clémentine. She understands that her mother and I don't make each other happy. She's much happier we're apart and wants to stay living with me. She wants me to be happy too. To find love.'

My heart lurches. Could he be talking about finding love with me?

'Rachelle wanted the château, but not me. Or the work involved in being a chatelaine. She could never do what you have done here.'

'Thank you,' I say. He's just complimenting me on the business.

'You've changed our lives, the villagers', mine, Clémentine's and Charlotte's.'

He stops. Then, 'I prayed you would decide to stay.'

'Really, you don't mind?'

'I could not be happier. This is a new beginning for us all.'

'You do know we met many years ago when we were children? My family and I came here, just the once.'

He grins. 'Of course. And thank goodness you came back.'

My heart swells with joy.

And suddenly there's a bang and a flash!

'Fireworks! I didn't organize those!'

He laughs. 'Every year at this time, midnight, to celebrate the end of the year, we used to set off fireworks in the orchard to awaken the spirits, thank them for the harvest and ask for a good new year.'

Little flakes of snow begin to fall from the dark sky. Tiny specks, as we watch the fireworks shooting upwards.

'A good new year!' I smile. 'A new beginning.'

Then, without words, the sides of our hands touch, our little fingers entwine and finally, my hand is in his as we gaze at the bright lights in the sky.

'Happy New Year!' he says. 'And to new beginnings . . .'

'A new beginning,' I say.

'Kiss her!' I hear a loud whisper from behind a tree.

'Thank you, Clémentine.' Jacques laughs and so do I as he kisses me on the lips, and I know that love has finally put me on the right path in the apple orchard. This is a new beginning for all of us. The snowflakes begin to fall fatter and fluffier around us.

'Thank goodness for the apple orchard and the cider,' I say. 'I wish it was ready for us to toast our hard work.'

'It will be ready in the spring, when the blossom is out in the orchard.'

He looks at me in the way I have wanted to be looked at for so long. As if I am the one person he loves, my whole future laid out in front of me.

'A beautiful time of year for a wedding,' he says softly, as the snowflakes fall like confetti, tumbling, floating and swirling, and he pulls me closer to him, the snow settling on his hair and lashes.

'Yes.' I swear I can hear the sound of happy laughter in the trees once more as my heart explodes, like the fireworks lighting up the château, its family, neighbours and welcome visitors from overhead; like me, full of life and love, looking forward to everything that life at the château will bring next year, laughter, challenges and celebrations in the apple orchard. A new year, a new list . . . and I think the hole in the apple orchard's wall will be at the bottom again.

EPILOGUE

Drip, drip, drip. I can hear it as I sit at the dressing-table in the big bedroom overlooking the lawns at the front of the house. The bridal suite, as we've named it. We've done it up, imagining everything we would want if it was our big day.

It's a long way from the cosy warmth of the bedroom I share with Jacques in the farmhouse. This room has high ceilings, and is painted a light blue, with white edging around the ceiling coving and panelling on the walls. There's a four-poster bed, with a view of the woods through the big windows, and an en suite, with a big slipper bath. There are candles and a huge bunch of white roses from the florist in town.

Drip, drip, drip.

I try to ignore it, but I can't. I have to go and investigate.

The sun is streaming in, pushing out the rain clouds from last night, leaving the huge sky blue, with soft fluffy clouds dotted across it. I swear I can smell the apple blossom with the window open.

I stand up and follow the sound up the next flight of stairs, running my hand along the polished banister, remembering when I first arrived here, when I fell in love with the place and the people . . . one person in particular: Jacques.

I go into the loft room and spot it straight away. There's a hole. We've lost a tile or two. There's only one thing I can do. I run down and get a bucket from the basement, and as I do, I see the neat lines of cups to be taken into the orchard after the ceremony. The pile of plates and pressed napkins for the table. Everything is ready: tick, tick, tick. I smile. Then I return to the attic and place the big bucket under the leak.

There. That should hold it for now. I dust off my hands. I'm glad I've caught it. I'll get someone in as soon as the wedding is over.

I hear a noise from behind me, a rustle.

I turn. It's Charlotte in a beautiful full-length dress, in peacock blue. The colour of Cedric's breast feathers. I hear him call on the lawn, and I know he's showing himself off to the guests arriving. Pegasus will be as excited as ever.

'What are you doing up here?' She tuts.

'I heard dripping. We've got a leak. It's okay. It should

hold until after the weekend. I've got a bucket and the weather forecast is fine.'

'A chatelaine's work is never done.' She smiles. 'I have a gift for you,' she says, and hands it to me.

I undo the curled ribbon around the soft tissue paper and peel it off.

'Because a chatelaine's work is never done!' She smiles wider.

It's a new notebook, with my initials, FC, in the corner, embossed in gold. I run my fingers over them. '*Merci*,' I say to her.

'You are welcome,' she says, and kisses me on each cheek. 'Now, be quick! Everyone is waiting! We cannot have the bride being late!'

'The bride.' I pick up the hem of my skirt and run down the stairs to the bridal suite. I look at myself in the mirror, straighten my headdress, check for any smudges on my face or dress and smile. The bride.

I put down the book on the dressing-table and open it. 'Mend château roof,' I write at the top of the page. I sigh. It won't be an easy job or cheap. We'll need to find the money. But that can wait until another day. Not today.

A chatelaine's lists are never-ending, hopefully like my marriage here today, in the orchard, under the apple blossom to the man I love. Jacques Cadieux.

ACKNOWLEDGEMENTS

This book was inspired by the Channel 4 television series *Escape to the Chateau*. I loved it. Devoured it. I recommended it to people. Discussed it as if it were the latest high concept drama to drop on Netflix. But it wasn't. This was real life, which made it even more exciting. It was Katie Fforde who first put me on to it and after that I lived and breathed it, in full admiration of Dick and Angel, the 'plucky Brits' prepared to take on and do up a château in France. And then, joy of joys, we had *Escape to the Chateau DIY*, a follow-on series of more 'plucky Brits' taking on châteaux all over France. Who knew so many people had the same dream. It was all about the dream. But in reality it was about the drama along the way. These châteaux owners inspired me. Not because they had managed to be brave enough to give everything up and 'live the dream' but it was that they risked everything. It wasn't ever a given that their lives in France would be a success. It was the hard work, the determination and throwing themselves into making the dream work, even if there were nightmares along the way. It was about what was at stake. It was about the risk of failure. Putting everything into it, heart and soul. It's also about their shared sense of community and all that they have in common.

I think lots of us have a dream.

I remember someone saying to me once 'What's the one thing you would do if you knew you couldn't fail?' I remember saying 'I'd be Jilly Cooper!' Well, clearly I'm not Jilly Cooper, Jilly is Jilly. But I am doing what I love, writing. And it hasn't been an easy journey to get there. No overnight success here. In fact, it took about ten years! But with help from the friends I made in the Romantic Novelists Association and the support I found there, when times were tough, when I thought about giving up, many times, I finally made it over the finish line. And wow! What a feeling! When my first book won The Joan Hessayon Award and then Best Ebook at the Festival of Romance, my friends were there to celebrate with me, who understood the dream and the struggle and it made it all worth while; the rejections, the feelings of failure and the digging deep and getting the job done. No one said living your dream was going to be easy. But I got mine, with the support of my friends I'd found in the RNA. I think if you have a dream, you'll find others with the same dream, who'll be there to reach out a hand and help you along the way. We all have to start somewhere, with a dream.

So this book wouldn't have been possible without the inspiring 'plucky Brits' from *Escape to the Chateau DIY*, who were brave enough to follow their dreams, and the RNA, who helped me follow mine.

I do hope you enjoy your time at the Château.

With Love
Jo
x

*Read on for
delicious
French recipes
for you to try
at home*

Normandy Chicken

Serves 4–6 people

75g butter
6 chicken breasts
12 shallots, finely sliced
4 eating apples, such as Cox's or Braeburn, cored and cut into wedges
Pinch of freshly grated nutmeg
Ground white pepper, to season
300ml cider
300ml chicken stock
200ml crème fraiche
3 tbsp chopped chives, to serve

1. Heat half of the butter in a large pan and colour the chicken breasts on both sides.
2. Remove the chicken from the pan and add the remaining butter.
3. Add the shallots and apples to cook for about 5 minutes until they start to soften.
4. Add the chicken breasts back to the pan and season with a touch of nutmeg and ground white pepper.
5. Add the cider and stock to the chicken, shallots and apples and cook over a low heat for about 30 minutes to reduce the liquid by two-thirds.
6. Add the crème fraiche and emulsify with the cider sauce. If the sauce seems too runny, remove the chicken and apples and reduce the cream over a low-medium heat.
7. Sprinkle with chopped chives and serve.

SERVING SUGGESTION
This dish is delicious with mashed potato, roasted broccoli and green beans.

Apple Tarte Tatin

Serves 6–8 people

50g butter
50g caster sugar
1 vanilla pod, seeds included
3 Braeburn apples
320g pack ready-rolled puff pastry
1 beaten egg

1. Preheat the oven to 180°C. Melt the butter and caster sugar in a 20cm ovenproof frying pan over a medium heat. Add the vanilla pod and seeds and continue to melt together until all the sugar and butter turns into a golden caramel.
2. Peel, core and quarter the apples. Place neatly in the pan so they fit in the base. Turn the heat to medium-low and cook the apples for 8–10 minutes or until softened slightly. Remove from the heat, discard the vanilla pod and leave to cool for 5 minutes.
3. Unroll the pastry and cut out a circle 2cm wider than the diameter of the frying pan. Carefully place over the hot apples and then press down the sides to ensure all the fruit is covered and the pastry goes to the edge. Prick all over a few times with a fork.
4. Brush with the beaten egg and then bake in the oven for 20–25 minutes.
5. Leave to cool for 5 minutes in the pan, then run a small sharp knife between the pastry and the edge of the pan, place a serving plate over the top and invert the pan.

SERVING SUGGESTION
Serve with scoops of vanilla ice cream, whipped or pouring cream, or hot custard.

Crêpes with Stewed Apples and Calvados Cream

Serves 2 people

Crêpes

128g plain flour
1 egg
250ml milk
Pinch of salt

1. Combine all the ingredients in a bowl. Whisk until smooth. Cover and set aside to rest for 5 minutes.
2. Heat a 24cm non-stick frying pan over medium heat. Spray with cooking oil. Using 4 tbsp of mixture per crêpe, pour the batter into the pan, tilting the pan from side to side so the batter covers the base in a thin layer. Cook the crêpe for about 1 minute or until the underside is golden, then use a spatula to flip it. Cook the other side for just under a minute until golden. Repeat with the remaining mixture, spraying the pan with cooking oil between crêpes.

Stewed Apples and Calvados Cream

2 cooking apples
1 tbsp butter
2 tsp cinnamon
1 tbsp dark brown sugar
175ml double cream
½ tbsp icing sugar
1 tbsp Calvados

1. Core, peel and slice the apples into wedges. Heat the butter in a saucepan over a medium heat, add the apples and cook for around 5 minutes until slightly softened. Stir in the cinnamon and dark brown sugar along with a splash of water and cover for around 10 minutes until the apples are soft and the sauce has a caramel-like consistency.

2. Meanwhile, make the Calvados cream. Place the cream and icing sugar in a bowl and whisk until it starts to form soft peaks. Add the Calvados and stir gently.

SERVING SUGGESTION

To assemble, place one crêpe on a plate and fill it with stewed apples and Calvados cream. Either roll the crêpe or fold it into quarters and top with additional apples and cream. Serve warm.

Coming next summer...

Retreat
to the
Spanish Sun

*Because sometimes
you just need to get away*

Other books by *Jo Thomas*

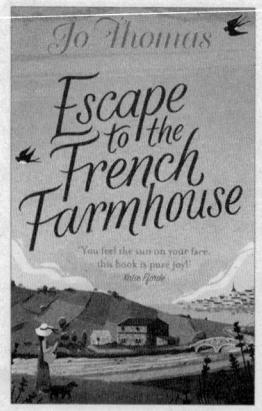

Available to read now